Only We Know

Only We Know

KAREN PERRY

MICHAEL JOSEPH
an imprint of
PENGUIN BOOKS

PENGUIN BOOKS

UK | USA | Canada | Ireland | Australia
India | New Zealand | South Africa

Penguin Books is part of the Penguin Random House group of companies
whose addresses can be found at global.penguinrandomhouse.com.

Penguin
Random House
UK

Set in 13.5/16pt Garamond MT by Palimpsest Book Production Limited, Falkirk, Stirlingshire
Printed in Great Britain by Clays Ltd, St Ives plc

A CIP catalogue record for this book is available from the British Library

HARDBACK ISBN: 978–0–718–17960–1
TRADE PAPERBACK ISBN: 978–1–405–91312–6

www.greenpenguin.co.uk

Prologue

Kenya, 1982

A woman lies in a field, sunning herself. The grass grows long around her, and from it, she hears the sibilant hum of unseen insects. Nearby, the children sit in the grass, restless and bored, but content to leave her be. Above her, the air shimmers with heat. It is almost noon.

She has flattened out a patch of grass with the tarpaulin they have used beneath their tent. It gives off a stale tang of sweat or mould, but right now that doesn't bother her as she stretches out, legs crossed at the ankles, a paperback novel unread and flattened against her belly, sunglasses covering her eyes from the white glare of the sun. For now, all she wants is to lie still and soak up the heat.

She breathes in the heavy air, feels the baking earth beneath her, and takes in the hush of the great meadows and plains that stretch out around her. The others left a half-hour ago, down the worn track towards the Masai village and she, Sally, has stayed behind to watch over the children. But the children are of an age that resists parental supervision. All summer long, they have held her at a distance, absorbing themselves in their new-found alliance, forming their own secret games, their own clandestine code. She feels driven out by their new demands for privacy. Even now, she can hear them stirring, getting to their feet, a resolve formed between them. She sits up and watches the three of them moving purposefully towards the downward slope of the field.

'Boys!' she calls to them, and when she calls a second time, they stop, Luke turning to look at her, Nicky mumbling something to Katie.

'What?'

She has to shade her eyes to see her elder son's face, and even though it is in shadow, she can still see the sullen set of his features, the suspicious look he has been giving her for some time now. Recently, whenever she is with him, she has the sense that the boy is faintly disgusted by her.

'Where are you off to?'

'The river.'

'No, Luke, it's dangerous –'

'Dad lets us.'

'Even so, I'm not happy with –'

'Oh, for Christ's sake.'

'Luke!' she shouts, enraged.

He opens his mouth to say something, thinks better of it and stands there chewing his lip, waiting. Sally feels prickly and uncomfortable, the vast heat rising around her. When she thinks of the trees that flank the river, the relief of shade there, she finds she hasn't the heart to argue with him.

'Oh, very well,' she says, trying to sound firm and purposeful. She wishes she wasn't seated. Her authority seems diminished, stretched out on her tarpaulin sheet, her son gazing imperiously down on her. Ten years old with the haughtiness of an aristocrat. 'But you're to be careful, do you understand? All of you.'

She casts her voice out so that the other two will take note. Katie glances back but Nicky keeps his eyes fixed firmly on the dusty ground.

'Luke,' she says sharply, as he turns to go. 'I'm counting on you to watch out for the others. All right?'

He gives her a look, closed and unreadable, and there it is again, the feeling she's had lately that he's holding himself back from blurting something out and confronting her.

'All right?' she says again.

He shrugs, then turns away. She watches him catching up with the others, overtaking them, his shoulders set with a grim determination, moving towards the shady banks with a purposeful air while the others lope along in his wake. How different they are, her two sons. Where one is bold and enlivened with a kind of animal energy, the other hangs back, dreamy and shy. Sally finds it hard sometimes to negotiate the role of parent to two such different children. If she is honest with herself, she knows she leans towards her younger son, finding she understands him innately, that she can identify with his dreaminess, with the rich inner life that occupies him. Her older son remains a mystery – an enigma – even though he lives his life so openly, almost aggressively, with an energy that sometimes baffles her. A wave of feeling takes her as she watches them until they reach the trees and disappear into the shadows – her two sons, her beautiful boys.

The sun is too bright, and the stifling heat makes it impossible to linger in the middle of the field. She can feel her body becoming desiccated, like the baked earth around her. Besides, there are things to be done before the others return. She gets to her feet and moves back towards the camp, leaving her book and the tarpaulin behind her – she will get them later, when Ken and Helen return with another driver.

The tents have been collapsed already, but the job of folding and packing them away was abandoned when Mackenzie came back and they discovered he was drunk. God, what a scene. Sally doesn't even want to think about it. She stops by the white van to check on him before she tackles the tents. Peeping in through the cab window she sees him stretched out on the seat, one arm thrown over his head, the other dangling down into the foot-well, the steady rise and fall of his chest as he sleeps it off. She cannot see his face as it is turned away, into the backrest.

'I don't like him,' she had said to Jim that first day.

They were in the office in Kianda, the two of them. Mackenzie had just left.

'Why not?' Jim had asked, surprised.

'I don't trust him,' she replied, and Jim had laughed, shaking his head, before returning his gaze to his paperwork, one hand tapping out a rhythm with his pen.

'You don't trust anyone,' he had said, but there was fondness in his tone, a light-hearted mockery that took the sting out of his words.

But it was true – she didn't trust the man, although she had nothing to base it on, only her own gut instinct. Within minutes of him stepping inside the office, she had felt the nudge of wariness. He was small, thin shoulders braced with tension, square-faced and flat-nosed, with nostrils that seemed permanently flared. She had watched him lighting up, puffing away on his cigarette the whole time they were making the arrangements, his small eyes flicking around the room but hardly ever alighting on her. He directed his comments to Father Jim, as if Sally wasn't even there. The whites of his eyes were tinged yellow, as if nicotine-stained, and he never once looked her clear in the face.

'He seems shifty,' she had said.

'Listen,' Jim was trying to sound reasonable, 'he knows the road well, and he knows the safari routes out there like the back of his hand. By all means, look for someone else, but you won't find anyone who can sniff out the big game like Mack, believe me.'

She had gone along with it. So, when they had woken on the last day of their three-day safari to find their driver missing, it had been, in a way, her fault.

It was mid-morning by the time the white van came skidding up the track, coughing up dust around it as it drew to an unsteady halt. She had known, as soon as Mackenzie stepped out, that he was drunk. The angle of his cap, the unsteady weave of his gait as he came towards them, the way he heaved in his breath as if trying to push down on the rising bile inside him.

'Oh, Christ,' Ken had said. 'He's pissed.'

And he was. Astonishingly and outstandingly drunk. He had staggered towards them, tried to string a few words together but they had emerged as an incoherent mash-up of an excuse. Helen, a witness to his inebriation, had blown up. Ken had lost all his patience, and Sally had felt rage ripping through her as if she wanted to kill someone. The row that ensued was awful. It was like the driver's drunkenness had put a match to a highly flammable atmosphere, one that had been smouldering for days, setting it ablaze.

In the searing heat of the midday sun, as Sally bends to begin folding away the tents, she feels suffused with a sense of shame. She should never have let it get so far. The words she had spoken, the things she had said – in front of her own children, in front of Helen's daughter – were unforgivable.

She would have to patch things up with Helen, although time was not on her side. They would drive back to Nairobi tonight – if they could find a driver – and the next day, Helen and Katie would board their flight for home. And then what would happen?

She packs away the tents, stacks the neat bundles alongside their bags, and looks around for any stray belongings. There is still no sign of the others.

Shouts erupt from the trees down by the river – yelps of joy and delight, alongside sounds of taunting. Helen's words come back at her – *You'll keep an eye on Katie, won't you?* She feels a small stab of guilt. The shouts draw her on, as does the need to get out of the sun's glare.

Even here, under the shade of the acacias, it's still hot as hell. Sweat beads on her brow and she wipes it away with the back of her forearm, looks down into the gloom, her eyes adjusting to the sudden plunging loss of sunlight. A great whoop of delight catches her off guard – shrieked out through the shadows, it causes her to step back involuntarily – followed by a deep splash. She looks down into the water, sees it ripple and rock in the half-light, before Luke's blond head emerges, then his naked torso. His skin glistens, and when she calls to him, for just an instant she sees unabashed glee on his face before the mask comes down, extinguishing the glittering light of his joy.

'What?' he asks sullenly.

'I told you not to go into the river,' she says.

'No, you didn't.'

'Luke, I did. It's not safe.'

'You said to be careful, and we are. But you never said not to go in.'

She hesitates — a fatal mistake. He lowers himself back into the water, keeping his eyes locked on her, challenging her.

'Where's Nicky?' she asks.

'There.' She follows the direction of his outstretched arm, sees the dark hair of her younger son a little way down. He is crouched among the shallows, and there are two girls with him, but neither is Katie.

'Hello,' she says tentatively, feeling her way carefully down to the bank. 'I see you've made new friends, Nicky.'

The boy doesn't look up, just stays there, hugging his knees to his chest and staring into the water, a strange little smile on his face.

'Hello, lady!' the girl next to him shouts up.

Sally laughs at the salutation, and turns to the girl — white blonde hair in bunches, two big square front teeth shining in their newness, gaps on either side where the adult teeth are yet but stubs. A rabbitty face busy with freckles, rounded cheeks. Her smile is open and warm but there is something about her that Sally is unsure of. Gormless. That is the word she alights on. Something in the girl's eye that is dull and slow. 'Not the full shilling,' as her father might have said.

'What's your name?' she asks brightly.

'Cora.'

'Hello, Cora.'

'And she's Amy.'

A jerked thumb indicates the presence of a smaller girl hovering behind her. A tatty dress tucked into knickers, the same white blond hair as her sister, but her eyes are sharper, the gaze more discerning. Sally guesses this child is four or five.

'Are you allowed to play here by the river?' she asks, wondering about the younger child, wary somehow of leaving her in the care of the older girl.

'Oh, yeah. Pops says it's fine.'

Sally glances behind the girl, up past the bank of trees on the other side of the river. There is a clearing there, the vague outline of some kind of house. Over the past few nights, they have seen the glow of a campfire through the trees, smoke rising into the night. When they asked him about it, Mackenzie had snorted dismissively. 'Gypsies.'

Sally takes in these girls with their washed-out dresses, dirty faces and feet, and feels a jab of uncertainty.

'Where's Katie?' she asks.

'Here I am.'

The voice, directly behind her, causes Sally to jump. She swings around, sees the girl sitting still in the shadows, sandalled feet together, hands clasped around her knees, and those big round eyes, solemn and staring up at her through the gloom.

'What are you doing?' Sally asks, unreasonably sharp, but she is still recovering from the fright.

'Nothing,' Katie says, her eyes fixed on Sally.

'Well, it's time to go back to camp now,' she says firmly.

'Is Dad back yet?' Luke asks.

'No. But he will be soon.'

'Ten more minutes.'

'Now.'

'Aw, please, Mum,' he says, a plaintive whine in his voice. It strikes Sally forcefully that, for the first time in days, he has addressed her as 'Mum'. Something inside her falters.

'All right, then.'

What's the point in arguing anyway? Best to leave them here playing, where they're happily entertaining themselves, than have them under her feet, whining and moaning and questioning her constantly about when the others will return.

She scrambles up the bank, stops to take one look back at them – Luke gliding through the water, Nicky turned to the girl with the buck teeth, whispering something to her, Katie sitting and gazing down at them, still and impassive. Sally watches them for no more than a minute, before turning away. And as she steps back out into the blinding heat, feeling the dryness of the grass brushing her ankles, she has no idea that this is the last time she will see them as innocent children, the last time she will feel such uncompromising love. She doesn't know it yet, but in less than an hour, her whole life will have changed.

Everything is packed and ready now, but still the others have not returned. Sally lies down again on the tarpaulin, resting on her front, and tries to read her book. But the words blur on the page, sweat running into her eyes; soon she gives up, rolls onto her back and closes her eyes.

She feels her body swamped in heat, imagines herself as a tiny insect trapped beneath the searing gaze of the African sun. Three years they have been here, and now that Ken is coming to the end of his contract, a decision must be made. Do they return to Ireland or will he push to extend his contract for another year? The boys are growing up and there is their education to consider. There is also Sally's own work in Kianda, and the growing pull it has on her life. She thinks of the house back in Ireland, remote in the Wicklow hills, each room crowded with inherited antiques, and tries to imagine going back there, picking up where she had left off. Africa has changed her. She is not the same person as the woman who kept house in those rooms. A door has been opened inside her and she fears returning to Ireland will mean slamming it shut.

Tiredness pulls at her limbs, dragging her towards sleep. She should go and fetch the children. Five more minutes, and she'll get up and go to the river.

A decision needs to be made – Ken will begin to push her on it soon. The truth is, she had hoped to know by now, had thought that somehow it would grow clear to her what she should do. But her thoughts are so muddy and opaque. And there is another decision that pulls at her conscience – an ultimatum delivered before they left for the Masai Mara, an ultimatum from someone else entirely.

'I have to know,' the man had said. 'I can't hang on here waiting for you for ever.'

The three days away on safari were supposed to be spent in thinking it over. But somehow, whenever she has a quiet moment to herself, the last thing she wants to do is think about it.

Sleep comes to her then, swooping down and taking her; under the burning sun, she lets it all go – the argument this morning, her decaying friendship, the ultimatum delivered, the indecision and dread that she has been dogged by lately – all of it obliterated by the blanketing darkness of sleep.

A scream.

The shrill note of terror.

It comes to her through her dream. Instantly, she opens her eyes, squints under the glare of the sun, feels the tightness of sunburn across her forehead and cheeks.

Another scream. She pulls herself up, head heavy and swimming with sleep. She looks about her, confused, the searing knot of a headache announcing itself at the back of her eyes.

Silence surrounds her. Only the gentle hissing of a breeze through the grass, the click and hum of insects. Birds in the trees. And yet the absence of any other sound strikes a chord of urgency within her. She cannot hear the children now but, remembering the scream, her heart gives a sudden lurch of fright. She knows it wasn't imagined.

She stumbles to her feet, scans the empty field, and turns towards the river. She moves swiftly, the ground hard and unforgiving beneath the soles of her feet, propelled by a fear that has come alive inside her.

The silence seems to deepen, to gather density as the dark clutch of trees looms in front of her.

A voice whispers in her head.

The boys, it says.

And then it starts, the stream of frightening possibilities – a fall, a broken limb, a gashed head, a snake-bite – all of it running through her as she pounds a ragged path through the bush. The silence seems to roar around her now, and a warning voice sounds in her head, a voice that tells her to hold steady, to steel herself for whatever is to come.

Another scream – this time from the opposite bank – stops her in her tracks.

And it comes to Sally then, with a striking clarity, an insight so clear that she knows it to be true.

The river.

A child under water.

Momentarily the fear drains away as she reels from the impact, coldness flushing through her body. It lasts but a second. Then, she starts to run.

PART ONE

Dublin 2013

1. Katie

It starts with the pictures.

A Thursday morning, much like any other in the office, three of us standing around Reilly's desk shooting the breeze while we wait for the deputy editor to arrive. The others are giving me flak on account of my appearance – last night's make-up slipping off my face, my hair still spiky with grips, the collapsed up-do that I haven't yet brushed out. I'm feeling like I'm only half present. The other half of me is biding my time until I can get back to my desk, finish writing my piece, then high-tail it home to my apartment for a shower and a long sleep.

Colm from Legal says: 'Jesus, Katie, the smell of booze off you would knock out a horse.'

Beside him Peter sniggers and I smile sweetly. 'Just doing my job, boys. Sacrificing my sobriety for the scoop, you know how it is.'

And he says, no, he doesn't, but it's all fine, really, despite the pain searing my temples and the weariness rising up my legs, like mercury in a thermometer. I've been here before. And then Reilly arrives, clearly harassed, as if he has something important to tell us. He sits in his chair, throws the pictures onto his desk and says: 'Get a load of these.'

The four of us lean in to peer at them and straight away I feel it start.

Pictures of a dead girl floating in a swimming-pool.

'They just came in,' Reilly tells us. A death at a party in the early hours of the morning. Drink, drugs, a bunch of students, a game that got out of hand.

Peter is spreading them out now so that they cover half of the desk. The water so clear. The girl, only a teenager, her hair fanning out in the water.

'Some sicko at the party took these with his phone,' Reilly explains.

'We can't print them,' Colm says emphatically. 'There's no way.'

'So fucking ghoulish,' Peter whispers, with an air of fascination. His eyes are soaking them up.

'Her parents probably haven't even identified her body yet, and here we are staring at these,' Colm says, disgusted.

'We can't print them, but there's a story nonetheless,' Reilly insists, 'about camera phones and the lack of morality governing their use.'

He's directing his comments at all of us. I'm listening to him, but I can't drag my attention away from the pictures. The creamy whiteness of her skin, the reddish cloud of hair spreading in the water. Clothes sticking to her limbs. Her body half turned as if in a slow farewell. Eyes open and unseeing, her mouth frozen into an O of surprise. I imagine all the water leaking into her, filling her, swelling her lungs to bursting point.

Someone says my name.

But I stare at the pictures, transfixed. Not a bubble of air. Just the stillness of that girl beneath a film of water. I look at her and feel the change come over me, that tender

16

place deep inside me prodded with a stick. My toughness vaporizes in a puff of steam.

'Katie?' Reilly says again, but I don't look at him. I don't look at any of them.

I reach down and grab my bag, urgency consuming me as I stumble away from the death spread on that desk. Without saying a word, I run from them, not stopping until I reach the lift.

I head out onto the grey blandness of Talbot Street, cross the road, without glancing left or right, and go straight into the pub.

'Whiskey,' I say to the barman, fumbling for change in my purse.

'Powers or Jameson?' he asks, his face betraying neither surprise nor judgement. It's not even midday.

'Jameson.'

It's that kind of pub, walls adorned with framed mirrors and dusty trinkets, horse-racing on the telly, a smell of damp clothing in the air. No matter how early in the day, there's always some solo drinker in here, hunched morosely over a pint. I take my drink to a quiet corner and wait for my nerves to calm. Nausea stirs in the pit of my stomach and it has nothing to do with my hangover. That girl in the water. A cold shiver goes straight to the soft spot inside me. I close my eyes and wait for it to pass, urging myself to get a grip.

I can feel it coming over me. The tightening, like a belt, around my neck. Every time something like this happens, I feel the belt tightening by a notch. Like when I heard that Ken Yates had been killed in a car crash all those years ago – a notch. And Sally's funeral last year – another notch. With each little piece of news from the past that trickles through – another notch.

Most of the time, I don't feel it – the vice about my neck. But then something will happen, like those pictures just now, coming out of nowhere, pictures of a girl and a tragedy completely unrelated to me. That's when I feel the tentacles of the past reaching out to grasp me so that I can't breathe, as if I'm the one under water. Only a few weeks ago, in this very pub, I'd felt the belt tighten.

I remember the night vividly. I was sitting with some of the other hacks, a quick pint after work having turned into a session, the telly on in the background. Someone said: 'Here, turn that up, will you?' I swivelled in my seat to see the screen, and there was Luke Yates making an impassioned plea to the general public from the sofa of a TV talk-show. Among a panel of entrepreneurs, economists and other talking heads, discussing the downturn in the economy and how we as a nation needed to encourage growth instead of austerity, Luke seemed to be going off-script as he urged the viewers to stop focusing on their own misery, and start looking further afield to see what real suffering was like.

'This country has always punched above its weight,' he said. 'In terms of international standing, in terms of international aid, we have never turned our backs on those whose need is greater than ours. Generations of Irish people have given to help the poor of other countries – from the Trocaire boxes during Lent, to Live Aid, and well before that. When it comes to putting our hands in our pockets to help our fellow man, this country has not been found wanting. But now the storm clouds have gathered, and the bogeymen are here, the IMF, the Troika, and all we talk about is austerity, budget cuts, mortgage arrears, job losses. Fear has taken hold of Ireland. All around me I see people turning in on themselves. And the worst thing about the fear is what it does to us as a nation. It makes us insular. We no longer look out, we seek to protect ourselves, batten down the hatches and hold on to what we've got. To hell with everyone else. The fear extinguishes our generosity, it suppresses our collective conscience, it makes us hard, mean and grasping and that, to my mind, is not who we are. That is not who the Irish are.'

On and on he went. The host and some of the others on the panel interjected with talk of job losses and creeping poverty, but Luke would not be silenced.

'Jaysus, he's getting a bit worked up,' someone said.

And it was true. I could see the colour rising in his face as he leaned forward in the seat, barely able to contain himself. Where had it come from, his passion, his social conscience? Like those around me, I'd had no inkling he held such strong principles or beliefs. As I watched, I noticed something else. Everyone had fallen silent. The whole pub was watching: pints were left untouched, each drinker's attention arrested by the man on the screen, with his smart suit and his media-friendly features, pounding the table and berating us for our failings, urging us not to allow this depression to change our fundamental values, not to allow our human decency to crack under the strain. The studio audience had fallen silent, too, and I had a sudden flash of memory: Luke as a boy, waist deep in the river, vines hanging down from the trees overhead. I felt it then

19

as I watched him up there on the screen – the tightening about my throat – which was strange, because we hardly knew each other now, not really.

He finished what he was saying and there was a pause. Into the brief silence, a man at the bar raised his pint to the telly. 'Hear, hear.' As the studio audience broke into applause, people around me raised their glasses, nodding, and for the rest of the night, it was all anyone could talk about.

The next day, the airwaves were clogged with news of Luke and his *Late Late Show* performance. The papers were full of it. Unlike some stories that have a brief moment, then fade from the public consciousness, this one seemed to stick. It was no surprise when word came down from the editor-in-chief that someone had to write a profile of Luke for the paper. I just hadn't realized the job would fall to me.

I finish my drink, pick up my bag and go out into the afternoon sun. The rain has cleared and I have the half-formed intention of taking a walk along the canal, knowing that the fresh air and exercise will help clear my thoughts. Instead I sit at a picnic table outside the Barge and email the office, telling them I've gone home, sick. After that I switch off my phone and spend the afternoon sipping Coronas and eavesdropping on the conversation at the next table, until the shadows start to lengthen and the air grows chilly. Reggae drifts down from an open window nearby, with traffic noise rising from the streets beyond.

This time yesterday I was applying make-up and pin-ning up my hair, a red dress laid out on the bed, with an evening bag containing my invitation. A fund-raiser at the

Morrison. Not something I desperately wanted to go to, but Luke would be there, with some others I was supposed to be researching. It was out of duty more than pleasure that I headed into the city.

By the time I arrived the party was in full flow, well-dressed and -groomed bodies pressing against each other, imbibing champagne, waitresses in starched white shirts and aprons passing among them with trays of canapés. All of us crammed together in a room on the top floor of a hotel, the windows giving onto the roofs, spires and cranes that punctuated the city's skyline. Luke and Julia Yates, the glamorous couple, were in the midst of the throng, and I watched them from afar: their practised smiles, the way they worked the room together, in a carefully choreo-graphed routine, their sheen of confidence and privilege. I felt a creeping sense of envy. No, not envy. Rather, it was as though I was confronted with a mirror reflection of myself: a thirty-seven-year-old woman with nothing of permanence in her life. No husband, no children, no home of her own. An apartment she rents – just another in a long list of places she has tried and failed to make into a home. Her job the one constant in her life that keeps her tethered to the earth. There have been times lately when she's felt that sense of displacement nudging into her work. Even in the office, where she feels safe, she is still in danger of slipping off.

I kept my smile bright, and made my way through the crowd, escaping onto the terrace for air, to suck oxygen back into my body and try to calm the shaking in my hands. I sipped my champagne and felt fury curdle within me, fury at myself. Why had I come to this party? How on earth did I think I might fit in here? At this stage of my life I should know by now when to leave well enough alone.

'Penny for your thoughts.'

I turned. He was standing outside the glass doors. He closed them behind him so that the noise of the party was contained, and I watched as he came towards me, grinning. My heart was beating fast as he approached. Neat and unruffled in his black tuxedo, hair smoothed off his handsome face, he had a glass of champagne in each hand and offered one to me. 'Looks like you're running dry.'

The air had done nothing to dispel my unease. Luke smiled but I couldn't make out whether it was genuine or just that he was better than me at covering up his discomfort.

'I was waiting for you to come and say hello,' he added.

'You could have come over to me,' I said, defensive.

'True.' He stood alongside me and looked out across the city.

'I had the feeling we were studiously avoiding one another, Katie.'

'I don't know what you mean.'

And yet I felt the pull between us, and knew he felt it too, just as I knew he was equally aware of the past, which threatened every contact between us. Even the most casual encounter seemed charged with fear, regret or some other elusive emotion.

'I didn't think you'd be here,' he said. 'After our last conversation, I thought you'd keep your distance.'

His tone, initially jokey, had softened. We were standing together as the last of the sunset cast the roofs of Dublin in a soft glow. I saw the glint of gold on his finger, and watched his hand move to cover my own.

He left it where it was and I made no attempt to move mine. Further down the terrace, a group of smokers were sharing a joke. Their laughter reached us as we stood on the balcony, the shadows deepening in the streets below.

'It sounded like it might be fun.'

'You don't look like you're having fun, Katie.'

'But what about you?' I said, slipping my hand out from under his. 'The golden boy. The man of the moment.'

A flash of disappointment crossed his face. Then he laughed and made a swatting gesture, as if to bat my words away. It was hard to fathom. At one moment he was a businessman who'd had a couple of lucky breaks. At the next he had been catapulted into an exalted position – man of the people, champion of the masses, his finger on the public pulse. All it had taken was one high-profile interview on national television. The right words spoken at the right time.

'So where will it all lead?' I asked, watching him over the rim of my champagne flute. 'Leinster House? A seat in government? Or how about the presidency? You know, I can see you and Julia settling into life in the Phoenix Park.'

I was joking, of course: there was too much in Luke's past for him to pull off a successful political career.

'Jesus, Katie, come off it!' He laughed. 'Politics isn't my bag, you know that.'

But there was something in the way he said it that made me look closely at him. Faint shadows under his eyes, tension in the way he held himself. I wondered whether he had bitten off more than he could chew. But before I could ask him about it, he said, 'I heard from Nick.'

His brother.

'Oh?'

'He rang a few days ago, out of the blue.'

Anxiety stirred in the pit of my stomach.

'Is he still in Nairobi?'

'Yes.' He nodded, then said, 'Did you know he's getting married?'

My mouth went dry.

'An American he met over there, apparently. Another hippie drop-out by the sound of it. They've known each other about five minutes.' He drank some champagne. 'The wedding is tomorrow.'

Before I could answer, there was movement behind us. The glass door opened and someone came out. Luke instantly drew away from me.

'Christ, it's hot in there,' the man exclaimed, coming towards us and giving Luke a friendly slap on the shoulder. I recognized him at once – Damien Rourke, a self-made multi-millionaire who still resembled a rumpled grocer. He had taken a white hankie from his pocket and was mopping his brow with it, before turning his attention to me. 'You, is it?' he asked, in an unfriendly way.

I had once penned a not, entirely, flattering piece about him. 'In the flesh.'

'Still writing for that rag, are you?' he asked, with a grin.

'A girl's gotta make a living somehow.'

He snorted, and the conversation moved on. For a while, we talked about politics and the economics of the European crisis. A ribbon of grey cloud hung above the horizon as the sun dipped low. I tried not to glance too much at Luke, conscious of his quiet confidence and the contours of his handsome face. *Nick's getting married.* Nick: dark hair falling over his forehead, that introspective gaze and the shy smile, as if something funny or touching had just occurred to him that he didn't wish to share.

I smiled and nodded along with the conversation, sipped from my glass, all the while feeling numb and telling myself there was no reason why this news of Nick should get to me in this way.

Now, as I sit drinking another Corona, watching the swans gliding along the canal, I think of Nick and try to imagine him waiting at the top of the aisle for some nameless, faceless woman. There had been a bond between us once, Nick and me – I have the scar to prove it. Yet we're strangers now. I have the urge to text him, to tell him that I'm happy for him, though that doesn't come anywhere close to describing the emotion passing through me.

Get a grip, I tell myself sternly. Don't indulge yourself with this maudlin bullshit. I get up from my seat and leave my half-empty beer bottle. Walking briskly back towards the city, I pull my jacket about me, crossing my arms over my chest, as if a cold wind is blowing, even though it's still warm and, although night has fallen, there's barely the whisper of a breeze coming off the canal.

I climb into bed and fall into a sleep that feels like oblivion.

When I wake to the sound of someone banging on my apartment's front door, it feels like the middle of the night. I get up and go to open it, my head still swimming with fatigue. Reilly's familiar bulk stands under the halo of light cast by the bare bulb above his head.

'Reilly? What is it? What are you doing here?'

'I tried calling but your phone is switched off.'

'It's the middle of the night, for Chrissakes!'

'It's eight a.m., Katie,' he says, a wrinkle of concern in his voice. 'Are you okay? I can't say you look it.'

'I'm fine,' I reply, embarrassed now, pulling my robe tight around me.

'You didn't come back to the office yesterday.'

'I was sick.'

I turn away and let him follow me into the flat, hear him closing the door, before he joins me in the kitchen. I flick on the coffee machine, then rest my head on the counter, feeling the ache that stretches from my temples to the small of my back.

I can feel him watching me, so I straighten and busy myself with making coffee because, even though I like him, it feels strange to have Reilly in my kitchen. He's unlike most of the men who have witnessed me making morning coffee in my bathrobe. Thick hair the colour of oatmeal, a reddish tinge to his beard, which fails to hide the deep lines on either side of his mouth, or the amusement that animates his face. Black leather jacket, grey shirt, faded blue jeans – the hack's uniform: all of it out of place on him, somehow. I like to imagine that when Reilly goes home, he dons a smoking jacket and velvet slippers.

He accepts a mug of coffee, then casts his eyes around my apartment. It's all pitiful enough – two rooms painted in pastel shades, a galley kitchen and a bathroom the size of a cupboard, books stacked precariously against the wall and house-plants at different stages of decay. This has been home to me for the past four months, two rooms in a three-storey Edwardian red-brick villa, its façade tired and unloved, in the heart of Dublin.

'When did you start doing house-calls, Reilly?'

'You're my first patient.'

'Lucky me.'

'I was worried, Katie. The way you left yesterday –'

'I was sick . . .'

He fixes me with a look that reminds me suddenly and painfully of my father.

'Listen, Katie,' he says, his voice lowered. 'What happened yesterday . . . We were all appalled, repulsed by the thought of some sicko trying to squeeze a few quid from us for pictures of a corpse. But you . . . you were white as a sheet. And while the rest of us were discussing it, you bolted from the room, hardly stopping to pick up your bag. Eddie at the door said he'd never seen anyone take off out of there and across into Mother Kelly's as fast.' He pauses. 'But, they were just pictures, Katie. And not the worst you've seen. You're a tough cookie. Why did they upset you so much?'

I couldn't tell him. It would mean peeling away all the layers until we got to the one dark place I didn't ever want to shine a light on. 'Listen, Reilly,' I say. 'I appreciate your concern, really I do. But I'm fine. Honestly.'

He looks at me in that considering way of his. 'There's something else,' he says. 'Luke Yates.'

The way he says it makes the words dry up inside me. I see the hesitation on his face and it sends a jolt of alarm right through me.

'What?' I ask.

'You haven't heard.' A statement, not a question.

'Tell me.' My heart is pounding.

'I'm sorry to do this, Katie,' he says softly, 'but Luke Yates is dead.'

2. Nick

The cufflinks, slightly tarnished, sit on a bed of cushioned black velvet in a matching black box. They're old, but the box is new and this makes me think of Julia. My guess is that it was she who packed them so carefully for their journey, even though the gift is supposedly from Luke. Had it been up to him, I'm sure my brother would have slipped them into an envelope, sealed and addressed it, then hoped for the best. I hold them up to the light, my hand shaking a little. I see my father's initials engraved in an elegant script on the flat gold discs and remember an evening on the veranda at the house in Lavington: Dad – just home from work – sitting with Mum, loosening his tie and taking off his cufflinks, the clinking sound they make against the hard surface of the table as the screen-door opens and Jamil brings the drinks.

The memory slips away, blotted out by the sounds from the streets. Outside, the city is raucous. Car horns blare. I can hear the whine of a scooter, and the crash of something heavy spilling onto the ground. Nairobi is at full throttle, vibrating with life and urgency. But in this room, just for a moment, the world seems to be holding its breath.

The package arrived yesterday, a padded envelope containing the box and a note:

Wear these on your big day, Nico. And be happy. Your brother, Luke.

Today is my wedding day.

The door opens. It's Murphy. He brings with him a gust of energy.

'Well, now,' he says, clapping his large hands together and rubbing them briskly. 'How are we set?'

'Good,' I say, trying to steady myself.

'Here, let me do that.' Before I can protest, he takes the box from my hands. 'Show me your cuffs.'

He fixes the cufflinks in place, his fingers firm yet gentle despite their size, his brow gathering in a frown of concentration. I can't help thinking that it should be my father here, steadying me. But Dad is long dead.

'Not nervous, are you?' Murphy glances at me with his small, shrewd eyes.

'No,' I say, though I've felt uneasy since I read Luke's note.

'Good. You've nothing to be nervous about. You have your whole life ahead of you.'

He clasps my shoulder, holds it for a moment. I can sense his restless energy. He takes my jacket from the chair-back and holds it up for me to slide into.

'We're in plenty of time, so there's no panic,' he says.

Beyond the window, Nairobi's skyline is swathed in mild sunlight. I nod.

'The weather is good,' Murphy says. He means well. And while I'm ready for this day, something is nipping at me.

Murphy has known me long enough to realize when

something's up, but before he can say anything, we hear whistling from the hall. It's Karl. He flings open the door. 'Hello! Hello!' In his hand, the box that contains the rings.

'You remembered them,' I say drily.

He grins and shakes the box next to his ear. 'Would I forget? Come on.' He closes the door behind him. Karl is small, slight and fair. His hair is cropped close to the skull. Already the energy in the room has changed. It fizzes with his presence. This morning, he is wearing a blue suit that fits neatly, a skinny black tie, and Vans on his feet. His pork-pie hat sits far back on his head. He's clearly made an effort – he looks like he's even shaved. No sooner has he closed the door than he's fishing for smokes in his pocket. As he pops one between his lips, Murphy comes forward to protest.

'None of that now,' he chides. 'Can't have the groom turning up stinking of smoke.'

Karl pretends to be offended, but he does as he's told, not questioning the priest's authority, not cowed by it either.

'Hey, Father Murphy,' he says, his eyes shooting to Murphy's hairline. 'I see you've been to my barber.'

Murphy laughs. He had until recently sported a head of greying but still thick unruly hair that he never seemed able to keep neat. It was a shock to see him with stubble. It drew attention to his cheekbones, giving him a puritanical air.

'Well, now,' Murphy says. 'Your parents would be very proud of you today, Nick, making this commitment. I know it's difficult for you not to have them here.'

My phone rings. Murphy seems a little embarrassed at his show of emotion. He reaches for the phone on the table, but instead of handing it to me, he answers it.

'Murphy here,' he says jovially. 'Ah, hello.'

I look at him expectantly, waiting for him to hand me the phone. 'Yes, he's here . . .'

He glances in my direction and turns, his shoulders hunched. Something in his demeanour suggests he is put out by whatever he is hearing. He grunts. I wait for him to turn, but instead he raises a finger and leaves the room.

'What's that all about?' I say to Karl.

He shrugs. 'Wedding arrangements, no doubt. He doesn't want you worrying about anything. You know Murphy, he'd rather shoulder the whole mountain.'

'Show me the rings,' I say, to dispel the unease left in Murphy's wake.

Taking them from the box, I weigh them in my hand. 'Heavier than I remembered.'

'They'll weigh you down,' Karl jokes. 'Come on, let's have a smoke while Murphy's not here.' He opens the window, lights a cigarette and passes it to me. 'We'll spray you with air freshener or something.'

Side by side, we lean against the windowsill, sharing the cigarette like a couple of truant schoolboys.

'Keep the speech short, Nick, right? I mean, as best man, I'd like to be able to say my piece, and I know what you're like, hogging all the air-time. People don't like speeches that ramble.'

I drag on the cigarette and smile. The truth is I'm the quiet one. Even as a child, I hung back, preferring others to do the talking for me. There was always Luke who had plenty to say – enough for both of us. When I was eight I didn't speak for a whole year. It was like something had stuck inside me. Post-traumatic stress disorder, I suppose you'd call it. Back then, we didn't call it anything. My parents, for reasons of their own, chose not to have it closely investigated. They preferred to wait it out. I drew a lot of pictures and listened to a good deal of music. I spent hours at the piano. It took Luke to bring me back to the world of the speaking. 'It's my birthday,' he said, one morning, standing in the doorway to my bedroom.

'Happy birthday,' I said hoarsely, forgetting myself, the words making a croaking sound in my throat. Luke ran to tell Mum and Dad I had spoken and that was the end of my self-imposed silence.

Now I prefer to let my music do the talking for me. And even though I'm not one for words, when I'm at the piano and Karl has his sax, what passes between us is the most soulful discussion I can imagine.

When Murphy gets back, he says nothing about the call, but seems perturbed. He hands me the phone.

'Who was it?'

'Nothing to worry about right now,' Murphy says, straining to sound upbeat. He waves his hand about. 'Boys, boys, boys. Really! Do you have to smoke?'

'Nothing to worry about?' I ask.

'I'll tell you later,' he says, checking his watch. 'Right, put that out, Karl. Time to go.'

Karl makes some comment about the condemned man, gives me a friendly thump on the back and ducks out after Murphy.

Before I follow them, I glance at my phone to see who has called, but under 'incoming calls', nothing is listed.

A few nights ago, I'd called my brother. When he answered, I could hear the noise of a party in the background. Almost immediately, I felt like hanging up.

'There's something I wanted to tell you,' I said, hearing him step away from the clamour. 'Luke, I'm getting married.'

There was a pause. Luke coughed. 'That's great news, Nick. Congratulations!' Even though he tried to sound happy for me, he couldn't hide his surprise. 'When's the big day?'

'Next week . . .'

'Next week? Well, now,' he said. I had taken him off guard. 'And the lucky girl?'

'Her name's Lauren.'

I gave him some details, although it was difficult because she was lying next to me, listening to every word. I thought that by telling him about her I would break the spell. There was a nagging fear that Luke might say something that would shed a drop of poison into the one thing I held dear. That he might have balked at my marrying her after we'd been together such a short time – that he might even caution me against it. When Lauren and I are together, the love between us seems ancient and solid, but while I was talking to Luke, it felt fragile and bare.

'It would be nice to meet her some day,' Luke said. He sounded agitated. 'And the wedding – it's in Nairobi, I take it?'

'Yes,' I said.

'You know I won't make it. Not at such short notice.' The noise of voices and music grew in the background. He must have been making his way back closer to where the party was, keeping an eye on it.

'It sounds like you're celebrating yourself,' I said.

'A little shindig here. Nothing to top a wedding.'

My brother could be the life and soul of the party, and there had been many times when I'd heard his school pals laugh at his jokes when they came back to our house after school. Their playful banter was not for me, though – as the younger brother I was excluded, watching from a distance or overhearing what he shared with an inner circle that had not included me since we'd left Nairobi.

'I'm sorry,' I said. 'We didn't decide to get married until a few days ago. It's kind of a spontaneous thing.'

Whatever script I had planned was faltering. My words petered out.

'Spontaneous,' Luke repeated. I imagined him shaking his head.

'No invitations, nothing like that,' I said. It wasn't supposed to be a party. It was just me and Lauren, and a couple of friends, simple and low-key. None of Lauren's family was coming over either. She'd made the call to them and received the kind of stunned response she'd expected. But we'd kept our promise to one another: create as little fuss as possible. I wanted our marriage to be an intimate affair, not like Luke and Julia's society wedding, which had made the Sunday supplements and glossy magazines, but once Karl had got wind of our plans, he had told others. Before we knew it, a party had been planned, with a venue, a band and a guest list. I told myself that Luke wouldn't have come anyway, but in the brief pause in our conversation, I imagined what he would have said of it afterwards if he had.

'It's the principle of the thing,' I could hear him saying to Julia.

Why hadn't I sent him an invitation? Because his presence would stir up too much? Or because he might have felt obliged to come even though he might not have wanted to return to Nairobi?

The truth is, I didn't want him intruding into my world, into a reality I had made for myself, into something that had nothing to do with him.

'I never saw you as the marrying type, Nick, but I do hope you and your bride-to-be have a lovely day,' he said, and sounded like he meant it, which only made things worse. I wondered what he meant by 'not the marrying type'.

'I'll be thinking of you. It's . . .' He hesitated.

'What?'

'Nothing. I want the best for you, Nick. I always have.'

I felt a lump in my throat. I wanted to say 'thank you', to say 'sorry', but what I said was 'Murphy will do the honours.'

'Murphy? Your wedding, Mum's funeral . . . What would we do without him?'

The sarcasm was there, but I chose to ignore it. Luke slurred his next words: 'You left so quickly after the funeral . . .'

'You know me, Luke. Not one for goodbyes.'

'I suppose not,' he said.

The party was louder now as he moved closer to it, and

further, it seemed, from me. I could hardly make out what he said next: 'I suppose there's never a right time to say goodbye.'

He thanked me for calling, offered his congratulations again, and said something about meeting up in the not-too-distant future, but it was all a blur, words running into each other as a seam of panic threatened to open inside me. I mumbled goodbye, put the phone down on the bed-side table and turned to Lauren. She pulled me to her, but said nothing.

Club Iguana looks bereft in daylight, decrepit and forlorn. It is a small space, already filling with an expectant mur-mur: friends of Lauren's from the university, friends of mine from the music scene. There is the clinking of bottles and glasses. A barbecue begins to smoke. Smiling faces greet us. Murphy leads me into the growing mêlée where people clap me on the back and embrace me. Despite my awkwardness, I'm moved by how happy people are for us.

I've not been there long before there's the honk of a car-horn followed by a resounding cheer. Karl takes my arm. 'She's here,' he says, pulling me outside just in time to see my bride arriving on the back of a pick-up truck with lilies in her hands.

There's a tremor in the smile, a lowering of the eyes: a mix of shyness and nerves that's not like her at all. For a moment, I'm taken back to that night in this club, sitting at a piano, when I first saw her, standing at the entrance. Above the din, through the miasma of smoke, I was so aware of her, trying hard to concentrate on the music while she wove her way through the tables until she found a seat. My eyes sought her out as if she were drawing me to her through the shadows. I couldn't wait to finish the set, pull up a chair next to her and begin a conversation. When I closed the lid of the piano and stepped away, when I went up to her – surprising even myself – a beer in each hand, and offered one to her, she accepted it as if our conversation had started long ago. She smiled at me, nervously, unsure. We began to talk, and it felt to me as if we were picking up where we had left off, even though we had never met. That was how easily we slipped into it, how natural it seemed.

I experienced a strange, easy comfort in Lauren's company. I didn't feel I had to try to impress her. We'd both travelled around the world, estranged from the rest of our families. I guess we shared the unanchored quality that brings drifters like us together.

When I held her in my arms that first night, it was as if meeting her was more like a slow remembering that, deep in my bones, I knew her well, that I had known her all along.

She was scared by how rapidly we were falling for each other. I was too. But she didn't pry or push or question me. Lauren's own vulnerability meant I knew somehow that she wouldn't try to prise me open, as others had wanted to, until I surrendered to her the things I kept to myself.

'Are you ready?' I say to her now.

'Ready,' she says nervously.

There is no altar. Instead, Murphy stands by the piano, waiting for us. He clutches an old prayer book in his trembling hands. After some prayers, come our vows.

I say mine, then look at Lauren.

Murphy asks: 'Do you take Nicholas to be your lawful wedded husband?'

The words catch in her throat. Someone makes a joke, something like 'no regrets now' and she says, 'I do,' and I feel sudden relief.

We eventually sign the register and there is a cheer. Karl picks up his saxophone: the room fills with the caramel tones of 'These Foolish Things'.

'Okay?' I ask Lauren.

'Okay,' she answers, laughing. She smiles in happy disbelief. I take her in my arms and kiss her. I want to tell her I can't believe it either, but that it feels so right.

Across a stretch of grass, a few kids are riding an ostrich. We have drifted outside where the sun has risen higher in the sky. I sip a beer and feel a lightness come over me. The rest of the band members have taken out their instruments: they cluster around Karl – Bill on double bass, Philly on trumpet, Pierre on the drums. Another friend, Sam, is filling in for me at the piano. 'Can't have you working on your wedding day,' Karl had said to me, with a broad smile that, for an instant, resembled my brother's.

And even though I haven't invited him, I miss him. In fact, ever since the summer when we left Kenya, I've missed him. Even if, ever since, Luke and I have felt awkward around each other. As if, after everything that had happened, we simply don't know how to act in each other's company. There's no malice in our estrangement, just a deadening in the closeness we once had.

So, today my happiness is tinged with regret – the pure note of my wedding day slightly off-key. But I relax into the evening as best I can and watch my wife, who has not stopped dancing, her hair and dress swirling about her as she gives herself to the night.

'When will it be my turn?' I shout over to her, my inhibitions loosened by beer and love and all this goodwill.

She blows me a kiss.

I want to thank Murphy for doing the honours, but can't see him anywhere. A cake appears and there are cheers. Someone has placed a single candle on it. Karl thrusts the knife into my hand and beckons Lauren over. She scoops up a mound of icing and smears it over my cheek. Then she kisses me passionately.

I'm already looking forward to our honeymoon on Île Sainte-Marie.

'What are you thinking?' she asks me.

'I'm hoping the bike is up to the drive to Mozambique.'

'As little luggage as possible,' Lauren reminds me.

I pull her to me, whispering: 'When can we get out of here?'

'Soon,' she says, and I feel the erotic charge between us again – something so compulsive it feels out of our control, like an improvised jam gone wild.

We dance then to the jittery rhythms of the Benga band, which has come on now. Everyone is watching, dancing alongside us. I feel their gaze on me and soon enough I exit the dance-floor, leaving Lauren to it. I walk to the bar where Karl and Murphy are talking. Karl is telling some story, but the older man seems despondent, disinterested, nursing a glass of wine, acting less like a priest and more like a jilted blind-date.

'Hey, my main man!' Karl says, wrapping me in his

warm, solid embrace. 'A drink for the groom!' he shouts to the barman.

Three whiskeys are lined up in front of us. We drink deeply, and return our glasses to the counter.

Murphy sighs. 'I'm sorry,' he says hoarsely. 'I'm very tired. I'll go to bed now. We can talk in the morning. And congratulations to you, Nick, and to your lovely wife.'

'Thanks, Jim. And for the ceremony,' I say, then remember something. 'But before you go, you never said what that phone call was about.'

Karl has moved away, his attention hooked by the sway of a young woman's hips. I watch as Murphy briefly closes his eyes, a small gesture that indicates the depth of his fatigue.

'Leave it until tomorrow, hmm?' He scratches his forehead, glancing about the room as if for the nearest exit.

'Jim,' I say softly, taking his arm.

He turns to me. I see at once the seriousness of it. All day, it's been at the back of my mind, but now it comes to it, when I see the worry on his lined face, the fear in his eyes, I find myself drawing back.

'It's Luke,' he says.

'What about him?'

'It was Julia who called earlier. She was wondering if you'd heard from him, spoken to him . . .'

I think of the cufflinks, his note, *be happy* . . . 'I don't understand.'

He takes a handkerchief from his pocket, and dabs his brow. 'Nick. It's your wedding night.'

'To hell with that, Jim. Just tell me what's going on.'

He tells me about a party in Dublin, about Julia going to

bed alone, about how the next day she discovers Luke has disappeared, leaving his phone, his wallet and keys behind. It's only when he tells me about Luke's office, about the broken glass and the blood on the carpet that a germ of fear rises in me.

'Is he dead?' I ask, the word like a cold, hard stone in my mouth.

'I pray to God he's all right,' he says simply, but his answer angers me.

'You should have told me, Jim, straight after you got the call –'

'Nick, I was trying to protect you.'

The light in the bar is too bright. Its harshness makes Murphy appear older than he is. I ask him again what he knows.

'I don't know,' he says – again and again.

With the music blaring and the whole stretch of the day behind him, Murphy appears tired to the bone. 'Please, I don't want you to worry yourself over this,' he says, his hand on my shoulder. 'Not tonight. Let's not jump to any hasty conclusions. It may all be easily explained.'

It's been a long day. I let him go. For a moment, I sit by myself, absorbing the shock of what I've learned. Night is drawing on. Somewhere far from here, my brother is lost and alone. The thought brings with it a great roll of sadness and regret. Something else too: the painful tug of the past.

'There you are,' Lauren says, taking my hand, her voice inflected with breezy American optimism. 'Come on,' she urges, dragging me into the cooling air outside.

Twilight. The musicians are teetering on the brink of

collapse. If they were a train, they would have slipped the tracks. The lights from houses and hotels shine in a blur of light. Without warning, a stream of gold and green fireworks lights the sky, bringing the guests outside. Many are cheering. Lauren is so beautiful that I want to freeze this memory of her in my mind and hold onto it for ever.

Out of the corner of my eye, I see Murphy slipping away. Only he and I know, for now. He turns, catches my eye and mouths, 'Sorry.'

3. Katie

'Luke Yates is dead,' Reilly says.

For a moment it all falls away – Reilly, my surroundings, even the throb in my head seems to still itself for that instant.

Then Reilly speaks again: 'At least, that's the rumour.'

'What?'

'His wife came home yesterday lunchtime and found the house had been broken into, blood everywhere, no sign of her husband. She hasn't seen him since the night before.'

'Missing? But not dead?'

'Well, there's no body yet but –'

'Jesus, Reilly! That's not the same thing at all!'

A wave of nausea comes over me, and I put a hand to the counter to steady myself. I feel light-headed, over-whelmed.

Reilly grasps my shoulders and steers me towards an armchair. 'I'm sorry, Katie. That was insensitive of me. I had no idea you'd take it this way. I didn't think you two were close.'

'We're not,' I say quickly, trying to cover up the collapse within me. 'We knew each other as kids. My folks and his were friends. I knew his brother in college too.'

Uncomfortable beneath his stare, I get to my feet and mumble something about getting dressed.

'I'll wait for you,' Reilly says.

'There's no need –'

'You'll need a lift out to Dalkey, and you're in no fit state to drive.'

'Dalkey?'

He frowns a little. 'This is a story, Katie. And you know the guy. You were at that party too, right?'

'Yes.'

'So you need to get out there and find out what happened.'

Leaving Reilly to survey my book collection, I stand in the shower and allow myself to cry a little under the ferocity of the hot jets. Afterwards, I put on jeans and a sweatshirt, grab my bag, and soon we're driving towards a village on the south-east coast of Dublin, whose humble fishing roots have been subsumed by the mega-wealth of the Celtic Tiger.

Reilly's car – an old Merc – reeks of coconut. My stomach, still tender from the excesses of the last two nights, rebels against it. I sit up, tug down the dangling air freshener and shove it into the glove compartment. Reilly observes this without protest. It is only when I take my cigarettes from my handbag that he holds up his hand. 'Sorry, Katie. Not in here.'

'What's this?'

'I quit.'

My eyes widen. 'You quit?'

'Three months ago,' he says, a grin of pride brightening his tired features.

'Why?'

'To get healthy, of course.'

I regard him now, taking him in properly for the first time in months, and notice a new leanness. He is slender and fit. The meatiness of his hands and in the bearded line of his jaw remain, but he looks neater somehow. I say, in a speculative manner: 'You've lost weight.'

He nods, keeping his eyes on the road, and bites down on an embarrassed smile. 'Stop eyeballing me, Katie. It's unnerving.'

'Is it just the smokes, or have you gone the whole hog?'

'Cigarettes, alcohol and red meat.'

'Don't tell me – you've also found God?'

He widens his open shirt-collar and flicks out the crucifix on a chain. Grinning, he says: 'Jesus loves me, Katie.'

Reilly and I go way back. He gave me my first job at the paper, and has always been supportive, particularly since he became deputy editor. We know each other well but only on a certain level. There is something deeply private about Reilly. Sure, he goes for drinks after work and is always convivial and warm, yet I've no idea whether he has a partner or children tucked away somewhere, or whether he prefers to live in grand isolation. Rumours have flown around the office about him over the years, but somehow nothing has stuck, and I can't help but think he enjoys the enigma that surrounds him.

I feel light-headed, and try to ground myself while Reilly talks.

'I met him once,' he says now, 'Luke Yates. Some years back, before he became the great man.'

'What did you think of him?'

He squints out at the glittering sea as we drive along the coast road. 'He struck me as someone who had a great facility for sounding sincere.'

46

'You don't think he is?'

He spreads his hands on the steering-wheel and smiles. 'Who knows, Katie, what's real and what's fake? What about the brother? What's he like?'

'He's . . . well, he's just different,' I say quickly, astonished to find myself flustered and hot.

Reilly spots my discomfort, and asks, with interest: 'Oh? Is there history there?'

'God, no! We were like brother and sister, me and Nick, back when we were kids. And then in college we hung around in the same group for a while . . .' I hear my voice, the uncertainty in it, and cut myself off. 'Anyway, that was about a million years ago now.'

'You're not that old, sweetheart,' he says, and I can't help but smile. 'So where is he? The brother?'

'Africa,' I say, and all at once I'm back sitting in a field of prickly grass, dizzy from the sun, and Nick is running towards me, helter-skelter across the lawn, water sploshing in the cup as he skids to a halt and falls to his knees beside me, offering the cup to me, like some kind of prize, dirt beneath his fingernails, hair falling into his eyes, the shy smile that he can never seem to erase – it's even there while he sleeps – and I'm hearing his voice, low-pitched and gravelly for an eight-year-old, saying, 'Here, Kay', his name for me. No one else has called me that since.

'Do you think he's dead, Reilly?'

'Perhaps.'

'Murder?'

He shrugs. 'There was a rumour about him some years back, that he smashed up a hotel room.'

'I never heard it.'

'It was hushed up.'

'So what happened?'

'Nothing, really. The guy got drunk, went a bit berserk and totted up a massive bill.'

'Was anyone else involved?'

'Nope.'

'You're saying he has a self-destructive streak?'

'What do I know, Katie? Often these things amount to nothing. They were at a party, right? So maybe the wife went to bed and he fell over and smashed a glass coffee-table or what-not, gave himself a nasty gash in the process but was so drunk he barely felt it, then decided in the wisdom of his inebriation that he'd be best off taking himself elsewhere before herself woke up and saw the mess. He could at this very moment be happily bleeding out on the floor of some whorehouse in the city.'

'Perhaps,' I say flatly, staring out the window.

It's been a while since I've been out in this neck of the woods, and the place feels kind of sleepy this morning as the car noses around sharp bends through narrow streets. A misty drizzle is coming in off the bay although there is a little heat still in the air, making it muggy and close. I take in the tall walls and heavy gates with intercoms that line both sides of the road, the houses tucked away from prying eyes. The place seems so snug and safe, that it seems hard to imagine any kind of violence happening behind the closed doors – no domestic nightmares, no fists raised, no black dogs rubbing against walls done in expensive paint.

Reilly pulls up outside the house where a small scrum has formed. I can pick out at least three hacks I recognize.

Magnolias in full bloom flank the gate, and behind it, a short distance from the road, sits a glass and concrete monstrosity. Massive windows, black frames around reflective glass, white walls dazzling, despite the grey weather.

'No sign of the weeping widow then,' Reilly says, peering out through the windscreen.

For a moment, we stare up at the mansion, and for the first time since this started, I think about the scene inside that house: the plush carpet splattered with blood, the broken glass, the terror . . .

'You all set?'

I nod, but the truth is I feel like shit. Coffee has made my stomach churn and my eyes are dry from lack of sleep. The thought of violence has left me feeling queasy.

'Thanks for the lift, Reilly,' I say, leaning across to plant a kiss on his bristly cheek before collecting myself into some semblance of professionalism and sliding out of the seat.

I join the others at the gate, where a burly guy with a neck like a rhino's is holding up his hands and imploring those gathered there to disband and give Mrs Yates some privacy. He has broad shoulders and a cool-eyed, strong-jawed appearance. Dealing with all the pestering queries looks like a penance to him. The questions are all the same: *Has Luke Yates been found yet? What's the story with his missus? Is it true the place is awash with blood?* (This from the tabloid hack, always on the sniff for gore.) After a while, he stops answering, closes the gate behind him and withdraws to the house. The rain gets heavier, and some of the rubberneckers peel away, the hacks too. I'm considering whether it's worth my while to knock on the doors of

49

the neighbouring fortresses in search of anything worth printing, but the high walls bristling with security cameras tell me to save my shoe leather.

Reilly has gone, so the logical thing is to catch a train back into the city, yet I feel the desire to linger for a while. I walk through the rain to the strip of beach that runs along the backs of the houses. I have no hood, no umbrella, but the rain is not heavy and the air is warm, and the quiet hush of the sea calms me, settling my troubled mind.

The weather was much like this the last time I saw Nick, a year ago. A grey day in Dublin, a crowd of mourners spilling out of a church, flecks of rain falling. Luke and Julia were standing on the church steps to greet us as if it was their wedding we'd just attended, not Sally's funeral. And there was Nick, some way off, standing with his hands in his pockets next to the hearse, listening to the conversation of an older man I didn't recognize. There was something so forlorn about him, but when I stepped towards him and he raised his head, he looked at me as if I was someone he didn't know who had just walked in on something private. I stopped, and something about his expression changed, a warning sharpening his stare that seemed to say, *Not now, not here, with all these people around us.* So I turned away, feeling let down and somehow ashamed, which was stupid, I know, given the circumstances – his adored mother was lying dead in the hearse, after all. 'You'll come to the grave?' Luke had said, clasping my hand in both of his. 'And back to the house afterwards?' But after the look Nick had given me, I couldn't. Too cowardly to face him.

The wind whips at my hair and I feel the rain on my

face. My legs ache as I trudge through the sand and I resolve to walk past the last house, then turn back, but before I reach that point I see her.

A small figure perched on a rock, watching me. Grey jeans and flip-flops, the hood of her parka pulled over her head, but I recognize her and, for just an instant, I hesitate before approaching her. The wind draws a thin line of cigarette smoke from her mouth, her eyes fixed on me as I get close.

'The vultures circle,' she says, her voice glacial.

'Julia.'

'Come to pick over the spoils, have we?'

I stop a couple of metres from her and choose my words carefully. 'I came because I was concerned, and because I care about Luke.'

'Do you indeed?' Her voice sharp with sarcasm.

'Okay. So we're not exactly close, but there was a time when we were children, our families . . .' Something about the way she is watching me makes my words dry up.

Her eyes narrow as she puts her cigarette to her lips and inhales. 'You and those boys.' Her voice is dead flat but I feel the spike of an accusation.

Her eyes flicker over me, cool and assessing, and I can't help feeling self-conscious. Even now in the grip of her anguish, Julia Yates remains the same well-groomed, sophisticated woman she was two nights ago in the Morrison. Her feet are partially buried in the pale sand, toenails peeking out – a vibrant red to match her fingertips – and strands of ash-blonde hair escape from beneath her hood. But there is a tightness about her face now, her mouth pinched into a grim line, and her face looks raw.

Her glittering charm has taken flight, leaving a cool creature with narrowed eyes laden with suspicion.

'When I saw you just now coming up the beach, I felt a sudden flash of disappointment,' she tells me. 'You see, I thought perhaps Luke was with you.'

Her eyes are unblinking. 'I saw the two of you together. At the Morrison. I saw you on the terrace, Katie Walsh, taking the night air, and holding hands with my husband.'

A beat. My mouth is dry. The statement sits heavily between us. She brings the cigarette to her lips again, waits.

I want to tell her that it wasn't what she thinks it was – but how can I explain it? How can I describe how it feels to be bound to another person by something so awful that you have to put distance between you? Still, I'm drawn to him because he is the one person who knows . . .

'Look, Julia. Whatever you saw, there was nothing going on between us. It was nostalgia, that's all. A childhood affection . . .'

She frowns and shakes her head, dismissing what I said. 'Oh, I don't care. Really. Right now, I couldn't give a damn. Ridiculous, isn't it?' she says, giving a burst of dry laughter. 'I'm at the stage now where I would almost be happy to hear that he was off with some other woman, rather than what I'm imagining.'

'What do the guards think?' I ask.

'A couple of them came from Forensics to take samples – fingerprints, carpet fibres.' She enunciates each word clearly with almost a trace of bitterness, and beneath her cool veneer I'm surprised to glimpse a bubbling fury. 'As for the detectives, they're remaining tight-lipped. Giving me the usual spiel – they're following a couple of lines of enquiry, keeping an open mind, blah, blah, blah. They come here with their questions – just like you, I suppose – and draw their own conclusions. Only, they have the decency to call to the front of the house,' she adds pointedly. 'They don't come prowling around the back.'

'I didn't expect to find you here, Julia. I wanted to get some fresh air before heading back to the office.'

'How lucky to stumble across me, then.' She smiles up at me but it's an angry grimace that fades quickly. Dropping her head, she looks about her at the rocks among which she is sitting and, her voice quieter now, somewhat subdued, she says: 'This is where I come for a sneaky cigarette.'

Her softened tone encourages me a little, so I move closer and perch on a rock near her.

'We quit smoking, Luke and I. It was our New Year's resolution.' Glancing down at the pack of Marlboro Lights in her hand, she lets out a hollow laugh. 'He's better at it than I am. More disciplined. So when I want to smoke, I come down here.'

'He doesn't know you haven't quit?'

Her eyes flash. 'I can have my secrets too.'

Something about the way she says it, guarded yet provocative, pushes me to ask: 'And Luke? Did he have secrets?'

She frowns again and turns towards the sea, its grey-green flatness, so still and benign this morning. 'I suppose. Luke is quite protective of me. He likes to shield me from bad news. We have an old-fashioned marriage, in that sense. Any problems he has, he likes to deal with them himself.'

'Were there problems?'

She shrugs, biting her lip. 'There are debts. Business debts I'm not supposed to know about.'

'And are the sums significant?'

'I don't know. I suppose they must be. Enough to keep Luke awake at night. And then there's this thing with the media, the publicity, Luke getting political . . . that night on *The Late Late Show* . . . I thought it was a mistake.'

'Why?'

'It's so nasty. Ruthless. And once you step into that arena, they seek out every flaw, every misdemeanour.'

Her eyes meet mine and the cool facade slips a little. I take out my own cigarettes and offer her one, then light up myself.

'Julia, what happened that night, after the party?' I ask tentatively.

She looks as if she's weighing up the wisdom of speaking to me, but I can feel it in her: the temptation to talk. She takes a deep breath, briefly closes her eyes, then begins, her voice low and steady, and I get the feeling she has gone through this countless times in her head over the past forty-eight hours.

'We left the party around one and came straight home. We were both a little drunk and Luke seemed distracted. Moody. But I didn't think too much of it. He can be like that sometimes, particularly after social events. Sort of deflated, you know? I've learned that it's best to leave him alone when he's like that. He said he needed to make a phone call so I went upstairs to bed. I took a sleeping pill and was out cold until almost nine a.m. When I woke, he wasn't beside me and I could see he hadn't slept there.'

'Were you concerned?'

'No. It's not unusual. When he gets like that, he kind of goes in on himself, needs to be alone. I assumed he'd slept in the spare bedroom or fallen asleep in his study.'

'Did you check on him?'

'No. I figured he needed to sleep it off. So I went for my run. It was only when I got home that I realized something was wrong.'

'How so?'

'The spare bedroom was empty. His car was still there, but I thought he might have taken the train into the office. I went to ring him, but his phone was on the kitchen counter. That was when I went into the study.'

She pauses, biting her lip. Her eyes are fixed on some point in the middle distance and I try to imagine the horror of what she's seeing in her mind's eye. When she speaks again, there's a ripple of distress in her words.

'He loves that room, all the old furniture in it. I call it his man-cave. He had all these photographs framed some years ago and hung them on the wall behind his desk. And there's a cabinet where he keeps various things – awards, trophies, framed certificates and newspaper cuttings, stuff relating to his work, objects of pride. When I stepped into that room I saw that the cabinet was open, the entire contents strewn on the floor. And every single picture on the wall was smashed to pieces.'

I watch her sucking in her breath, composing herself, and I see for the first time how upset she is.

'There was such anger in that room. Such violence. Whoever had done it must have been deranged with fury. I saw all that glass, those broken frames and lumps of granite, and I felt afraid. And that was before I noticed the blood.'

She closes her eyes, squeezing them shut as if trying to block out the image. When she opens them again, she doesn't look at me. 'Luke is . . . well, he's more fragile than you'd think. He has a vulnerable side.'

I think of Reilly's story about the hotel room, the destruction. 'Could he have done it himself?'

'He suffers from depression,' she tells me in a flat voice. 'Did you know that?'

'I had no idea.'

'He hides it well,' Julia says. 'And it's intermittent. And never this bad. Never enough to suggest . . .' she falters, but she's said enough for me to understand.

'Is it possible he did this?'

Her eyes meet mine. 'No,' she says.

'Is he happy?' I ask her then.

Briefly, confusion crosses her face. 'Yes. For the most part. Although this past year has been difficult. Since his mother died, it's been hard for him. He would have done anything for her. Even though their relationship was complicated.'

'Complicated?'

She frowns, leaning forward, trying to formulate the words to express her meaning.

'Yes. You see Luke is so different from his mother, in looks and in personality. Not like Nick, who never had to try very hard with Sally because he's so like her in almost every way. There was a natural bond between them. Luke and Sally . . . well, it was different. He loved his mother, of course, and she loved him. But it always seemed to me that he was forever striving to please her and yet, no matter what he did, she held him at a distance. Not in any overt way, just this very subtle coldness despite her love for him.'

As she talks, a scrap of memory surfaces from nowhere. I was nineteen years old and sitting in the kitchen of the Yates' house up in the Wicklow hills. It was some time in the first weeks when Nick and I were reviving our friendship. Ireland can be funny like that – you lose touch with someone, assume you're never going to see them again, until one night you're in a student bar with your friends and across the room you see a face through the smoke and gloom, a face from childhood, a face that brings with it a jolt of recognition so strong that you just stand there, transfixed. That was how it was with me and Nick. That first reunion, so awkward and clumsy, Nick with his habitual shyness, barely able to look up at me while I jabbered away, simulating casual confidence, and all the while a great hole of uncertainty was opening inside me. And then it was like we couldn't stop running into each other – parties, discos, on campus at UCD.

Now, in retrospect, I wonder how much of it was coincidental, or whether we had sought each other out. But the day I'm remembering, a group of us from college were out hiking in the hills, when a sudden downpour sent us all running for cover and Nick suggested we go to his parents' house. I can still recall the sickness I felt as the nerves gathered in my stomach, reluctance holding me back. The house was not far and we could dry off there and get something to eat. Everyone else was going along with the idea so I couldn't object – it would seem odd, and I would draw too much attention to myself. So I had sat with the others in that house, trying to relax, trying to pretend that it was not strange to be there, Nick making sandwiches while the others lounged around the kitchen table, chatting and smoking, and all of a sudden Sally Yates walked in. Hair shoulder-length and still dark but with a glamorous streak of grey at the temple, her body thickened now in middle age yet still curvy and louche, the same easy sway of the hips. Her clothes had the chic I remembered from childhood, a cardigan thrown over her shoulders, shoes that were strappy and heeled. And she greeted us with a smile so hazy it seemed almost medicated.

'Oh, how lovely!' she had said. 'To meet my Nicky's charming new friends.'

Nick blushing furiously while his mother's gaze drifted over us.

And then she saw me. Her smile tightened and she said, her voice cool with astonishment: 'Katie Walsh. I don't believe it.'

The last time I had seen her was at the airport in Nairobi with my mother, a witness to their stiff farewell.

'Hello, Mrs Yates.'

'Well, now. This is a surprise.'

I could see the struggle going on inside her, and I knew the others saw it too. A silence had fallen over the table.

'And how is your father, Katie?'

'He's fine.'

'Good. Good. Please remember me to him, won't you?'

'Sure.'

Not a word about my mother. But, then, Sally had said everything she had wanted to say about her. I remember the card that had come after Mam died, icy in its formality, not a trace of tenderness in the neat hand, the carefully chosen words of condolence.

And there was Sally Yates, smiling tightly at me in the kitchen of her home, turning on her charm and departing gaily with a warm word for everyone – but just before she left the room, I caught her glancing back at Nick, caught the anxiety in her eyes, the flash of warning, and I had the sense that later she would pull him aside, question him about me, and then, in that silky way of hers, advise him to stay away from me – that it was for the best.

'She was a complex woman,' I say to Julia now, hearing a little ice in my own voice.

'She was. I keep forgetting you knew her.'

'Well, I didn't, really. At least, not in recent years. But when I was a child – '

'You spent that summer with them. In Kenya.'

She says this suddenly, and I'm momentarily taken aback. I hadn't realized she knew this. Instantly, the question pops into my head: *Does she know what we did?*

'Yes. That's right.'

She sits still, the breeze blowing strands of hair across her face, her eyes never leaving mine. There is a challenge in them; she's waiting for me to tell her something about that time, about what happened, and I have no idea how much she knows of it, how much Luke has shared with her, but either way I don't want to get into it. In my head, the iron doors come sliding down, cutting off the route to that memory.

'Come up to the house,' she says, after a minute, getting to her feet. 'There's something I want to show you.'

I follow her up the path, and in through a side door. A

narrow passageway opens suddenly onto the living room where the seaward wall is made of glass. Through it I can see the trees in the garden dripping from the recent downpour, and beyond them the green swathe of a briny sea, the sky a dim metallic grey bearing down heavily. The décor is all angles and hard surfaces. An echoey silence hangs heavily in the vaulted space. I follow Julia, wondering what's happened to the heavy who was guarding the gates. Marble floors, high ceilings, a great deal of wrought iron curving around the staircase.

Just before we reach the vestibule and the two massive old doors, she stops and turns to a mirrored cabinet against the wall, and from it she takes something. When she turns to me, there is a photograph in her hand. 'When I went into the study yesterday morning and found that – that mess, I also found this.' She turns the picture over in her hands. 'It was on his desk, propped up against the computer monitor.'

She takes one last look at it, then hands it to me.

As soon as my gaze falls upon it, I feel the belt around my neck.

The colours are faded, and there is a crease down the middle as if the photograph has been folded for some time. Three youthful faces captured in the golden light of a summer's day from the distant time of my childhood. Luke, Nick and I are sitting on a wall, the yellow-green of high grass in the background, a blue sky flecked with clouds above. Luke wears a black U2 T-shirt and he is the only one of us staring at the camera. Smirking. Nick wore his hair long that summer, and he is looking at the ground, his face almost hidden. He is smiling but, unlike his brother, seems bashful, secretive even. I am sitting next to him, face turned to my right, my attention caught by something off camera. My hair is long and raggedy, bleached golden by the sun, and my bare arms are brown, my face a riot of freckles. I am the only one who isn't smiling.

'How old were you when that was taken?' she asks.

I answer straight away: 'Eight.'

I know instantly. It was the summer when everything changed. 'This was on his desk, you say?'

'Yes.'

'But why?' The air in the hall feels suddenly chilly.

'I really couldn't say,' she answers, her eyes level and examining. 'All I can tell you is that until yesterday I had never set eyes on that picture.'

I examine the photograph again and see that my hands are shaking.

'You know, until recently, I was barely aware of you,' she goes on. 'And yet, in the last few days, you keep cropping up. What exactly is your relationship with my husband?'

'Not that,' I say quietly. 'It's not what you're thinking.'

I can't bring myself to return her gaze, but I can feel her eyes on me, the air between us pulled taut.

'And the photograph?'

'I've no idea why it was there,' I say briskly, thrusting it back at her but she holds up her hand.

'Keep it. Please.'

I pull my notebook out of my bag, then stuff the picture into it, trying to cover up how shaken I am.

She holds the door open for me and watches as I walk out.

On the step, I turn to her. 'That phone call Luke made – who was it to?'

She shrugs in reply.

'Nick is coming,' she says then.

I pause on the step. 'Nick? Nick's coming here?'

'You seem surprised.'

My heart is hammering. 'When?'

'Tomorrow.'

With that she closes the door softly, and I am left standing on the limestone step where the sun finds my feet and travels up to my face. Beyond the walls there is silence from the street, and someone in the house must have pressed a button because the gates slowly open of their own accord. The scrum of journalists has gone, dispersed as quickly as the rain. The warm air holds the sweet, heavy scent of some flower I don't recognize, and standing there by the closed door, a strange vertiginous feeling comes over me. For Nick to return brings home to me, with crushing certainty, just how serious this is. Then I cross the cobblelock driveway, walk out into the street and hurry away.

4. Nick

I'd intended never to go back. Ever. When I sat on the plane after my mum's funeral and felt it making its steep ascent, I closed my eyes and released my breath – I felt as if I'd held it the whole time I was home. Never again, I told myself.

Now here I am, barely a year later, another flight, another intake of breath, only this time I'm not alone.

Lauren sits beside me, quietly absorbing the great expanse of sky. It seems like the first time we have been alone since our wedding. The past couple of days have been a blur of anxiety and activity – booking flights and hotels. In a way, I'm glad to be on this flight. I can be still and quiet for a few hours and I know I can do nothing until the plane lands and the whole thing cranks up again.

The plane dips a little as it hits a pocket of air and I give Lauren's hand an involuntary squeeze, shoot her a smile of reassurance, which she returns before settling back in her seat, eyes closed. The truth is, I'm nervous as hell. I've barely slept since I heard the news. My body is swamped in fatigue and I'm too hyped up to rest, nerves jangling, anticipation dancing through every fibre.

'You'll let me know,' Murphy had said hoarsely, 'as soon as you hear anything?'

His face was lined and swollen when he saw us off at the gate, passing his cap from one hand to the other.

'Of course.'

'Come here.' He'd pulled me into his embrace and I'd briefly dropped my head to his shoulder, felt the coarse weave of his cotton shirt against my face. 'He'll be all right, Nick. You'll see. Chances are he'll be waiting for you at Arrivals.'

'Yeah. I'll bet you're right,' I'd said, but we both knew that was a lie.

As the plane bumps from one pocket of air to another, the captain announcing that the turbulence will soon pass, all I can think of is the blood. It was the one detail that had jumped out at me when I'd finally got to talk to Julia.

There was blood on the floor, Nick.

Around me, the other passengers are bracing themselves. I'm not the only one to grip the arm rests. I take a deep breath and wait for the next side-swipe from the elements. My stomach quivers. I close my eyes, press my head back against the seat and wait it out.

The whole time I was back, I seemed cloaked in a sense of disbelief − numb to the reality of the situation. Nothing about it felt right, from the suit I was wearing to the press of people's hands against my own: the words spoken, condolences offered, a box with a body in it − my mother's − her withered limbs, her shrunken frame. A brief moment alone with her, masking my shock at her papery skin, the groove worn into the tissues of her nose where the tube had entered her nostril, her ribcage protruding like that of a malnourished child, her flesh having wasted away. One last kiss before they closed the coffin − and, Jesus, how I didn't cry out in fright at the stone coldness of her forehead as I pressed my lips to it . . .

Murphy said the Mass. He spoke fondly of Sally, of how she had touched the lives of many, but the words seemed to string together and buzz in my ears, as if something were wrong with their rhythm, something that made me shift in my seat. I remember Luke walking to the edge of the grave after Mum was lowered. He bent down, picked up a handful of earth and threw it onto her coffin. I can still hear the echo of the stony soil, like a melancholy snare drum.

I push away the memory and, gradually, the plane levels off as we find a smooth line. People sigh with relief. The nervous energy is still there, but it's venting itself now in movement and chatter.

'You okay?' I ask Lauren.

'Fine,' she says, but I know that this whole episode is not what she'd expected. She's still jittery and nervous.

'Hey, I'm so sorry about this – all of it. I'll make it up to you. I promise.'

'I know you will,' she says.

'This is supposed to be your honeymoon.'

'*Our* honeymoon,' she corrects me.

'We'll still do it – Madagascar, the whale-watching, the whole thing – I promise.'

She raises my hand to her mouth, places a kiss on my palm. 'He's going to be okay,' she says.

I shrug, unsure how to answer. 'I hope so,' I say.

'We're together, that's all that matters,' she says. 'Everything will be fine.'

Part of me wants to believe her. Part of me almost does. But the way she says it, earnest and sincere, makes her seem so hopelessly young. My twenty-three-year-old bride is still brimming with youthful optimism because she hasn't lived long enough for something to shake her confidence in the world.

The plane lands to ripples of applause. We disembark, collect our luggage and find our way through the airport to the taxi rank.

In the taxi, Lauren talks to the garrulous driver while, through the window, I watch the city slide by: the mangy pubs, the foul-smelling butchers, the convenience stores and fast-food joints of my memory. There are new sights too: Polish grocers, the halal shop and Asian markets. Dublin has changed in a short time, even if the crooked curve of houses are the same. The hymn the city hums goes something like 'Dirty Old Town'. The streets have a familiar meanness; like an aunt's kiss, they say, 'Welcome back.' The winding roads and church spires say, 'We knew you'd be back.' And so, I suppose, did I.

We make it to the coast road and I ask the driver to pull over at the top of the hill. We pay the fare and the taxi takes off.

'Where's the house?' Lauren asks.

When I point towards the bottom where grand houses cluster near the shore, she looks at me, a question in her eyes.

'I didn't feel well,' I say. 'Needed some air.'

We begin to walk. The road is steep. On one side of the road, houses are dotted along the hill; on the other, the land falls away to a magnificent stretch of coast. On this sunny morning, the sweep of Dublin Bay sparkles, its beauty calling out to me in a way that I find painful.

I remember Dad bringing us out here some Sundays, to

the beach in Killiney, Luke hanging back to talk to him about the latest rugby results as I ran ahead. There was something about the coast Dad loved in autumn. Maybe it was the air or the light or just the lonely pleasure of walking with no real destination in mind. Either way, I wanted to collect shells and stones on those walks. Dad said something about hearing the ocean when you held a shell to your ear. 'And when you hold the right one – you can hear the waves crashing far off.'

I spent years trying to find the right shell to hear those waves. Luke, on the other hand, kept talking to Dad about tactics and transfers. 'What do you think of . . . ?' was his insistent refrain. By then, it seemed he paid me hardly any heed at all – vying as he was for all of Dad's attention.

On the way home from those windy walks, Dad bought us ice-cream at Teddy's in Dún Laoghaire. 'Don't tell your mother,' he'd say, even though she never came on those walks and rarely asked about them. But, still, it was a secret we shared, and it was a bearable one. Some of the happiest moments of our life after Africa involved standing dumbly on the pier licking ice-cream, shivering, glad to be around Dad as he hummed old show-tunes to himself.

I doubt he could have foreseen Luke living here, Luke going missing. Or me here waiting to hear any news of a brother who is by now a stranger to me.

Lauren walks on ahead. I can tell from the way she holds herself that she's breathing in the sea air gratefully after all those hours on the plane. At the same time she's trying to calm herself for the situation she finds herself in. As we near the foot of the hill, where my brother has his home, Lauren slows, then stops, her attention snagged on something below. I come up behind her.

The beach, pebbled and craggy, is lapped by the blue-green sea. Three men in luminous yellow jackets walk along it, the intervals between them wide and evenly spaced, their pace deliberately slow and measured.

Lauren puts out her hand to steady me. She doesn't say anything – she doesn't need to. On this bright morning, we stand watching the guards conduct their search, sweeping the beach for the presence of a body.

Julia is standing in the doorway as if she has been waiting all morning. 'Nick,' she says, coming forward with her arms outstretched. I step into her embrace. She feels so small and insubstantial against me, as if she is made of air. We hold onto each other for a moment and I feel the heave of her body as she gulps back tears. When we pull away I notice the dark shadows beneath her eyes, the kind that no amount of make-up can hide.

'Why is it that you and I only ever see each other on sad occasions, Nick?' she asks, holding both of my hands in hers. Her smile, for all its bravery, is thin and pained. She is barely holding herself together.

Lauren is beside me. I make the introductions and the two women embrace as if they've known each other for years. We follow Julia into the house; a man wearing an earpiece carries our luggage. When she instructs him to put our suitcases into the spare room, I find myself awkwardly stammering that we have our own accommodation.

'What?' she says, pausing on the step. 'Why aren't you staying here?'

'I'm sorry, Julia. We just thought it would be better . . . We didn't want to be under your feet.'

'But you wouldn't be.'

'And we're only a short taxi-ride away, if you need us to come out here quickly.'

She bites her lip, her eyes searching my face, and I can see the fight going on inside her head. My cheeks burn with shame.

'Of course,' she says. 'Whatever you want.'

I can't help but feel that already I've let her down. Julia leads us through the hallway into the expansive living area. I glance around at the high ceiling, the wide, cool space. I remember this house from my mother's funeral. Today it feels even bigger, more cavernous, than it did then: an echo chamber of domestically troubled conversations. If it ever had a soul, it's gone. There's no warmth, and the welcome we have received is a frightened one.

My sister-in-law directs us to the cluster of sofas and asks if we want tea or coffee; even under such testing circumstances, she remains the perfect hostess.

'Julia,' Lauren says, laying a hand on her arm, 'sit down. You must be exhausted.'

Julia turns to me and in her movement there is the suggestion of defiance and despair. 'Please,' Lauren says, her tone gentle but insistent. 'Let me make the tea. I'm sure I can find my way around your kitchen. You two should talk.'

Julia smiles, then sits on the sofa. I sit a short distance from her while my wife leaves us alone.

'She's lovely, Nick. You're a lucky man.'

'How are you holding up?' I reach across to her.

Instantly she crumbles, her defences falling away at my touch. 'Oh, God, Nick,' she says, 'what's happened to him?'

For a moment, I sit there, my hand resting on her shoulder, a tremor of fear in my fingers. She leans her head back and opens her eyes. 'I just keep expecting the door to open and him to walk in.' She wipes the corners of her eyes with her fingers. 'It's been three days.'

Three days, I think. What good can come of this? 'What do the guards say?'

'They have a tape,' she says. 'A security camera at the end of the road caught him staggering down the street, disoriented, holding a hand to his head. Then he gets into a car. Now they're looking for it and the driver.'

'A taxi?' I say.

'They're asking so many questions,' she says, 'about the business, money, Luke's behaviour. I hardly know what to tell them.'

'When I spoke to him on the phone the other night, he sounded a little downbeat.'

She glances at me. 'Things haven't been right with him for a while, Nick. Your mother's death hit him hard.'

'I know,' I say, my voice almost a whisper.

'He's been very up and down these past few months.'

'How do you mean?'

'Mood swings. Erratic behaviour.'

'Like?'

'Well, like that outburst on national television,' she says. 'It seemed to come from nowhere. And there's been speculation that it was all calculated, all part of some grand plan to kick-start a political career, but if it was, then I never knew about it. I mean, Luke never expressed any desire to go into politics. Even the charity, which everyone points to as an example of his social conscience, even that didn't have much to do with Luke. It was always Sally's project. Luke just provided her with a steer. And when she died and the directorship passed to him, it was a burden, a nuisance, not some kind of vocation.'

'What about your man out there?' I ask, inclining my head. 'Who's he?'

'Gary?' she asks. 'That's more of it. He was Luke's idea. This paranoia he had that we needed security, protection. I said to him: "Protection from what? What is it we're supposed to be afraid of?" But he wouldn't tell me. He just became evasive and moody whenever I pushed him on the subject.'

'How long has he been here?'

'Not long. We took him on shortly after the *Late Late Show* appearance. God knows what I'll do with him now. Just him and me in this house – it creeps me out. Are you sure you won't stay?'

She's pleading, which almost makes me give in. I offer a smile to take the sting out of it.

A hush then, nothing but the far-off sounds of industry in the kitchen. Then: 'Did you see the guards out there?' she asks quietly. I nod, thinking of the yellow jackets, the deliberate spread of them moving over the beach.

Julia is twisting a hankie between her hands. Something drops inside me – with it a shiver of unwanted nostalgia. I want, more than anything, to get away from this house – this mausoleum – the widow on the couch, but then the door opens: Lauren is there with a tray. Setting it on the

71

table, she begins passing around cups and saucers and I welcome the distraction, seizing my chance. 'Would you mind if I took a look at the study?' I ask.

'All right,' Julia agrees, getting to her feet, but I stop her, telling her I remember where it is.

I leave them, the two women, the clink of their teacups and their soft conspiratorial whispers echoing behind me.

When I open the door to his study, I feel as if I'm trespassing. I pause on the threshold, unsure and nervous. The air smells sterile, as if the place has been scrubbed with an industrial cleaner, all traces of a struggle erased.

I step into the room, allow the door to close behind me and, in the quiet dimness, I take it all in: the books, the golf clubs in the corner. The desk occupying the centre was once my father's — solid and mahogany, a stern piece. The armchairs that cluster around the fireplace came from my parents' house too, along with the oil painting above the hearth. In fact, it's as if this one room has taken on the life, the charm, the personality that once persisted in our home in the Wicklow hills, a house that has been sold, abandoned, and is now overrun with weeds and dust. All that remains of it seems to be here in this room, so utterly out of place in the rest of this house.

At first glance, everything appears normal. Untouched. But a closer look reveals disturbances. The wall behind the desk is blank where it had once been filled with framed photographs. In a cabinet is an assortment of awards — slabs of Perspex engraved with words I haven't the heart to read; chips have appeared in a couple, a great fissure passing through another that speaks of an episode of violence. A chair that had once sat by the desk has been moved. I peer down at the floor, the heavy pile of the carpet, and see the mark made by the rub of a soaked cloth. It was here that the blood must have been.

On the desk lie reams of papers, files neatly stacked. The room is cluttered, claustrophobic with work, but more than that I feel something else: a presence.

I remember him here, the day of Mum's funeral, sitting behind the desk, a tumbler of whiskey in his hands, watching as I stood by the fireplace. From beyond the door came the low hum of voices, the house crowded with mourners. We had escaped for a few moments, and it was to be the only time in that whole long day that we were alone.

'So, Nick . . . what are you going to do now?'

I felt a familiar nudge of irritation. 'What do you mean?'

'With yourself. With your life,' he said.

Already he was assuming the parental role. But that wasn't the only reason for my irritation. Asking me these questions, as if what I was doing was not real – as if playing music was a pastime, not a career; a hobby instead of a vocation.

'Head back to Nairobi, I suppose,' I said. I was reverting to a moody teenager, but I couldn't stop.

He seemed to sigh, as if I had disappointed him. He stared at me for a minute, tipped his whiskey down his throat and set the tumbler firmly on the desk. 'I think you should know that there's no money in the will,' he said.

I was shocked by the crassness of his statement.

'She's left it all to the charity. Every penny of it.'

'I don't care about the money, Luke,' I said, in a low voice.

He caught my eye, my tone, and gave a quick smile.

'Yeah, I know. Did you know she's made me the sole director?'

'Oh?'

'Fucking poisoned chalice.'

'I thought you'd relish the opportunity.'

'Oh, please. I don't have the time. It was fine for Mum – she liked nothing better than flitting off to Nairobi to inspect a new water-pump or whatever. Where am I going to find the time for that?'

'Employ someone,' I said. 'Have Murphy do it. He's already involved.'

Something changed in his face then. He grew quiet, swinging his chair slowly from side to side. 'He laid it on a bit thick today, don't you think? All that talk about Mum and Dad. And did you see him out there just now?' he continued, gesturing to the room beyond. 'Sitting in a corner getting quietly sozzled, as if he's about to burst into tears.'

'That's Murphy,' I said. 'You know what he's like. He wears his heart on his sleeve. He loves the grand gesture.'

'What he said during Mass – about Mum, the trials she went through. What do you think he meant by that?'

'Her illness. Dad's death. I dunno.'

'You don't suppose he knows, do you? About what happened back then?'

I felt a tilt of sudden emotion. We never spoke about it. Never. And I heard again my father's words in my ears: *Not a soul. Ever. Do you hear me? You must never tell anyone.*

'No,' I said, hearing the sternness in my own voice. 'He doesn't know. No one does.'

'Just you, me and Katie now,' he said, in a wistful kind of way.

'You're right,' he said, conceding something, getting to his feet and picking up his empty glass. 'Let's have another drink. Then you can play us a few tunes – liven up this party.' Clasping an arm around my shoulders, he squeezed me to him. 'Make you sing for your supper, eh, Music Boy?'

The stains to the left of the desk, caught on the tiny barbs of the tufted carpet. They have been scrubbed, and the thick woven carpet has been steam-cleaned, but the blood, its density and weight, is still there.

I bend down to touch the place: as my fingers brush the carpet fibre I know it's Luke's blood and my ears fill with an unnatural humming.

A shadow falls over me and I almost cry out in fright.

'Nick? Are you okay?' Julia asks.

'I'm fine,' I say, straightening and leaning against the desk to try to stop the trembling in my legs.

'It's weird, isn't it? The atmosphere in here,' she says, hugging herself.

'A bit, yeah.'

She glances at the empty wall, then bends down to pick up a cardboard box I hadn't noticed. Now I see that it contains the fallen photographs, rent from their frames; the glass that was shattered has been swept away and discarded. She sifts through them, then picks one out and holds it up. It's of Luke and me as kids. 'I don't know why he had that hanging in here,' I say.

'He loved you,' she replies, referring to Luke in the past tense. 'There was another I found. Not on the wall, but here, on the desk. Taken that same summer, but it had Katie in it.'

'Katie Walsh?'

'Yes. I gave it to her.'

I'm so tired, I have difficulty focusing. I can hardly grasp what she is saying. 'You gave it to Katie?'

'She was here yesterday. Or was it the day before? It's been so hard to keep track of time since it happened.'

She's unsettled, worried and upset. But she gives off something else too, something that suggests she knows more than she's letting on. Or am I dreaming? I'm jet-lagged, dazed by being in Dublin. My surroundings are familiar yet odd; it's as if I'm remembering something I dreamed, not something that actually happened.

'She asked me whether Luke could have done this.'

This quiet room, the mess all tidied and cleaned away, retains a shadow of the violence that was done to it. And when I think of my brother, brought to such a state of anguish that he could inflict it, I feel weak with sadness and fear.

'He was having one of his turns,' she says softly. 'You know how he can get . . . It's like a shadow comes over him and all his confidence falls away. The light goes out in his eyes and he's somehow vacant.'

'I know what you mean, but I haven't seen him in so long . . .'

'Only last month he was out late at a meeting. After-wards, he had too much to drink and when he got home he couldn't get the key in the lock so he punched through the glass of the front door. I took him to the hospital and he stayed in for monitoring . . . He was shaken, Nick.'

'But had anything happened lately? Anything that might have triggered it?'

'I don't know,' she says. 'He's been under some pressure with the business, but —' She breaks off.

I sense she's holding something back. 'What is it?' I ask gently.

'It only ever happens when something from the past comes up . . . You know what I mean, Nick. That's the only time he's vulnerable.'

I feel the closeness of the room around me, but say nothing.

'Nick,' she says. 'What did happen back in Kenya?'

I try to imagine what Luke might or might not have told her. How he might have hinted at what had happened, alluded to it or even made some drunken, confused confession. But I don't know what. How could I?

Julia loses patience. 'Your wife is waiting,' she says, her voice flat and stern. 'You should go.'

5. Katie

'It's not that it's bad,' Reilly says hesitantly. 'It's just not really enough. There isn't anything new here.'

He seems tired this morning, a little crumpled, bruised from the editorial meeting he's just come from. The editor, a notorious exploder, doesn't pull any punches and it's not the first time Reilly's been on the receiving end of his verbal abuse. Still, I feel bad that he's had to take a bullet on my behalf.

'Was it awful?' I ask.

'Not the worst.'

'Give it to me straight, Reilly. What did he say?'

He sighs and leans against my desk. 'That it's dull and ponderous and it reads like an obit for the fucking *FT*. That most of it could have been gleaned from Wikipedia.' His eyes pass over me, searching for signs of distress.

I raise my eyebrows, lean back in my chair and exhale. 'Wow.'

'Don't take it to heart, Katie.'

'An obit for the *FT*?'

It strikes a note of fear in me. I hadn't intended to make it sound as if Luke is dead. For the first time since this began, the dark sliver of that possibility opens before me.

The post-boy is doing the rounds with his trolley and stops to drop some letters on my desk, glancing at me and Reilly, then moving on. My face is burning, the sting of those words bringing the blood rushing to my cheeks. I lean forward, pluck a small package from the pile and turn it over in my hands.

'Could you go back to Julia Yates? See if she'd open up to you a bit more?'

'I doubt it.'

'And you're sure there's nothing else from her interview? Nothing at all?'

Instantly my mind goes to the photograph – Luke, Nick and I sitting under the African sun, just before it all changed. It's been hovering in my consciousness since Julia gave it to me, questions like bees buzzing at the back of my mind. Why had he kept that picture of us? Leaving it there to be found, what message had he meant to convey? I can feel Reilly's eyes on me, something in me inclining towards his wisdom and intelligence, and I almost tell him. But the urge passes, overtaken by the dominant voice inside my head that insists I suppress it, keep a lid on it. Words shoot up painfully from the past: *Don't tell anyone.*

'There's nothing,' I say, turning the padded envelope over in my hands.

'What about your man at the gates?'

'I dunno. Security, doorman, whatever.'

'He didn't look very *Downton Abbey* to me. Anything worth exploring there?'

I don't try to hide my disgust and he smiles, saying: 'I know, I know. You don't need to say it.'

We've had this argument before, about the risks involved in slipping into murky tabloid territory in a bid to sell newspapers. It kills me because Reilly has such integrity that I can't bear to watch his ideals being compromised.

He's giving me the company line now in his softly reasoned tones: circulation, sales figures, blah, blah, blah. I'm half listening to him as I examine the package in my hands, my thumb hooking under the flap. The competition of the tabloids, he's saying, and of the internet, of every twenty-four-hour rolling news agency. And how else are we supposed to survive when anyone with a Twitter account can write the news?

'You may not like it, Katie, but scandal sells. We can't afford to sit in our ivory towers.'

But I don't say anything.

I'm staring hard at the open envelope in my hands. It's small enough – no bigger than A4 – manila in colour and padded. My details have been scrawled in blue marker. English stamps, but I can't make out the postmark.

'What is it?' Reilly asks, as I slide the contents out onto the desk.

For a moment, neither of us says anything. We just look at it. A sparrow, perhaps, or some other small bird. Ornithology is not one of my strong suits. There is something tender about the way it lies so small and still – even without touching it, you can sense the silky softness of its feathers, a flare of orange at its throat. Tender, apart from the angle of its neck – a sharp break, blood on the feathers from a deep gash that has almost taken the head clean off.

'Jesus,' Reilly says.

Still I can't speak.

He's on his feet now, shouting for Janice, and the pitch of his voice betrays his alarm, so that heads pop up from other desks, interest stirred. His secretary comes running.

'Get onto the guards,' he tells her.

'Oh, my God,' she says, spotting the dead bird, her hand going to her mouth.

'Reilly, there's no need for that,' I say quietly, still reeling.

'It was sent to you here at the paper, Katie. We have to take it seriously.'

'It's probably just some crank.'

'Course it is, but we still have to deal with it properly,' he says. 'Is there anything else? A note?'

'No.'

'And the postmark?' He picks up the envelope, squints at it.

'Smudged.'

'Brilliant.' He lets out a sigh, apprehension coming off him in waves. When he reaches out and I feel the weight of his hand steady on my shoulder, I swear it's all I can do not to burst into tears. The bird lies in front of me, a grim message. But what meaning is it supposed to convey? And why have I been singled out? Something comes to me then – a sound tunnelling up through memory: the beating of wings against the bars of a cage. Afternoon sunlight reaching the veranda, a heavy burden of bougainvillaea blossoms hanging down. On the lawn a revolving sprinkler sending out jets of water in hoops and swirls. The flutter and twitter of those sparrows in their cage.

No, I tell myself. It couldn't be that. It's not possible – nobody knows . . . Mentally I shake myself to shrug off the memory. Still, the strangeness of the past few days presses down on me. I pull my hands away from the desk, tuck them under my thighs so that Reilly can't see them trembling.

'Listen, don't let it get to you,' he says quietly. 'This

happens to everyone once in a while. You'd be amazed at the kind of cretins out there with time on their hands, fucking idiots with no imagination who think it'll be great gas to send something ghoulish to a journalist, put the frighteners on her.'

'You're lucky it's just a bird,' Janice adds. 'Kieran Fox was sent a turd.'

'Kieran Fox *is* a turd,' Reilly says brusquely. Then swiftly, before I have a chance to object, he plucks the bird from the desk and the queasiness rises to my throat. Without a word, he slots it into the envelope, taking possession of it. Janice has hurried away, and the hush that had briefly fallen over the office breaks up, phones ringing, movement entering the space.

'You all right?' Reilly asks me, and I nod quickly.

His hesitancy is back, but it's something different now and I feel my cheeks grow hot again. I try to smile. 'Really,' I say. 'I'm fine.'

I spend the next couple of hours trying to sex up my article, the words scattering like ash over the screen. A female guard comes. We sit in the canteen and I answer her questions.

Do you know who might have sent this? *No.*

Have you received similar threatening messages in the past? *No.*

Do you know of anyone who might have a grudge against you?

I waver a little over the last one. In my profession, there are always people whose toes you've trodden on. But when she asks me if there was anything else I could think that might be significant – anything at all – it's there again: the nudge of memory, that sound in my ears, the flapping of wings. I feel the tightening around my throat, the pinch of another notch. *No, there's nothing.*

Something about this is making me deeply uneasy. And it's not just the dead bird. It began with those photographs of a drowned girl, like some portent of doom, yet still I didn't see it coming. But now Luke is missing and Nick is coming back and I can feel myself being sucked in. Nostalgia is creeping over me, the strings of the past drawing us together again, tightening around the three of us.

The guard's visit leaves me feeling worse. Instead of reassuring me, her careful questioning seemed more like she was sticking her fingers into the wound and having a good poke around in it. Afterwards, I can't sit still. I grab my things, leave the office, and pretty soon I'm driving out to the coast. The stale smell of the car rises up around me. It's no triumph of modern engineering but I don't really give a damn, and as I drive down the quays alongside the widening river, I ignore the detritus of paper coffee cups, old newspapers and other junk that furnish the back seat, as well as the straining sound the engine makes every time I change gear. The drive-time radio shows are kicking off and I flick through the stations, searching for news of Luke, but there's nothing so I switch it off.

Before long, I draw the car into a space at Sandymount Strand, turn off the engine, and silence fills the air around me. I could have gone to a pub, but I can't bear the thought of human contact right now – the noise and distraction. I want to sit alone in my car, watching the night coming on.

I know what has drawn me back here: Luke, of course. Less than a month ago, now, I had contacted him to arrange a meeting. He was still riding high on the wave of his successful *Late Late Show* appearance and I had been assigned to do a feature on him for the paper. I was reluctant, what with the whole freight of family history between us, yet something had snagged my interest – an itch I had to scratch.

My request must have seemed like a bolt from the blue. We had seen each other at Sally's funeral, briefly, and on a couple of other occasions, Dublin being the size it is, but I always felt he was wary of me. However warm his greeting, I couldn't escape the thought that, behind the friendly exterior, he was dying to be rid of me. So it came as a surprise when he responded warmly to my email, agreeing to meet me, and within his response, I read a degree of interest on his part in our becoming reacquainted. We arranged to meet for coffee in a hotel near Spencer Dock but, an hour beforehand, he rang to suggest we meet instead out at Sandymount Strand.

'It's such a beautiful morning,' he had said, his voice confident and optimistic. 'Let's make the most of it.'

And I had found myself in the car park by the strand, a paper cup of coffee in each hand, leaning against my car and waiting for him to turn up. I was nervous in a way I couldn't quite figure out, for what was there to be nervous of? As his car swung into the car park – a black Range Rover gleaming in the morning sun – I caught his eye and saw the grin already on his face, felt the jump of my nerves as I pushed myself away from my car and went to meet him.

'Great minds,' he said, coming towards me with two paper cups of coffee held aloft.

He leaned forward to kiss my cheek and we laughed while awkwardly holding our twin coffees.

'Mine are from Dunne & Crescenzi,' he said, glancing sceptically at the cups in my hands. 'What about yours?'

'Petrol station.'

'Ah, Katie! Throw that muck away and take one of these!' he said, in a voice that might have sounded brash and bullying were it not for the charm of his accompanying smile. And I, surprising myself, did just that, telling myself it was best to get on his good side if I wanted any information out of him but, really, that was a lame excuse, for it had always been that way between us – him giving the orders, setting the pace, and me reluctant to disappoint, not wanting to be the one to show resistance.

The tide was way out that morning, the brown sand skimmed and marbled and stretching for miles, occasional breezes blowing in little eddies over the hard surface, sending up brief clouds of dust. We walked together, Luke and I, out across the strand, past the Martello tower, veering south in the direction of Bray Head. The sky above us was a brittle blue. We drank our coffee and chatted, and it was surprising to me how quickly and easily we settled into a pattern of conversation. It was a knack he had, I realized, of putting people at their ease, the openness he had that made you feel you were an old friend with no barriers or secrets between you and him.

We talked at length of his business and its success. Two pubs, a restaurant and a half-share in a country house that was being converted into an exclusive weekend retreat – he had made a name for himself as one of a handful of entrepreneurs who were responsible for the transformation of the Dublin social scene, developing venues that were casually chic, modern enough but with a nod and a wink in the direction of the traditional Irish pub. There was no doubting Luke's success, his Midas touch and innate understanding of what passed for 'cool'. And when the crash came, he seemed to escape unscathed. Not everyone was as lucky. And when I put it to him that it was unusual he had managed to remain untouched by the downturn in a business that relied heavily on a thriving economy, he gave a belting laugh, then sent me a sideways look, saying: 'Prudence, Katie. Prudence saved me.'

Snatched glances at him as we walked side by side showed him to have aged well. He was thirty-nine – two years older than me – and his sandy-brown hair was cut smartly, with only a peppering of grey at the temples. He wore jeans, Converse shoes and a green parka – casual clothes, but you knew they were expensive. There was something of the ageing Brit-pop star about Luke. His wedding ring appeared to be platinum and was the only flashy thing about him, if you could even call it that.

'What about luck?' I asked.

'Luck?'

'It could easily have gone the other way.'

He frowned then, a pinched line of confusion running between his eyebrows.

'If you consider the rest of your peers, other entrepreneurs in the pub and club scene, all of whom played a part in the regeneration of the economy –' I listed a few '– they haven't all been as fortunate as you. Some of them got badly burned.'

Young guns with a pioneering attitude that in hindsight seems like borderline gambling; borrowing heavily, they had pressed ahead, transforming Dublin from a dingy urban backwater, tired and neglected in the post-colonial years, into a vibrant, youthful city, pulsing with money and music, culture and excitement. Luke nodded, sanguine, as I spoke of some of those who had fallen.

'Poor fuckers,' he intoned. 'They hadn't a clue what was up the road waiting for them. Thought it was going to be champagne and oysters till Doomsday. They pushed it too far, took on too much. It was madness.'

'Do you see them much now?'

He shrugged. 'Mulvey, the odd time. Farrell's a basket-case since he lost all his money, and the others have left the country.'

'They must hate you,' I said jokingly, but he glanced at me sideways and I felt his confidence slip.

'Why do you say that?'

'Because they're in hock for millions, and you're still afloat,' I said, laughing at his expression. He seemed genuinely affronted.

'I suppose.'

I asked him whether any of his peers had commented on his TV appearance, but he waved away the question, as if embarrassed by it.

'I have to ask, Luke: was it planned, your speech that night?'

'No,' he said firmly. 'Honestly, it wasn't. To tell you the truth, I don't know where it came from, what came over me.'

'You seemed so passionate.'

'I was livid! Christ, all that self-important bullshit the others were coming out with, the faffing around in the studio beforehand . . . It just got to me, and I kind of exploded. It was funny in a way, thinking back on it. My philanthropic side coming out.'

'Your mother would have been proud.'

'Yeah, well . . .'

We had reached the edge of the shore now, the water starting to turn back on itself. The tide comes in swiftly over the strand, and there are signs warning you to avoid being trapped. But we lingered for a moment, the sea lapping the toes of our shoes.

'So what has you working on this story, Katie? I don't give interviews to just anyone, you know,' he said, in a jokey voice. 'Did you beg the editor to let you have it? Wave our old connection in his face? Claw away the other slavering journos who were grasping for it?'

I laughed, but it was a hollow sound, and he was waiting for an answer. It would have been so easy to make a joke of it, make some glib remark about a catfight in the boardroom or sleeping with the editor. It was the kind of flippancy that came effortlessly to me. But instead, surprising myself, I told him the truth.

'I didn't want to do it, but it was foisted on me. I didn't want to interview you, Luke. The thought of it scared me.'

'Scared you?'

I turned to him then. 'I was scared of what it might stir up, afraid of waking old ghosts.'

Maybe it was the way he was watching me as we paused at the edge of the water. The stillness that had come over his features and the softening in his voice. Maybe it was just that he had stopped talking about himself and his own concerns and was now focusing on mine. Whatever it was, I read it as an opening – a small, truthful space for me to slip into and for once speak plainly about my feelings. But I have never been very good at judging such moments. What I see as openings for honesty are often something else. And when I gazed up at Luke's face that sunny morning, I saw something slip over it: a guardedness.

He said, 'Nothing to be afraid of,' and something inside me seemed to plummet.

I don't know what I expected of him, but it was more than that. 'Don't you ever think of her? Don't you ever think about what happened and wonder whether –'

'No.' He looked me full in the face, his mouth set in a stern line, anger in his eyes. 'No, I don't think about it, Katie. I don't allow myself to think about it. That's my choice. That's how I get through my day. And if you're wise – if you want to make something of yourself, do something with your life – then you'll do the same. Stop dwelling on the past because thinking about it won't change a thing. All it will achieve is your own destruction.'

I was startled into silence, overwhelmed by the sudden change in him – his charm had fled, leaving in its wake that shell of a man cloaked in anger and fear.

'What about Nick?' I asked quietly, compelled somehow to press on. 'Do you ever talk to him about it?'

He laughed then, a small harsh burst that contained little amusement. 'What would be the point, Katie? You know what he's like.'

I didn't say anything after that, and neither did he, the

two of us just standing at the water's edge, taking in the ripples in the hard sand, bubbles gathering in the shallows. After a moment's silence, he said: 'We'd best turn back.'

For the rest of the walk to the car park, I tried to push down the wave of disappointment that kept rising within me. Our conversation turned back to his business. In one way, I suppose, my opening up to him had seemed to produce a corresponding openness in him: on the way back to our cars, his comments took on a new candour. But there was no further mention of what had happened when we were kids or anything it might have stirred up, and for some reason, this seemed to crush me in a way I couldn't begin to understand.

He spoke about his father, how he had always been an inspiration and a guide when it came to economic matters. How when Ken had died, Luke had lost his father, but also a mentor.

'It must have been such a shock,' I said, remembering my own reaction to the news. A vehicle crash in the Wicklow hills. No one else involved.

'It was. Even though it's been years now, I still miss him.'

I made some remark then about the accident, about the unfairness of such a death and about the treacherous way the road wends down into the Sally Gap. He focused on the sand in front of us, softening now where the marram grass sprouted in tufts, and his expression seemed to tighten. 'Depends on the state of the driver, I should think,' he said, distracted.

Something in me held back from pressing him on it, but it had struck a discordant note in me, the suggestion of intent that cast a cool shadow over my memory of Ken Yates, sketchy as it was.

He walked me to my car, and stood waiting while I unlocked the door and threw my bag onto the passenger seat.

'I meant to get in touch with you,' he said, 'after Mum's funeral. It was good of you to attend.'

'That's okay.'

'It meant a lot to us – to me and Nick – that you were there. You should have stuck around afterwards, though. We never got to talk. You could have come back to the house.'

'I didn't want to intrude,' I said, shy all of a sudden.

It occurred to me then that, with Sally's death, there was no one else who had been there that summer – only the three of us remained. Perhaps he thought it too, because he said next: 'Are you in touch with Nick?'

I shook my head: no.

He nodded, his eyes passing over my face. 'I don't hear from him much myself,' he admitted. 'Not once since the funeral.'

'No?'

'You know how it is.' He shrugged, then laughed, looking back towards the sea, but there was something sad about the way he had said it that got me thinking of the brothers and what might have happened between them.

Then, just before we parted, he turned to me and I thought he was going to make some remark about old times, but a shadow crossed his face and he said: 'You don't really think they hate me, do you? Mulvey and them?'

I laughed – I couldn't help it. He seemed hurt or put out somehow, which was ridiculous. I'd only been winding him up.

'Jesus, Luke. No. How the hell should I know what they think?'

He nodded again briskly, then recovered himself, laughing even at his own seriousness. 'Well, goodbye, Katie Walsh,' he said, and leaned in towards me. I'd thought he was going to kiss my cheek, but instead he put his hands on my waist and pulled me to him and I felt his lips press against my own. He drew back and I stood there, too startled to say anything, watching him walk away from me.

As I left the strand that day, heading back into the city, I kept thinking of that kiss – the surprise of it, the firmness of his mouth against mine, how purposeful it had felt. I was so busy thinking about it that I never stopped to consider what he had said just before it. Too distracted by all that was stirred up within me to remember how troubled he had seemed – the worry in his face – and all that it might mean.

I think about him now and what he had said. Keeping my eyes trained on the line of the horizon, navy against the lavender grey of the evening sky, his words come back to me: *Stop dwelling on the past because thinking about it won't change a thing.* For people like me and Luke the past is a closed door, a sliding bolt to contain that tentacled thing.

My phone rings and my heart leaps in fright. My hand is shaking as I answer it.

'Katie?'

'Yes?'

'It's me, Nick.'

I suck in my breath and feel the fluttering in my chest cavity. 'Nick. Is there news?'

'No. He hasn't turned up yet.'

A sinking feeling then; the clamour of my heart quietens a little. I feel the strangeness of the silence between us.

'You're home, then,' I say, trying to keep my voice level, hoping it doesn't betray any of the myriad emotions that are pulsing through me right now because it's strange hearing his voice after all this time, its soft timbre, the low, gravelled tones – pebbles under water.

'Yes. We got in earlier today.'

'Right. I heard you're married. Congratulations.' The word comes out flat and I rest my forehead on the steering wheel, sick of myself and the tone of sarcasm that leaks into my conversation no matter what.

'Listen,' he goes on, like I haven't mentioned anything, the same old Nick, always turning a blind eye. 'I think we should have a talk. Can you meet me?'

'Sure,' I say. 'Where?'

'Grogan's. I can be there in half an hour.'

The arrangement made, I hang up, throwing my phone onto the passenger seat. In the fading light of the day, I breathe deeply, trying to collect my thoughts. Beyond the strand the headland of Shellybanks seems crushed by the weight of industry – cranes and chimneys and stacks of shipping containers all cast in a pinkish glow from the dying sunset. I watch the last of the evening walkers along the promenade and realize I'm looking for Luke among them, hopeful of catching a glimpse of him even though I know he's not there. And when I think of his expression on the day we met, the word that comes to mind is 'fearful'. That thought blots out any memory of the kiss, leaving a chill at the back of my neck as I start the engine and move my car away.

6. Nick

The taxi pulls up outside our hotel and we are greeted by a liveried doorman, with a top hat, then ushered inside the revolving doors. Inside it's all marble floors and mirrored walls, chandeliers suspended high above us. As we walk to Reception, I can see a drawing room to the right, soft carpeting, aproned staff, armfuls of flowers in oversize vases, the room populated with elegantly dressed women sipping tea. My wife is wearing flip-flops and torn jeans, the rucksack on her back her only luggage, and it hits home how conspicuous we are, like fish out of water.

In the lift, we stand side by side. The air between us is prickly, and it's only when I close the door of our bedroom behind us and Lauren dumps her bag on the floor that she breaks the silence.

'Say it,' she says, in a voice that is soft but challenging. 'Go on. Say it, Nick.'

'What?'

'This hotel. You hate it. You think I shouldn't have booked it.'

I feign ignorance, but we both know she's hit the nail on the head. To me the hotel is too upmarket for what we're doing, but I don't want to say so to her. The last thing I want, right now, is to get into a fight. I move past her, put my bag on the low bench at the foot of the bed, and stroll to the window which opens onto the public park that is St Stephen's Green.

'You'd rather I'd booked something cheap and out of the way, right? Some hostel for backpackers where we could bunk in a dorm with half a dozen others? I mean, it's supposed to be our fucking honeymoon!'

'Lauren –'

She sweeps past me, having worked herself up into a rage, goes into the bathroom and slams the door behind her. I collapse into an armchair and drop my head into my hands. From the bathroom comes the sound of water running, the hum and hiss of the shower. After a minute or two, I get up and find the mini-bar, pour myself a gin and tonic, and by the time it's finished, my nerves have calmed and my irritation has died away. When my wife emerges from the bathroom wrapped in a white robe, she is flushed and sheepish.

'Feel better?' I ask gently.

'Yeah. You?'

I hold up my empty glass. 'Much.'

We smile at each other then, a kind of shyness between us, and not for the first time, I wonder how much there is that we still have to learn about one another, about how we behave together, the rhythm of our marriage having yet to establish itself.

'Fix me one?' she says, sitting on the bed, one leg drawn up underneath her, towel-drying her damp hair. 'We can find somewhere else tomorrow,' she says, in a conciliatory tone, taking her glass, but I put my hand to her chin, tipping her face up gently so we are eye to eye.

'Lauren, this place is great.'

She smiles and I lean in and kiss her, feeling a crackle of electricity in my lips as our mouths meet. Then I lie down on the bed beside her, clasping my hands behind my head and watch as she continues drying her hair, pausing to take occasional sips of her gin and tonic.

'Do you think we should have stayed with her? Julia, I mean,' she says.

'No.'

'I feel bad for her, knocking around inside that massive house, all alone.'

'They have lots of friends. If she's on her own, it's because she must want to be.'

She swirls the drink in her glass, then asks: 'How come they don't have kids?'

'Lots of people don't have kids, Lauren.'

'True. But how long are they married?'

'I dunno. Six, maybe seven years. Why?'

'You'd think they'd have kids, that's all. So what's the deal? Can they not have them? Is that it?'

'I don't know. It's not the kind of thing you can ask.'

'He's your brother.'

How to explain to her that there are many things Luke and I can't discuss? 'I just don't think Luke was ever really interested in children of his own.'

'What about you?' Lauren asks. She has stopped drying her hair, and is sitting very still. 'Do you want kids?'

Outside, the light has faded. From my place on the bed, I can see purple clouds drawing in, the night sky coming on. I hear noises from the streets beyond and try to tune into them, the music the city makes, its own distinctive beat, but there is something wrong with my hearing – as if a bubble of air has caught inside my inner ear from the flight. The room has grown dim around us, making it hard to see her expression. But I can sense its concentrated intensity.

'Not yet,' I say softly, my heart beating slowly.

The words hang between us. If she senses my evasion, she doesn't comment on it. There is so much that we haven't talked about yet. I think of the commitment we have made to each other and feel a tingle of fear along my spine. The alcohol has gone straight to my head. I hadn't expected such a confusion of emotions. Lauren leans closer to me. Her towel lies to one side, discarded, along with her empty glass. I feel her gaze dwelling on me, and a small smile drifts onto her face. I need to focus, I tell myself. I need to find out what has happened to my brother. She moves closer, lifting her body, and I can feel her breath on my neck, the glance and brush of her hair against my face.

After we make love, she falls asleep. I feel the weight of her head resting on my arm, but I can't close my eyes. Thoughts whirr in my head, words echoing along the corridors of my mind. I think of Luke's study, the box of photographs and remember what Julia asked me: what did happen back then . . . in Kenya?

Gently, so as not to wake her, I slip my arm out from under Lauren's head and dress quietly in the dark. In the corridor outside, I make the call. Katie's voice sounds strange – there's a rasp to it that I don't remember, as if she's been chain-smoking Turkish cigarettes since we last met.

'Can you meet me?' I ask, and she says sure, although there's frost in her voice.

'Where?'

'Grogan's,' I tell her. 'Half an hour.'

I'm there before her, squeezing into a corner beneath a wall crowded with dubious artwork. The place is heaving with people and I feel lucky to have snatched a small space on a bench, hooking a stool with my foot for Katie. Despite the smoking ban, Grogan's reeks of cigarettes and stale alcohol, as if it's seeped into the upholstery and is trapped there for ever. The bartender's hair falls long and limp down her back, past her hips. I'm kind of entranced by it, so much so that I don't even notice Katie until she's standing right in front of me.

'Hello, you,' she says, a smile pulling at the corners of her mouth.

'Hey,' I say, getting to my feet. We lean towards each other, kissing on the cheek, then draw apart, the air between us awkward and stiff.

'I'll get us a drink,' she says, dumping her jacket on the stool. As she walks to the bar it's as if the years have fallen away and we're students again.

At first glance she seems hardly to have changed. She wears jeans and a tight T-shirt, her hair falling loosely to her shoulders – girlish, studenty, not the professional image I'd imagined she'd have cultivated. She holds herself with the same composure, the same self-possession, and it is only when she turns back to me, a pint in each hand, that I observe the dark shadows around her eyes, a tightness about her mouth.

'Thanks,' I say, taking the pint, and waiting as she settles onto her stool, flicking her hair.

'I suppose we should toast your marriage,' she says, a smile on her face, 'or is that inappropriate under the circumstances?'

At first, I'm too stunned to reply. I'm so tired I'm not sure I can trust what I might say, but at the same time there seems to be an edge to her words, a hidden barb, that throws me.

'Your health,' I say.

'Chin-chin,' she replies.

For a moment, neither of us says a word. I can't think of how to begin this conversation. It's been so long and I feel the gulf between us; perhaps she feels it too. She drums her fingers against her glass and jiggles a knee, casting glances at the door. It's strange to see her again – awkward yet something of a relief: as if all our lives we have been revolving around each other, only now and then coming together before being propelled away again.

'This is weird,' she says at last.

I can see the twitching of muscles in her jaw and the effort this is costing her. 'I know.'

'I can't believe you got hitched . . . Where is she – your wife?'

'She's asleep at the hotel. Her name's Lauren.'

'Lauren,' she says, smiling.

I don't know if there is a hint of jealousy in her smile, or a tinge of bitterness, as if she thinks my marriage is absurd. 'She's tired. It's been a long day,' I say.

'When did you get home?'

'This morning. We went straight out to see Julia.'

'Julia . . .' Her eyes widen.

'I heard you'd been to visit.' I let a silence drift around that, a silence that prickles with disapproval.

She picks up on it straight away. Rolling her eyes, she lets out a sigh. 'I was just trying to help.'

'Help who?'

'Look,' she says, the hardness creeping back into her tone, 'I saw Luke the night before he went missing. He and I had met up a few times recently. You know my editor wanted me to do a feature on him – Luke Yates, mover and shaker? So I sought him out.'

'You sought him out?'

'Nick, I didn't ask to do a piece on your brother. I was told to.'

'And you always do as you're told?'

'So, we met up,' she says, ignoring my antagonism. 'And we talked about his success and his luck at escaping unscathed from the crash when many of his peers had not.'

'Lucky Luke.'

'So, when I called over to see Julia, yes, I was doing my job. I was there in a professional capacity. But I was concerned too, Nick. I wanted to help.'

I listen but it's a blur because all I can think about is her and Luke, meeting up, talking, spending time alone.

She sips her pint, and into the pause, I say: 'Were you having an affair with him?'

The look she gives me: it's like she's been slapped. I can't quite believe I've spoken those words aloud. When she answers, her voice is icy. 'No, Nick. I wasn't.'

Shame comes over me, like a wave of nausea. 'Sorry,' I say. 'Things are just so fucked up right now.'

I hold my head in my hands, staring hard at the manky carpet, blood pounding at my temples. Then I feel her hand touch my knee. 'Can we start again?' she asks, and I nod.

She puts her glass down and gets to her feet. I do, too, and we lean in towards each other. She wraps her arms around my neck and I fold her into my embrace and we stand there holding each other like the old friends we are, and even though I can feel people staring at us, I don't give a fuck, because I know that this is what I've needed.

'It's so good to see you, Nick,' she says, against my cheek. I feel the conviction in her words. All malice between us has vaporised.

'It's good to see you too, Kay,' I say softly. She pulls away and I see something move behind her face, some push of emotion, of recognition. Kay – my old name for her.

It's easier now. The air between us is clear. We can talk freely, and for a while we do – discussing Luke, his recent behaviour, what she has learned of his business dealings, what Julia has told me.

'What about the photograph?' Katie asks. 'The one on Luke's desk – of the three of us.'

'I don't know, Katie,' I say. 'I don't know why he'd be looking at photos from so long ago.'

She thinks about that for a minute, biting her lower lip in a way that is painfully familiar to me. 'I wasn't being completely honest with you, when you asked about me and Luke.'

I wait for her to explain.

'It wasn't an affair – nothing like that. It was more a flirtation. A light-hearted thing. Can you imagine that?'

I can't help but notice the dark circles, like bruising, around her eyes, the taut pull of the muscles in her face, as if something angry and pained is lurking at the back of her expression. 'Kay, I can't imagine you doing anything light-hearted right now.'

It's honest – maybe too honest – and instantly I regret saying those words. But they can't be taken back.

She fiddles with a ring on her middle finger, turning it like a worry-bead.

'You don't think . . .' she begins '. . . you don't think this – Luke's disappearance, I mean – you don't think it has anything to do with what happened back then? In Kenya, when we were kids. Do you?'

'The past is the past,' I say.

'It makes me uneasy, Nick. Luke's missing, and now you're back.' She spreads her hands in a gesture of futility. 'It's the three of us again, isn't it? And then when Julia gave me that photograph –'

'I think Luke's overstretched himself,' I say in a rush. 'I think he's taken on too much and it's all got to him. I think he's still grieving for our mum and needed to get away for a while to be by himself. It's all just got him down. That's what I think.'

'That's a big speech from you,' she says wryly, and I know that she's teasing me but, still, I see the doubt in her eye.

She has almost finished her pint, and stares at the dregs in the bottom of her glass. Her voice so low, I can hardly hear her, she says: 'Do you ever think about it? About what happened?'

My heart gives a dull thud of fear. The dread that always lies at the pit of my stomach, like a sleeping dog about to stir.

'No,' I say, my voice thick with fatigue and stout. 'No, I don't.'

I don't ask her whether she does – I don't want to – though she seems to be inching towards talking about it. Then my mobile buzzes – a text – and I busy myself with checking it, grateful for the distraction. 'It's Lauren,' I say. 'She's awake.'

Katie smiles and drains what remains of her pint. 'Best run along then,' she says, turning to get her things.

When I get back, Lauren is not in the room. Her latest text says: *Need fresh air. Gone for a stroll in the park.*

I climb into bed and fall into a deep sleep. I sleep all night and wake early, feeling dazed and weary. At first I don't know where I am. The bed sheets feel strange to my touch. I open my eyes and reach for Lauren only to find that I am alone. I sit up and call her name but there is no answer from the bathroom.

I reach for my phone on the bedside locker. There's a missed call from Julia. As I swing my legs out and get to my feet, the door opens and Lauren enters. As soon as I see her I know that something has happened. She's agitated and there is an urgency to her movements that is foreign to me.

'Look,' she says, holding a newspaper up to me. I feel a sudden plunge of dread as I take it from her, steeling myself for the news I've been waiting for.

But when I study the paper, the headline and photographs,

there is nothing about Luke, nothing at all. Instead, it's a piece about a terrorist attack.

'It's in Westlands,' she says. 'They don't know yet how many are dead.'

'Nairobi?' I say, confused, as she crosses the room and switches on the TV, flicking rapidly through the channels until she finds Sky News.

'A gang of terrorists armed with AK-47s and grenades have taken over a shopping mall.'

I try to arrange my thoughts, clear them of the fug of sleep, picturing in my mind's eye that part of Nairobi with the nightclubs and shopping malls, an area of opulence and excess.

'God knows how many people they've got in there,' she says, concentrating on the words flashing across the screen. 'Nick? Honey, are you okay?'

I sit down on the bed, spots dancing in front of my eyes, and let the paper fall to the floor. A needling sound rises in my ears – a sharp tinnitus – and with it comes pain.

'Jesus, Nick, you're white as a sheet.'

'When you came in just now, the paper in your hand, I . . .'

Her arms wrap around me, and she pulls me to her. 'Of course you were thinking of Luke. I should have realized.'

I draw away from her embrace, take hold of her wrists and tell her I'm okay, even though I'm still shaking with nerves.

'Let's get out of here,' she says.

'All right. We should call over to Julia, I suppose.'

'No,' she says, with a degree of force. 'You need a break,

Nick – we both do. Let's get out of the city. I want you to show me where you grew up.'

'Really?'

'Come on. We'll hire a car, take a picnic, make a day of it. It'll be good for you.'

There's a hesitation within me, but I feel I have something to make up to Lauren. And maybe she's right – maybe it would be good for me, for us. So I dress quickly, and by the time we're having breakfast and the coffee has kicked in, I'm feeling like it's a good idea. It will take our minds off the search. It's been a hectic week; we need the break. The hotel arranges a rental car and, in no time, we're on our way.

Lauren's mood lightens as we leave the city and head towards the Dublin mountains and beyond to the Wicklow hills, and so does mine. Even with the nagging urgency I feel to find my brother, it's a relief to be leaving the city.

The traffic lightens as we pass Harold's Cross, drive through Terenure and begin the climb up the Grange road towards Kilmashogue. As I drive, Lauren busies herself sending emails and texts to our friends in Nairobi, trying to find out if anyone we know could be caught up in the siege. The responses are jittery and panicked; a sense of the shock that has taken over Nairobi drifts through the car. On the radio, a talk-show host is discussing the end of the bail-out, the forthcoming budget, and some changes to inheritance tax at which I zone out.

Then, after an ad-break, there is a piece about Luke.

'He'll turn up,' says one of the jaded pundits. 'He's like Houdini. He's always been able to get himself out of a fix.'

The host laughs. 'But where is Luke Yates and what has

happened to him? He was on with us, listeners, if you remember, only two weeks ago to talk about the wonderful work his charity ALIVE does in Kenya, building homes for the less fortunate.'

Before I get a chance to, Lauren switches the channel. She doesn't say anything, just stares resolutely ahead. The sound of stringed instruments fills the car. A violin lifts the heavy mood into some other-worldly trance.

We reach the outskirts of south Dublin and Ticknock where the road steepens. The engine strains, and the tyres bite into the ground beneath us. I stop at a junction on the Tibradden road.

'Take a peek,' I say to Lauren.

From here you can see the whole city; you can see from Howth Head all the way into the city centre where the Spire gleams, like a shining needle. You can see the red-and-white twin-stack chimneys of Poolbeg standing out like two sticks of candy rock. You can see Dublin in all its beauty.

Lauren takes it in with a deep breath of pleasure.

I keep on into Wicklow, past Bray, heading south towards the place I had once known as home. As soon as the house comes into view, I feel pressure building in my inner ear – the bubble of air threatening to burst. My tinnitus, pinging on a high, shrill note, makes me want to turn the car around. Coming here was a mistake, I want to say. I don't want to reveal the secrets that lie behind these walls. I don't want to disturb the sleeping ghosts.

But Lauren is expectant and full of excitement. Her wonder at seeing the house I grew up in makes me feel a little sad, but I can't bear to disappoint her.

'It's beautiful,' she says, taking in the elegant sweep of the drive, the high walls, the grandeur of the eaves.

'It was once,' I say to her. Then I explain that it was sold to a developer after my father died. 'He was going to knock it and the neighbours' houses down and build a bigger estate, only he went bust.'

She places a warm hand on my thigh as I drive. She is trying to reassure me, but all I feel is a dull panic. Lauren wants to invest this moment with too much significance. Tiredness creeps over me, and with it a confusion of emotions. I'm worried for my brother, but there's a whisper of anger too – at the senselessness of his disappearance, at his dragging me back here when I wanted to stay away – and with the anger comes a clinging shame.

Some of the stones in the driveway have come loose, weeds growing among them, making the surface crooked and uneven. The splendour of the sash windows remains hidden, plywood hammered over the frames. The garden is overgrown, bindweed choking everything. We're far from anything. The idyllic, once bustling family home is gone.

I park the car and turn the key to kill the engine.

'Come on,' Lauren says, stepping out.

She approaches one of the boarded-up windows, stands on a couple of stacked blocks, attempting to peer in. My eye is drawn upwards to the eaves where gaps have appeared, ripe for nesting house martins. I notice the holes in the woodwork and the fissures in the walls and think of the draughts whistling through the house, and feel a shiver of loneliness.

'What now?' I ask.

'Let's go inside.'

'Lauren,' I say patiently, 'the place is all locked up. There *is* no going in.'

She doesn't seem to hear me. Instead she walks around the side of the house and I trail after her, through the overgrown kitchen garden, a gnarled mess of shrubbery, nettles and weeds, and round to the back where the door into the scullery has been blocked off with two planks nailed across it. I watch her pulling at them, one half of me concerned at her insistence, the other half curious. All at once there is a rending sound as the wood gives way and she pushes the door open, turning to me with a grin of triumph that I can't help but laugh at, her excitement is so infectious.

'Congratulations,' I say, following her as she ducks in under the remaining plank and enters the dark space. 'You've a shining career as a house-breaker ahead of you.'

There's a dank smell of rot and damp. Lauren is one step ahead of me.

'Look at this place,' she says, her voice hushed with wonder, and I can see the thrill in her face – the thrill of the illicit, the forbidden. I'm full of warnings and words of heed, like a good husband, but she doesn't answer. In the kitchen, someone has built a small bonfire, which has gone out now. The walls are charred black in one corner. The picture of the Sacred Heart still hangs on the far wall, faded now. Somewhere in the cavern of my memory, I hear the ghostly echo of voices calling to me from the past.

'Oh, wow, check this out,' Lauren says, reaching the staircase, which has retained its elegant sweep despite the decay.

I watch her climb, her hand recoiling at the grimy touch of the banister.

'Be careful,' I tell her, worried that at any moment the wood under her feet might give way and she could crash through the stairs.

I watch her until she disappears, but I don't follow her. Instead, I step through into what had been the living room. A murky half-light fills the space. I can see that the fireplace has been ripped out and carried off, along with all the other furnishings. There is a stripped-out, forlorn quality to it, as if the room itself is in mourning for its past glory. A swarm of voices ghost through my head. They seem to echo with warning. I didn't think coming here would affect me so deeply. A well of emotion rises in me and I feel dizzy, as if I'm standing at some great height and looking down.

Lauren calls my name but I don't want to go up there. I've seen enough. I shout up to her that I'll wait for her outside. She calls me again. This time I hear a shrill note of panic in her voice. I take the staircase two at a time and follow the sound into the front bedroom.

She turns to me, her face pale with shock. I look past her to the quiet and stillness of the place.

The dimness is broken by a beam of light that has escaped through the cracked boarding of the window.

The light catches his feet and ankles – black patent shoes, socks with a diamond pattern, the cuffs of his black tuxedo trousers.

'Oh, God,' Lauren says quietly to herself, over and over.

I stand still, ears ringing painfully, pricked by a thousand stinging needles. If there are words to say, I cannot say them. Not here, not now. I feel Lauren's hand on my back, but I can't look at her. Instead I stand in my parents' house, transfixed, staring up at him: my brother, the beam above him creaking as he swings gently from the end of a rope.

PART TWO
Kenya 1982

7. Sally

'I don't like him,' she says.

They are in the office in Kianda, the two of them. The driver has just left. Sally stands at the door, watching the small figure oiling his way down the alley, the casual roll of his step.

'Why not?' Jim asks, and she turns to see him looking up at her, surprised.

'I don't trust him.'

He laughs, returning to his paperwork, one hand tapping out a rhythm with his pen. 'You don't trust anyone,' he says softly.

She turns away and looks out of the door again. The driver – Mackenzie – has paused at the corner to light another cigarette, shoulders hunched forward in his denim jacket. The whole time he was in the office he kept puffing away, cigarette pinched between stubby fingers, grime around the fingernails. Sally has a sudden glimpse of a lurching journey in a tin-can minibus, the stale smell of that cigarette smoke making her nauseous.

'He seems shifty,' she says, and feels again the push of her irritation. The way he had snubbed her, directing all his comments to Jim as if she wasn't even in the room. Occasionally, the conversation had drifted into Kikulu and Sally, who cannot speak the language, could only stand by and dumbly observe their exchange. Jim speaks it fluently, yet carries the current of Irishness through his vowels and inflections. She had shifted her weight from one foot to the other, arms crossed over her chest, and Jim, noticing her impatience, had drawn the conversation back into English. Once the arrangements were made and a fee settled on, the two men had shaken hands. She had come forward to offer hers but he had nodded at her and stepped past her out onto the street. Her anger had risen.

'Listen,' Jim says, trying to sound reasonable, 'he knows the road well, and the safari routes out there like the back of his hand. By all means look for someone else, but you won't find anyone who can sniff out the big game like Mack, believe me.'

He's right, but she doesn't say anything, watching silently as Mackenzie rounds a corner and disappears into the vast clogged wasteland of the Kibera slums. Today, in the heat, the stench is worse than ever. Sewage chugs through open channels and a lively commerce of shoe-repair and laundry takes place outside steaming tin huts. Overhead, the sky is a dull white, with heavy clouds, and the miasma of heat beats down oppressively.

Once, flying over Nairobi in a small aeroplane, Sally had peered out of the tiny window to the sprawling slum below.

'It's like a great big smear of shit on the landscape, isn't it?'

This from her neighbour – a fellow passenger she'd never met before. She'd glared at him, aghast and furious, but he had stared past her, his deadened gaze fixed on the land below.

Sally's is a familiar face in this part of the slum, having been a fixture there for the best part of a year. She is well practised now in suppressing any feelings of revulsion that rise to greet the monstrous filth of the place. Sometimes it seems to her that she is more at home among the alleyways of red-brown mud than she is in the lush and verdant setting of Lavington – all those sanitised homes on the hill with their intruder alarms and their guards, perimeter walls crowned with shards of glass.

'I suppose you're right,' she murmurs, pushing down on the uncertainty that keeps surfacing insistently.

Outside, Luke is kicking a plastic bottle around with two local boys, who wear shoes that seem huge, their narrow stick legs emerging from them and rising to swollen dark knees. Sally doesn't know why he has chosen to come with her today, instead of staying behind with the others. She suspects it has something to do with the friendship that has sprung up between his younger brother, Nick, and Helen's daughter, Katie. Their alliance seems to have thrown off-balance the bond that previously existed between her two sons. Sally feels ambivalent towards the quiet, mousy girl. But to watch her beloved Nicky become bewitched in his own quiet tender-hearted way has made her feel a kind of sadness that she cannot account for, as if his growing affection for the girl is somehow diminishing the love between mother and son.

Silly, she tells herself, as she watches Luke duck beneath the arm of his opponent, eyes fixed on the makeshift ball. Ten years old and already his body is becoming lean and rangy. Square shoulders, all the puppy fat fallen away now, and in the past month she has noticed, with a degree of alarm, the changes in her elder son's face – a strengthening in his jaw, the lengthening of his features – so that she can glimpse the adult face waiting for him. She does not want this boy to grow up – not yet. She is not ready to let go. And yet what worries her most, what keeps her awake and staring at the ceiling some nights, is the look that she has found him giving her lately when he thinks she can't see – a cold glance with a question in it, as if she's on the cusp of failing him and he is waiting expectantly for her to fall. Even now, this trip to Kianda and Luke's decision to accompany her, she cannot help but feel that he is doing so not because he is bored, or because he feels estranged from the others, no: he is there to keep an eye on her. For all his affected nonchalance, his refusal to look her in the eye, still he won't let her out of his sight.

'You're quiet today,' Jim remarks.

'Am I?'

'Unusually pensive.'

He is seated at his desk, his wide shoulders stooped forward. A big man, in the small, cramped office he appears awkward, a kind of balled-up energy rolling around inside him seeking an outlet. He doesn't look like a priest: a wooden cross on a thin leather strap around his neck is the only visible sign of his vocation. She cannot imagine him bent in silent prayer. What was it she had said to him once? That he bore hardly any resemblance to a man of the cloth, unless you were to count John the Baptist.

'It's this trip to the Masai Mara,' she tells him. 'I feel uneasy about it.'

'How come?'

'I don't know, really. I suppose because I feel like I'm being forced into it.'

'By whom?'

'Ken.'

He keeps his gaze fixed on her, waiting. His eyes are bright blue, disarming sometimes in the way they seem to convey a troubled history. And yet Sally knows there are deep wells of goodness within the man.

'We had a row last night,' she admits, turning towards the wall as if to examine the notice-board behind him. 'He says that Helen and Katie have stayed too long. He thinks that Helen is running away.'

'What do you think?'

She shrugs, surprised by the sudden tears that spring to her eyes. Blinking them away, she swallows hard and thinks of all the hours she has spent with her friend, the two of them poring over the hole at the centre of Helen and Michael's marriage, re-examining the details of every harsh word spoken, every bitter little dispute, the various slights and dismissals. She can feel Jim watching her, sitting back in his chair, thumbs ruminatively circling each other.

'He accused me of meddling in their marriage,' she says softly.

Jim sighs, then says, his voice low and soft with understanding, 'You're a good person, Sally. You care about your friend. Whatever you may have done, your intentions were good.'

She thinks about this, briefly contemplating that word 'good'. It is a word more easily associated with him, she thinks, than with her. His goodness seems to have been fostered not within the cool, lofty spaces of churches but to have grown from the rich, loamy earth of his people – generations that have farmed the land of County Antrim stretching back as far as the Elizabethan plantations – as if the richness of the soil that bred him has nurtured within him a great desire to draw life from the arid lands of this blighted place.

'She's running away,' Ken had said the night before. It was not the first time they had discussed it.

In a whisper that carried across the darkness of their bedroom, he had urged her yet again to send Helen home.

'This can't go on,' he had told her, a rare snap of anger in his voice as she'd held her body tightly away from him, feeling the unwelcome heat of his breath. The anger was brought about not by Helen's continued presence, but by Sally's refusal. Moments before, he had reached across the crumpled sheets of their bed and, instinctively, she had drawn away.

'Christ almighty, Sally!' he had hissed. 'How long is this going to go on?'

'It's not a good time –'

'It's never a bloody good time. Not since she arrived.'

Slamming his head back into the pillow, she had felt his fury rising and whipping around the room in faster revolutions than the lazy whirr of the ceiling fan above them.

'Since they came into this house, we haven't made love once. Not once! It's like you don't want me to touch you –'

'That's not true.'

'Like she's infected you with the poison seeping from the unhappiness of her own marriage.'

'It's not like that.'

'Then what is it? Please, tell me.'

'I'm tired, that's all. Entertaining the boys and Katie, talking things over with Helen, listening to what she's been through . . .'

'What she's been through,' he repeated scornfully. 'She's a spoiled brat, throwing a tantrum.'

'That's not true! She's been so miserable, so depressed. You've no idea –'

'She's acting like a bloody adolescent!'

'She'll hear you!'

'I don't bloody care! This is my house.'

But the warning seemed to calm him, or quieten him anyway. For a while neither of them spoke.

Then, before he turned away from her in the darkness, he said: 'Michael's not a bad man, Sally. He's just dull, and she knew that when she married him. Enough is enough. They need to go home.'

The lingering ghost of that conversation stays with her now as she examines the noticeboard in front of her, feels the sweat on her back, the heat beating down through the flimsy roof. She feels fragile after the row, shaky inside – all of it is happening too fast. And then the phone call from Ken at the office this morning, telling her he had rung the airline, everything was arranged . . .

Jim is on his feet now, standing beside her, his hands in his pockets, and she can feel him looking at her.

'What is it, Sal?' he asks carefully. 'You seem troubled.'

She holds herself still, keeping her eyes on the wall.

'Ken says this trip to the Masai Mara is our goodbye to them. He booked the flights – they leave the day after we come back.'

'Ah.' For a moment he says nothing, and she can feel him watching her. Something is rising inside her.

His voice, soft in a way that goes right to the sore spot, says: 'They were never going to stay here for ever, Sally. And surely you wouldn't want them to.'

'It's the way he did it!' she blurts out, suddenly upset.

'Making the decision with absolutely no regard for what I want, let alone what Helen wants! Do you know he rang Michael this morning? Told him we're sending his wife back to him. Those were the exact words he used! Like Helen was lost property – a piece of baggage! And dragging me into it. He hasn't a clue, not a bloody clue!'

Her voice breaks, emotion lodged in her throat, tears clawing around her eyes.

He doesn't say anything, but she feels his arm going around her back, the firmness of his hand on her shoulder holding her against him, holding her firm and still, as they wait for this wave to pass.

'Foolish,' she says, admonishing herself, a furious shake of her head.

'Ah, now . . .'

Then, in a softer voice, she says, 'He's made up his mind, Jim – about his contract. He's going to turn down their offer. He wants us to go back to Ireland.'

She lowers her head, feels the flutter of panic. She could explain it to Jim and he would understand, but not Ken. He would react with disbelief if she told him that the woman he lived with, the wife who could throw a perfect dinner party, who could be serene in the face of her children's tantrums, who could be warm and welcoming to her husband when he came home from work in the evening, was a fake – a hollow vessel. That it was all exterior, for show, and underneath there was nothing, only a wisp of uncertainty floating in an empty space. How when she had come to Kenya, she had felt something change inside her, felt her senses respond in a different way: smells became more intense, colours were deeper and more vibrant, her sense of taste became heightened. And these were not the only senses to awaken.

'Sometimes I feel like I can't stay with him another minute . . .'

She takes a breath, the emotion brought under control, feels his arm fall away from her and, half turning towards him, she sees her son standing in the doorway. He is holding her bag and staring at her, his face a blank in the shadows, eyes wide with shock and hurt, as if he's been slapped.

'Luke,' she says, but he is already turning away, letting her bag drop to the ground.

She thinks of what she said – words spoken against his father – and is filled with remorse.

Jim says something now but she doesn't hear it, doesn't respond. She watches her son walk swiftly across to the other boys, hunkering down on the stoop next to them, his expression furious and deeply private, and thinks of what she will say to him, how best to explain it.

As the evening shadows come on, the air clogs with cooking smells. Back in Lavington, the lawn-sprinkler will be turned off now. Jamil will be going through the house switching on the lights, Nick and Katie grumbling about dinner. She feels flattened beneath the weight of her responsibilities and the evening ahead.

'I'd better go,' she tells Jim, and stops to smile briefly, before stepping out to tell Luke it's time to head back.

Their journey home is subdued, neither of them wanting to talk. Climbing the steps to the house, Sally hears the twittering of a pair of starlings. Their cage hangs from the beam that runs between the carved posts of the veranda. She listens to them absently, her gaze unseeing. Cloaked in grime, the dirt of the slums clinging to her, the need to cleanse outweighs her desire to greet her younger son, so she hurries upstairs, the cooking smells from the kitchen already filling the house, anticipating the jets of hot water with a kind of hunger. After her shower, when she comes back into the bedroom to dress, she is surprised to find her husband waiting for her. Sitting back on the bed, legs crossed at the ankles, he sips his drink, then draws her attention to the glass he has brought for her and left on the dresser.

'You're home early,' Sally remarks, as she takes her gin and tonic, and picks out clothes to wear for dinner.

'The office is quiet at the moment,' Ken says.

'That's good, I suppose.'

'Yes. A welcome respite.'

She doesn't look at him but can tell from his pensiveness, his very presence in this room as she dresses instead of reading the paper downstairs or playing table-tennis with the boys, that there is something on his mind; that his early appearance has little to do with a lull at the office and is about something else entirely. The silence sits between them, like a scab begging to be picked. She dresses quickly, furtively almost, self-conscious in front of her husband.

'Did you talk to Helen?'

His tone is measured and she can tell he has chosen his words carefully.

'Not yet,' she says, conscious of the tension that has sprung up between them. The low hum of unease from their row the night before seems amplified and very present within the room.

'Look, I'm sorry about last night,' he says. 'I shouldn't have lost my temper like that.'

'Me too.'

'I just want things to get back to normal around here,' he continues.

She turns back to the dresser and fumbles in her jewellery box for a necklace to wear. 'I just feel sorry for Helen, that's all. It'll be hard on her, going back.'

He looks at her, saying nothing and waits.

'I'm sorry, Ken. I know you think it's best, but I just can't help feeling awful at the thought of her returning to that stifling life in a small town, trapped within a dying marriage.'

'What's the alternative, Sally?'

'She could get a job.'

He's thrown by this. 'A job? What do you mean a job?'

'So that she can pay her way.'

His eyes widen. '*Here?* She wants to get a job in Nairobi?'

'Yes,' she answers, a little cowed now by his reaction. Confronted by her husband's evident shock, which suggests how ridiculous he thinks the suggestion is, a trickle of doubt assails her. She turns to clip on her earrings, hoping to mask the indecision that is visible on her face.

'Sally, that's ridiculous! You can't seriously be suggesting that they continue to live with us?'

'Why not?' she asks, shrugging her shoulders in a show of nonchalance, trying to lighten the atmosphere.

'For a whole host of reasons! For a start, she has a home

of her own but, quite apart from that, I don't want to share mine, my family – my *wife* – with that woman.'

'You were the one who said she should come out here –'

'No, no! Hang on a second! I said she *could* come out here, if that was what she needed to do. But I never said "should". And I certainly never meant her to stay indefinitely. Two or three weeks, fine. But, Christ, they've been here over two months! Enough is enough, Sally!'

He gets to his feet as he says this, bringing his empty glass down firmly on the dresser, so firmly that she flinches. Hands on his hips, he assesses her and she can see the workings of his jaw beneath his cheek, the grinding of teeth a flag to his emotion, and knows she can't push him too far.

'Besides, she can't stay here because we'll be leaving ourselves soon enough. Won't we, Sally?'

Something within her – the spark of recklessness that ignited her confession to Jim that afternoon – pushes her to say: 'Are you giving me an ultimatum? Is that what you're doing, Kenneth?'

The two of them, facing one another, the air between them charged with all the tension and fury that have built up over the weeks and months that preceded this hot summer.

'She's got to go home,' he says quietly. 'And if you won't tell her, I will.'

With that, he pushes past her, out of the door, his feet descending the staircase heavy and ponderous.

Turning away, she finishes dressing, in her mind their argument running on, formulating phrases laden with self-righteous indignation that she flings at him in her imagination. It continues in her head as she leaves the bedroom and shuts the door behind her. Downstairs she can hear Helen's voice, a rising tinkle of laughter, and pictures the two of them standing there with pre-dinner drinks, Helen laughing at some joke Ken has made, no idea of the dark thoughts he is entertaining.

As she reaches the top of the staircase, something catches her eye – movement behind a half-closed door. She goes to it now, opening it wide to see Nicky and Katie hovering above the bathroom basin. Their faces when they turn to her seem furtive and closed in a way that makes her step into the room, her voice brisk and hard as she asks them: 'What are you doing?'

Straight away, they pull their hands behind their backs, Nicky lowering his eyes, but Katie meets Sally's full-on, her expression flat but there is daring in it too.

'Hold out your hands,' Sally tells them, a pinch of alarm coming on as she witnesses their hesitation, the slight inclination of Nicky's head as he glances at the girl, seeking her permission. That look inflames Sally, so that she reaches behind his back and grabs hold of his arm, bringing it forward. Despite herself, she gives a small cry of shock.

His hand is full of blood. Beneath the wetness, she can see the gash – an ugly line amid the creases and folds of his palm.

She doesn't ask how it happened, doesn't say anything at all. Reaching for Katie's hand, she tries to suppress her alarm at the matching wound, the trickle of blood running over the girl's wrist. This child is a guest in my home, she thinks, feeling a stab of guilt.

Hunkering down in front of them, she feels her heart beating so hard it must be audible. She looks from one hand to the other and, from the corner of her eye, sees the open penknife balanced on the edge of the basin, a smear of blood on the ceramic.

'Whose idea was this?' she asks, her voice low and barely controlled. 'Whose?'

The question is pointless. The pact they have formed – she can guess whose idea it was. The question she should be asking is: Why?

'Mine,' Nicky says quickly, the word coming out in a rush, and from the way Katie glances at him sharply, Sally knows it isn't true. As she watches her younger son take the blame – volunteer for it – the small act of chivalry breaks her heart a little.

'You shouldn't have done this,' she whispers, feeling herself coming close to the brink again. 'You might need stitches.'

'It doesn't hurt,' Katie says stoically. 'Not really.'

But her eyes are smarting with tears and Sally finds herself letting go of the child's hand and reaching up to touch her cheek – the only tender gesture she has made to her since her arrival.

The children are silent as she washes their wounds, wincing as the cold water runs into their palms.

'Wait there,' she instructs them, as she goes to her room for the first-aid box.

When she returns, they are standing together with their backs to her, Nicky leaning against Katie, in their shorts and T-shirts, feet bare on the cool tiled floor. Something about the way they stand together – how small and vulnerable they look – makes her stop short, holding her breath. Katie has her arm around Nicky's shoulders as if comforting him. Sally, entering the room, disturbs them, and when her son turns to face her, his eyes are swimming with tears.

'What is it, love?' she asks tenderly. 'Is it very sore?'

'Luke says you're sending her away.'

'What?'

'Katie. He says you'll make her go. I don't want her to go,' he says, his face contorting with emotion, so that she draws him to her, whispering words of comfort into his hair.

It's not until a few minutes later, not until she has left the children alone with their bandaged hands to change for dinner, when she reaches the bottom of the stairs that Sally feels it.

In the hallway, she hears Jamil singing in the kitchen, and through the open door, she can hear the starlings flapping restlessly in their cage on the veranda. From the next room comes the low murmur of Ken's voice and the tinkle of Helen's laughter, and Sally feels the steel entering her heart, tastes it on her tongue. She knows now what will happen: she will join them in the living room and, calmly but firmly, she will tell her friend that they will go to the Masai Mara – a final trip – and afterwards Helen and Katie must go back to Ireland. Ken has given her an ultimatum, but that is not why she does it. She sees in her mind's eye the knife on the basin, the blood, her son's whimpering body, and feels a shudder go through her. The bond between the children, intimate, too close, sealed now with blood, hardens her heart to any possible protests. The decision has been made. Ready now, she puts her hand to the door, pushes it, and the others turn to greet her.

PART THREE

Kenya 2013

8. Katie

The day I found out about Luke's death, I stopped drinking. It wasn't a conscious decision, not really. I didn't suddenly decide to flip over a new leaf. It was more a feeling that rose up from my gut, a deep revulsion with myself and with what had happened, so dark and intense that I could hardly stand my own company. Something had to change.

Three weeks of sobriety have passed without much strain, but now, sitting in the airport lounge with Reilly, nursing a cup of coffee, I feel the fear inside me and with it the nudge of longing for a drink.

'Penny for them,' Reilly says gently.

I look up at him, see his chin resting on his hand, a thumb meditatively stroking his bearded jaw, a furrow of concern between his eyes as he watches me carefully. He had picked me up when dawn had barely broken over the city and driven me to the airport, insisting on keeping me company. Here, in this bustling, transient place, there is a firmness about him – a solidity – which makes me feel safe, but a bit panicky too. In a few moments, I will have to leave and Reilly will stay, and this makes me feel uncertain.

'I'm wondering why I'm here, Reilly – why I'm about to get on this plane.'

'Because he wanted you to,' he says.

'That's what's bothering me,' I say, leaning in closer to him. 'Why did Luke want me to come?'

'You must have meant something to him,' Reilly suggests.

'But that's just it. Including me in this group of intimates suggests a closeness between us that no longer exists. And why Kenya? It just doesn't stack up. His whole adult life, he never went back, yet he wants to be laid to rest there?'

I bite my lip, my eyes darting around. I can't seem to shake the twitchiness I've been feeling ever since I got the phone call asking me to attend the event – one of a very small and select group of people that Luke requested be present when his ashes were scattered on the wind.

'Christ, what must his wife think?' I run a hand over my eyes and, in the lidded darkness, I see Julia Yates's face, her eyes level and examining that day in her house when she gave me the picture. I've brought it with me, tucked inside my handbag, and now, on a whim, I take it out and pass it to Reilly. 'Julia Yates gave this to me. She found it on his desk the morning he went missing.'

His eyes travel over it, taking it in: Luke, Nick and I, sitting in the African sun.

'Look at you,' he says quietly, 'before you were corrupted.'

'That was a hell of a long time ago,' I say drily.

'Ah, now, none of that. Fishing for compliments about your age.'

He turns it over in his hand, peers at the back, then slides it across the table to me. 'Do you think it's significant?'

'Something happened. Back when we were kids. . . something happened and now I wonder, I can't help but think that . . .'

My eyes fill, the room a blur, and his hand is on mine, steadying me. I hear his voice telling me that I need to calm myself, that there is no point second-guessing why the man killed himself, that people carry around inside them all sorts of secrets, all sorts of pain, and that no good ever came of that kind of soul-searching. But all the time he is talking, I keep thinking of the little bird, and the shadow of something else: a cage on a veranda, the fluttering of wings.

'The last thing you need right now,' Reilly says, 'is to spiral off into some kind of introspective self-examination of some long-forgotten childhood act that means nothing to anyone but you, probably. Do you hear me, Katie?'

I feel the wisdom in his words, tenderness too. If only it were true.

'What are you doing here, Reilly?' I ask. 'Why are you being so kind to me?'

His hand, still on mine, feels suddenly heavy, and something changes in the air between us.

'Because I care, Katie.'

He says it awkwardly, then withdraws his hand.

Across from us, a little girl sits with her mother, swinging her legs and staring right at me. The mother is peering into a hand-held mirror and dabbing at her cheeks with a little sponge. Where is the father? I wonder.

Something about Reilly, how safe he makes me feel when I'm with him, the way he's looking at me now with a mixture of interest and concern, reminds me of my father, and all at once I'm back in my parents' kitchen, a weekend home from university, my father frying bacon, and I'm saying to him casually: 'Guess who I bumped into the other day? Nick Yates.' The way his back, curved then in middle age but still elegant, had seemed to stiffen at the name. But I pressed on brightly, telling him about my new friendship, feigning an ease I didn't feel, pressured as I was by his unspoken anxiety. He didn't say anything at the time. But later, when the weekend was over and he was dropping me back to the station to catch my train, he reached out to grab my wrist before I climbed out of the car, an urgency in his voice and a warning in his eye as he said: 'Stay away from that boy now, Katie. He's no good for you.' And that was the last we ever spoke of it.

Now, with my coffee cooling in front of me, and a voice on the Tannoy announcing the boarding of another flight, I say to Reilly: 'I'm frightened about going back there.'

His eyes flicker over my face. 'What happened, Katie?'

'We were just kids. We'd been playing. But then . . . something terrible . . .'

Reilly's mouth bunches into a pensive pout and I hear him exhaling. 'Do you want to talk about it?'

I feel the pull of him there, and in one way it would be so easy to tell him, the relief of just letting it out. 'No,' I say quickly, wishing I hadn't brought it up.

Still, I can't help but feel the creep of sadness now. 'What I don't get is why he wants to go back there,' I say. 'Why would Luke Yates want his remains scattered over the one place on earth that this awful thing in his life happened?'

'To atone?' Reilly suggests.

'Maybe.'

But the unease remains. It stays with me as I gather my belongings and, with Reilly to accompany me, make my way towards the security gates. As we reach the barrier, I stop. 'When someone's remains are flown to a different country, do you think they're packed in the luggage hold with all the suitcases and golf-bags?'

Reilly doesn't answer. Instead he takes my shoulders and leans in to kiss my forehead. I feel the brush of his beard and with it comes a lurch of fear, like a foreshadowing of something unseen but terrible. I want to hold on to him then and keep him close. But he draws back and gives me a smile of reassurance. 'You'll be fine,' he says then, and I can feel his eyes on me, watching me as I make my way up the queue, until I'm through the barrier and lost from sight.

By the time the plane touches down on the runway at Jomo Kenyatta International Airport my head is pounding. I have spent the entire flight hiding in my seat, painfully aware of the others on this plane – Nick, Lauren, Julia. I tried to work, reading over the notes I'd made following the autopsy report, but the words kept stringing together – *alcohol and narcotics in the bloodstream, evidence of self-strangulation, bruising, the bursting of blood vessels, traumas to the body*. Reading it made me feel restless, uncontained, the stirring of some deep-buried emotion inside me. After touchdown, I look outside and see the night sky purple and green where the floodlights colour the air. My limbs ache from the journey. As I come down the steps and breathe in the diesel fumes polluting the soft African night breeze, the tension in my body is morphing into some kind of swamping fatigue. All I want now is to get to my hotel room and collapse into bed.

Standing at a distance from the rest, I watch as one by one the others collect their luggage from the carousel and wander off to find taxis to wherever they are staying. No one makes any attempt to speak to me – not even Nick – which only compounds my loneliness on what is already a solitary journey. Nick and Lauren have their own home somewhere in the city. I picture a bohemian apartment in an old colonial house, rotating fans and hardwood furniture, framed posters and ethnic prints, a cocktail bar in one corner, a piano in the other.

I can't help but sneak a glance at her – Nick's wife. There's something very easy in her manner, the relaxed way she holds herself, the casual flick of her hair, as if she's blissfully unaware of her own power, her own beauty. I wonder what Sally Yates would have made of her, this blonde creature – shockingly young, as if she's barely out of school. Looking at her, after the long, difficult flight, I feel old. Old, wasted and unfulfilled.

Julia takes her bag and catches my eye. She, I'm sure, will not be staying at Nick and Lauren's, more like at the Hilton or the Safari Club. Drowning her sorrows in South African wine, and being comforted by her mother and sister. As for me, I've booked a single room at the Meridian. For the price I'm paying, my expectations are pretty low.

A single unclaimed suitcase rides the carousel with a grim determination. 'For fuck's sake,' I say, under my breath. My bag, it would appear, has been lost.

After an hour of wrangling and form-filling, I find

myself riding in a taxi towards Nairobi's Central Business District. The driver signals he doesn't mind so I smoke cigarette after cigarette and feel myself grow calm as I blow smoke out of the open window and watch as we pass through one more roundabout onto another unlit street, scrubby black bushes running alongside the road. An eerie feeling comes over me at being back here. As if I'm entering a place that is out of bounds. It's almost thirty years since I set foot in Kenya. I was, after all, only a child back then.

Just Mam and me. 'The two girls,' she'd said, creating an ally of me. Dad was back in Ireland, still shaken by my mother's announcement. 'We're leaving,' she had told him, her head held aloft in a challenging way, and then, recanting, she had added: 'For a while, anyway.' It was odd to be so far away from him. I remember feeling frightened that we might not go back, that this time Mam really meant it, but I also recall feeling unable to say so to her. She was so wound up – a tightly coiled spring. It didn't feel like we were going on holiday; nor was it like an adventure. It felt like something illicit and shameful, and the whole time we were away, I couldn't shake the thought that something terrible would happen to my dad in our absence. Like he was going to get knocked over by a car or something. Lying awake in bed during those hot nights away, I thought of all the ways he might die in our absence and that it would be our fault, mine and Mam's, for leaving him. I never suspected that the terrible thing would happen to me.

Gradually, the black bushes peter out. Buildings sprout at the sides of the roads, lit now by streetlamps. Road signs appear and the buildings grow larger and more dense.

Soon enough, the taxi pulls up outside the Meridian, with its large impersonal façade. I pay my fare, get out wearily and go through the hotel's doors.

It's late when I find my room. I look down from my window at the street below; horns honking and the whine of engines reaches me on the eighth floor and restlessness takes hold of me. It's too late to go out wandering, but I don't want to be alone, so I go back downstairs to the sports bar that flanks the lobby.

The place is loud with voices and the clinking of glasses. Muzak is piped through speakers. I'm looking for a quiet corner to hide, when my eyes alight on a young woman darkly dressed, hair pulled back to show a face that is small and pretty, a woman who is regarding me with suspicion. I know who she is – her picture was in one of the tabloids after Luke's death, part of a montage of various shots of the women in his life. In the caption under Tanya Clarke's photograph, some sub-editor had added the caption 'Stalwart assistant'. Before I approach her, I wonder how she feels about being pinned under that label and then, as I step towards her, I see a hint of something in her that I recognize – loneliness, desperation. My spirits rise a little at the glimpse of an opening.

'Can I join you?' I ask, indicating the empty chair, and she shrugs, saying, 'It's a free country,' in a nonchalant manner, but her flickering eyes betray her.

A lounge boy passes and I order a club soda for me and a refill for Tanya, who is beginning to thaw a little – vodka and tonic.

'To steady the nerves,' she says quietly. 'Long flights make me anxious. I always need a drink after them . . .'

I take in her glossy brown hair, her perfectly mani-cured nails, her correct posture. But there is tiredness in the set of her shoulders, a kind of bewilderment at the edges of her gaze. And I feel her looking at me too, her eyes passing over me, and I imagine how tired and dishevelled I must appear. We exchange some small-talk about the flight, about the hotel. But Tanya also exudes a kind of practical ability, a hyper-organised profession-alism, that tells me she's not one for chit-chat, so I launch right in.

'It must have been a shock to see yourself in the paper the other day,' I say.

'My sudden leap to stardom,' she says drily, as our drinks arrive.

I watch her adding the tonic to her glass, giving it a brisk stir, then bringing it to her lips. 'From what I hear, Luke relied heavily on you.'

'Yes,' she says. 'I still can't believe he's gone.'

'You must miss him.'

'The office is so quiet now. I'm not sure what's going to happen.'

'Will you stay on?'

'I don't think so. It just wouldn't be the same.'

I can see that she's anxious, her hands fidgeting, and I know that she wants to talk but is wary of taking me into her confidence. 'You must have been close – you and Luke?'

'Oh, yes! He was great. I'd have done anything for him.' She catches me looking, and sits a little straighter in her seat. 'It's not what you're thinking. Luke wasn't like that – I mean, he was very charming, flirtatious even.

He loved the company of women but he would never take advantage.'

I wonder, not for the first time, whether she was a little in love with Luke Yates.

'Anyway,' she says brusquely, as if she feels she's said too much, 'he's dead now.'

I sense her closing down. Her drink is almost finished and so is mine, and the way she is shifting in her chair tells me she will leave soon.

'Are you going to the Masai Mara after the ceremony tomorrow?' I ask, and she nods.

'I've never been,' she adds. 'Funny, because it's a place I've always wanted to go. I just never thought it would be under these circumstances.'

'I've been,' I say. 'With Luke.'

She looks at me, surprised, and I catch the gleam of interest in her eye.

'It was when we were kids. His family were living out here – his dad had a job with the World Bank, and his mother was doing aid work of some kind or another.'

'You came out for a visit?'

'Sort of.' Then, leaning forward to create a conspiratorial circle of two, I say: 'My mother ran away from my father, you see. She took me with her and we fled to Kenya.'

Tanya's eyes widen. 'Why Kenya?'

'Luke's mother and mine had been friends since childhood.'

'How long did you stay?'

'Most of the summer. I've no real memory of Nairobi. But I remember the Masai Mara. We spent our last few days there.'

'It must have been amazing.'

'Yes,' I say carefully. 'Yes, it was.'

Carefully, because of the dangerous tangle of emotions those memories pull on. Carefully, because the joy of the trip was extinguished by all that followed.

'We all went,' I go on, not sure why I'm telling her this now, but propelled by some need to let the story out. To let it out so that I can let it go. 'Even Luke's dad. Six of us and the driver crammed into a HiAce van that seemed held together with rope and prayer, bumping and rattling over the worst road in Kenya down to the Rift Valley.'

How hot it had been in that van. The smell of sweat mingling with the peppery scent of the driver's tobacco. My bare knees knocking against Luke's and Nick's. I had lost the argument for a window seat, my mother snapping at me, afraid I might cause a scene. All that long afternoon, Nick kept pinching me, trying to make me squeal, tears coming to my eyes as I bit down the shriek that I knew would only annoy my mother more. Luke sat in a prickly silence, keeping his gaze fixed on the countryside flashing by, his expression unreadable.

The excitement at the first sighting of a zebra went a long way to alleviate my tiredness and discomfort. Then the sudden appearance of giraffes languorously tugging leaves off tall trees only yards from the road seemed to carry us through the last long hour of that journey.

'How long did you stay there?'

'Three nights. Then, on the last morning, when we were due to leave, our driver turned up drunk. He had been drinking all night with the Masai, and when the adults saw the state he was in, they hit the roof.'

I have a vivid memory of my mother throwing her hands up in a gesture of exasperation before turning her back on the others and walking away.

'After a while, someone decided a new driver needed to be found so my mother and Mr Yates went off to the nearest village to look for one. The rest of us were left to wait.'

Sally Yates was sunbathing and the driver had gone to the van to sleep it off. We children sloped down towards the river. In my mind's eye, I can see it – the stillness of the tall grass, yellow against the black clump of bushes and thorn trees that flanked the narrow stream; the low droop of branches, not a breeze whispering through the trees. No movement at all, but the sound of those girls on the other side, laughing. I hear their voices in my head and instantly draw back from the memory.

'So what happened?' Tanya asks, pulling me back into the present.

'Sorry?'

'After that?'

I'm momentarily rattled.

By the time they came back, it was done.

But I don't say this.

'They found another driver and we went back to Nairobi and the next day my Mam and I flew home to Ireland.'

I finish my drink, return the glass firmly to the table.

'Did your parents stay together?' she asks, and I see curiosity in her eyes.

'Yes. Although I wouldn't say either of them was very happy.'

'Oh.'

Not happy, but relieved. That is how I've come to think

of it. They had been given a glimpse of something terrible, and after that they clung to one another – and to me – fearful of letting go in case the terrible thing crept back. Sometimes, when she thought I couldn't see her, I'd find my mother staring at me as if she didn't understand me, as if I was a stranger to her, someone who'd slipped in during the night, and I was this unknowable creature, under her care but utterly strange to her.

'Do you think Luke was happy?' I ask her now.

She thinks about it for a moment, her brow furrowing with concentration. 'For the most part.'

'I know he suffered from depression,' I offer.

'From time to time. Luke was always very up and down. When he was up he was flying, but when he was down it was like he was lost in a fog or something. Every now and then, he'd have to take time off work to . . .'

'To what?'

'To walk the black dog. That was what he called it. The depression. I don't know. I suppose some people have it. When it got really bad, he would spend some time in a clinic: St John of Gods.'

'How was he in the last few weeks?'

She winces. 'Outwardly, he seemed okay. But there was something bothering him. You could see the signs. I found I was watching him, waiting for him to go into another slump.'

'What caused it, do you think? Did he have money worries?'

'Not exactly.' She draws out the word. 'There were a few problems. He felt like he'd overstretched himself with the country house he'd bought into. And if the banks called in his loans, he'd have been sunk. His mother's charity was taking up a lot of his time – he was concerned about it, and in recent months he'd asked an accountant to look things over. Sally, for all her good points, was not one for keeping the books up to date. But I don't think he was unduly worried about money issues. He seemed to have it under control.'

'What, then?'

I see her hesitation, the way her eyes pass over the table between us, the way she uncrosses then crosses her legs. She knows something. I feel the quickening of anticipation.

'One day, a few weeks ago now, I walked into his office and saw him sitting at his desk, looking like he'd just seen a ghost. He was so pale, his skin was almost grey. I thought he was ill. I asked if he wanted a glass of water, a painkiller, something – but he just sat there, not moving, staring at the desk in front of him. And that was when I saw it.'

'What?'

'A bird. A dead bird.'

My heart just about stops.

'Someone had sent him a dead bird in the post. It was lying there on the table in front of him, this tiny little thing, the claws drawn up like it had rigor mortis.'

'What kind of bird was it?' I ask, my voice cracking.

'I don't know. He didn't want me to touch it, or even come close to it. When I moved towards him, he put a hand up and told me he'd take care of it.'

'Do you know who sent it?'

'No idea. He wouldn't talk about it – just clammed up.'

'Do you think he knew?'

She shakes her head. Then, as if suddenly remembering, she says with conviction: 'He said something that made me stop. He said: "Tanya, my past is coming back to haunt me."' She glances up at me then, and if she sees the fear in my eyes, she doesn't remark on it. 'Strange, isn't it?'

'Yes,' I say, looking around for the lounge boy and signalling for the bill – I don't want her to see how shaken I am. I don't want her to witness the fear that is crawling up from my toes, the sickness and panic that are colonizing my whole body.

It's late. I'm tired and unprepared for the day that lies ahead, a day that's going to be hard. Besides, I'm afraid of what I might confess if I sit here much longer. Tanya has a weepy air about her now and I don't want to hear any of her confessions either, so I make my apologies, explaining that I'm dead tired and will probably sleep in my clothes, the shoes still on my feet. She smiles in sympathy and bids me goodnight.

But I don't sleep. Instead, I sit by the window high above an intersection that is quiet now, only the occasional purr of an engine rising to greet me, while I smoke cigarette after cigarette. My mind wanders along dark, lonely tracks, all of which lead back to the river. The girlish laughter; Luke saying, 'Come on,' the urgency of his excitement; Nick glancing over his shoulder to check for me. Then later, bouncing along in a different van with a different driver, a black ache of dread in my heart, all of us silent as we headed back to Nairobi. I remember the quietness of that space and how unnatural it seemed, as if it was something dangerous that might shatter at any moment. I got the window seat, but it was a hollow victory, and stared flatly at the zebras and giraffes, my eyes opened now in a way I didn't want them to be. Beside me, I could feel the gentle shake of Nick's body as he cried, his head down, tears falling onto his lap making dark circles on his shorts. I don't know whether Luke cried then, although he did later. He was staring at something out the window I couldn't see.

Nobody said a word.

I hadn't thought I would ever come back here. I had tried to put that part of my childhood behind me, yet still I had come to think of it as the defining moment in my life. In the dark hours, when I lay alone and unloved in my bed, salty tears of self-pity drying on my cheeks, I would turn to that moment, allow myself to peek at it from the distance of time, and think about how it might have changed me, how, if it had never happened, I might have become a different person and lived a different life.

I'd thought I was strong enough to come back. I'd told myself the memory of what had happened had diminished with time, lost its weight and significance. We had only been kids, after all. But sitting at the open window of a dim, unfamiliar room, absorbing the night smell of this foreign city, I feel the power of that event surfacing again. And this time I am alone. My mother dead, my father too, Luke and Luke's parents. All gone, all shadows now. Just me and Nick left. But Nick feels far, far away from me, even if what happened still binds us, and as the night grows later, it's as if a veil has been lifted, a door opened, and what it reveals I don't want to see. But it's there in the room with me, weaving its way inside, a dull insistent hum running through my head all night long.

9. Nick

It starts almost the moment I step off the plane – the sense of displacement. Something strange is happening. It's as if in my absence things have changed just fractionally, an imperceptible shift but enough to disorient me. Lauren feels it too. On the flight, we'd barely spoken, Lauren sleeping for most of it, while I was lost in my thoughts. Now, as we move through the airport, she turns to me and says: 'Check out the security.'

Her eyes travel in the direction of soldiers in fatigues, guns in their hands, the straps slung over their shoulders, their gaze hard and unrelenting.

'It's like a war zone,' she says.

The military presence persists throughout the building and outside to where the taxis and buses line the pavement.

'Let's get out of here,' she says, and we climb into the nearest taxi.

'What about Julia?' I say, as the taxi pulls away from the kerb.

'She's a grown-up,' Lauren mutters. 'She can take care of herself.'

Lauren is swamped by fatigue after the whole drawn-out rigmarole of my brother's death. Something has changed in her over the past few days, and while I can't place my finger on what it is, I know enough to draw back from asking her, not now, not yet, not with what lies ahead of us over the next few days.

The taxi turns onto familiar streets as we near home, and still the strangeness persists.

'It's so quiet,' Lauren says.

She's right. There isn't a sinner on the roads, no visible life apart from the dogs that roam the pavements, slinking against the walls, sniffing at the drains. Even after dark, these streets are usually alive with talk, movement and music, the vibrant nightlife spilling out of bars and clubs, but now it's all shut away behind closed doors, the air hanging still and quiet. There's nothing but the slow hum of fear.

'Curfew,' the driver explains. He pulls in to where Lauren indicates, and I fish for money in my wallet.

I take the bags and follow Lauren up the steps to our home – a few rooms above a bar, a front door with a missing number, only the ghostly outline of the lost digit fading a little more each day. Lauren jams the key into the lock and, with effort, turns it, throwing her weight against the sticking door so that we burst into the room.

The first thing I notice is that someone has opened the windows, which is a relief. Stepping inside and flicking on the lights, I see my wedding suit laid out on the table and wrapped in plastic, cleaned and pressed, and underneath it, Lauren's dress carefully folded. A note is propped against an unopened bottle of wine and Lauren reads it quietly, saying over her shoulder, 'Karl.' I smile to myself at my friend's thoughtfulness.

There are no plants in the apartment that needed watering, no pets that had to be fed; everything here is exactly as it was when we left. But it feels different now somehow, as if all the furniture has been moved around without our knowledge. Below us, the old man's bar is quiet.

Lauren takes her bag and goes to the bedroom. Through the half-open door I can see her emptying her case, putting clothes away. I fix us a couple of drinks and look about the place. These few rooms are a far cry from the space we had in the house in Lavington when I was a boy, where the rooms seemed endless and sunlight filled the kitchen. I can still remember how we cycled around it in a large loop and lost ourselves in its gardens. There's nowhere to hide in this apartment – not that I've ever wanted to. We've been happy here, Lauren and I.

When she comes out of the bedroom, and crosses to the sofa, she sinks into it with an air of exhaustion and kicks off her sandals.

'Drink?' I ask.

'Please.'

She takes the glass from me, swallows the full measure in one gulp and wipes her mouth. I don't think I've ever seen her do that before. But, then again, this week is full of firsts.

I sit down and see that she is holding something. 'What's that?'

'Haven't you seen it?' she asks. 'Julia had them done. All the guests got one.'

I study the card's black lettering, its elegant font, the itinerary of events listed as if it was a wedding we were all there for, not a memorial.

'Look at this,' I say, shaking my head. I read it silently:

At four o'clock, there will be a prayer service in the Safari Club,
after which I hope you will join us for a glass of champagne to cele-
brate Luke's life, a man who touched the hearts of so many.

I rub the paper between my finger and thumb, and stare
disbelievingly at the black border – it's out of the Victorian
era.

My temper rises.

'A prayer service in the Safari Club? Come on. A church
I could understand, but the thought of us all standing
around an urn in a hotel . . .'

'You okay?' Lauren asks.

I give back the card, run a hand over my face. 'Tired,
that's all,' I say, the blood pounding in my temples. 'I'm just
not sure this is what Luke would have wanted. It seems so
stagey, so formal.'

'What would he have wanted?' Lauren asks, watching
me with her clear eyes.

Something in her expression makes me draw back from
telling her. 'I don't know,' I say quietly.

'I'm exhausted,' she says, getting to her feet. 'You coming to bed?'

'In a while,' I say.

'Don't stay up late, honey,' she says gently. 'Tomorrow
will be a long day.'

I stretch out on the couch, rest my half-empty glass on
my chest and listen to the gentle creaking of our bed as
Lauren finds a comfortable position to sleep in. Funny
how quickly and easily you can adapt to another person's
ways, their routines, their very presence in your life. Part

of me knows I should join her, wrap myself around her and feel the warmth of her body in my arms as this day fades away. But the other part of me fears the oddness that seems to occupy this space, that it will follow me into the bedroom, and that is something I don't want to think about.

It feels as if nothing in the room belongs in it. Not the furniture, not the table, not the pots and pans, or any of the paraphernalia of a life lived together. The sepia photograph of Mount Kilimanjaro, which we had climbed together, hangs in an old antique frame as if it holds no relevance for me. The egg cups in the shape of old VW Beetles, the sofa we had dragged from outside a charity shop, the tapestry of the three African village women, one carrying a large pail of water on her head, the tribal masks we had worn when we were drunk and spoken through in voices not our own – the same unnerving shiver goes through me now as it did then – Lauren holding the mask over my face even as we came to one another to embrace and then make love.

She likes games, my wife, but that one had surprised me – that she would want to disguise herself, play at being someone else. Again, as happens frequently, I have the sense that I don't know my wife well. If I'm honest, it's part of the attraction that within our relationship we keep a part of ourselves separate from the other, enigmatic, unknowable.

Lauren asked me about my family, listened to my stories, probed a little but never pushed it. She, too, was sketchy with detail about hers – there was pain and disappointment, I could tell: her mother had been married before, but it hadn't worked out, so she'd remarried. Her father worked in a community college teaching history and she had a brother and a sister.

I sit up and let the alcohol do its work. Lauren has taken Julia's invitation into the bedroom, but something of its aftertaste lingers. I think of the events that lie ahead of me and feel the hours that are to come already dragging me down. The peculiarity persists. It's pointless to think I can dispel it now, not until all of this is done. I drag myself from the couch, enter the darkness of the bedroom, lie flat on the bed, and listen to the gentle rhythms of my wife's breathing.

I lapse into a half-waking, half-sleeping state, and I'm there again, at the coroner's. She, the coroner, walks ahead of me. 'Follow me,' she has said. And I do. My legs are weak as we enter the room; a heaviness fills my chest. The light is ghostly. There is a single table, a body covered with a sheet, which the coroner carefully draws back. I look at it, trace the lifeless limbs, the torso, and when I come to the face, I ask: 'The blood on his eyelids and lips?'

From the surrounding shadows, she answers: 'Hanging compresses the veins, but arterial blood flow continues. It causes small bleeding sites on the lips, inside the mouth and on the eyelids. The face and neck congest with blood and become dark red.'

I look back at the body. But what I see now startles me, because it is not Luke's face or Luke's body on the table in the morgue, but my face, my body.

I wake with a jolt. I'm covered with sweat. The room arranges itself around me and my heartbeat slows. I lie down again to await sleep, but it stays with me, the image: my own pallid face, lidded and blank.

In the morning I take a shower, then stand in the kitchen drinking the hot coffee that Lauren has brewed. It's black and tarry with a bitter tang, and I'm grateful for its strength. Lauren sits on the couch, legs curled under her, a mug of coffee in one hand as she sifts through the post.

'I think I'll go out,' I tell her, and she looks up. I say nothing of the dream.

'But the service?'

'It's not till four.'

'Right – but I told Julia we'd be there early to go through things with her. And we still have to pack for Mara . . .' She trails off, watching me as I reach up to the top of the press and take down my helmet. 'Where'll you go?'

'Downtown. Don't worry,' I tell her, as I lean in to kiss her goodbye. 'I'll be back in time.'

I keep the bike in a lock-up behind the bar below us. It's not the safest place in the world but it's close to home, and when I unlock the door, it's a relief to see the old KTM still there on its stand, bodywork gleaming as the sun breaks through the gloom. I'd spent a good deal of time getting it cleaned up before the wedding because it was meant to be our honeymoon transport, and as I put my lid on and wheel the bike outside, a strange feeling comes over me, a premonition, perhaps, that Lauren and I weren't meant to go to Madagascar.

I throw my leg over the bike, give myself a little shake, gun the engine and take off out of there, dust kicked up in my wake. My plan was to head out to Lavington and swing by the old homestead, but now that I'm on my way, something in me rears up against that idea. Instead, I turn the bike around and head south towards Kibera.

It's been a while since I've been out this way, but nothing much has changed. Still the same depressing poverty, the same tide of filth and waste. The sprawling mass of human tragedy is so vast, it splits into villages, and it is here, in the village of Kianda, that I have come to find Murphy.

For all the money that has come pouring into the coffers of ALIVE since my mother started it, little seems to have been spent on the premises. The structure is sound, a few steps above the makeshift corrugated sheds that line the streets here, but it's not much to look at. A block-built hut with a tin roof and a wooden door, iron bars over the windows. I pull the bike up outside and chain it to the post, casting an eye around the street for any possible trouble. Three young boys are sitting on the steps and jump up when they see me. I look down at them, their skinny limbs and infectious grins. One is wearing an ancient sweatshirt, the colours faded, although I can just about make out 'E.T.' on the chest.

'Here,' I say, giving them some change. 'Keep an eye on the bike, yeah?'

This sends them into whoops of ecstasy. I leave them, jumping and pulling at each other, and step in through the open door, my eyes adapting to the gloom of the room. Murphy is on the phone, seated behind his desk. He raises a hand to me, signals that he'll be with me in a minute. The walls of his office are plastered with posters warning about AIDS, clean water, immunizations, education, and a massive corkboard swarms with dozens of local community advertisements printed in a neat hand on various coloured postcards. A large map of Nairobi is tacked up on one wall, marked with coloured pins and flags, lines drawn in blue and red ink.

I take a seat at the second desk, and wait, swinging in my chair, my eyes roaming the room. Murphy is on his feet, anxious to finish his call. Finally he tells whoever is at the other end of the line, 'Look, I have to go,' and hangs up.

'Trouble?' I ask.

'No trouble, Nick,' he says, forcing a smile. 'You been up to the Safari Club yet?'

'Not yet.'

'Well, there's time enough,' he says, glancing at his watch.

I feel a twinge of guilt. I suppose I should have called to check on Julia, but a sense of estrangement has already crept between us. After the service, when I went to hug her and felt the thinness of her body in my embrace, a whole clatter of thoughts went through my head – that this was the body my brother had loved and worshipped and ultimately abandoned, that this woman and I were linked by name, and yet, without Luke, the bond seemed tenuous. I found myself wondering whether, after all this was over, Julia and I would ever speak to each other again.

'I do regret not making it to Ireland,' he says, with a look that is both intent and troubled. 'You know I would have . . . It's just that things here have been so busy and I didn't feel up to the journey.'

'It's all right, Jim, you don't need to explain. Luke would have been happier at the thought of you remaining here to steer the ship.'

'Yes, well . . .' He nods awkwardly. 'I wish I could have

been there for him. He meant the world to me. You both do. When you walked in that door just a few minutes ago, and I saw you, you reminded me so much of Sally. It was just like thirty years ago when she stepped over the threshold announcing her willingness to help.'

He smiles at me then, a grin tinged with nostalgia and the light that comes to his eye whenever he speaks of my mum and dad. 'What was it she said to me?' he says, almost to himself. 'Oh, yes – "I'm here to help." Like I should have been expecting her. You'd swear she was answering a job advert instead of just showing up here on a whim – ha!' He gives his sudden barking laugh. 'But that was Sally all over. Christ, but you're so like her, Nicholas.'

'Well,' I say, leaning against the opposite desk and raising my palms, 'I, too, am here to help.'

'You, Nicholas? You're not serious?'

'Why wouldn't I be?' I ask, with a grin to mask the surprise of hurt. 'There's no one else to do it.'

'It's very good of you to offer, Nick – it's the honourable thing to do. But it's a lot to take on, and you have your own life to lead – you and Lauren. Nobody expects you to yoke yourself to this place.'

I examine the laminate surface of the desk, my fingers going instinctively to the edge where it is starting to peel away. 'I feel I should. Luke wrote me a letter some time ago, asking me . . .'

'Of course, of course,' he says swiftly. 'If that's what you wish to do, then please, don't let me stop you. I'm only looking out for you.'

There is a sharpness behind his tone despite the kindness of the words. Exhaustion is etched into the creases of his face. Murphy is an old man now. It isn't fair to expect him to carry this thing alone.

'So, where do we begin?' I ask.

He takes a deep breath, collects himself and moves purposefully to the filing cabinet.

Onto my desk he piles several folders in different colours, each marked with text in Magic Marker. He leaves me with them and, for about an hour, I pore over the pages, trying to make sense of the columns of figures, the printed information, the projections and memos. The air in here is fetid and clotted with heat. The only air-cooling device is the open door.

Eventually I get up and stand with my hands in my pockets, staring out at the narrow streets shabby with rubbish and waste, effluent running along a channel at my feet. Two of the boys are sitting on the motorbike, one wearing my lid – outrageously oversized above his skinny shoulders, as if the weight of it alone might cause him to lose his balance and topple into the dirt. It's ten years since my mother began her campaign out here – Mum and Murphy battling the evils of poverty together – but with the vast sprawling slum of Kibera before us, I can't help but think that it hasn't made a bit of difference. With Murphy getting on in years, who knows how much longer he can continue, and then what?

'I don't know, Murphy,' I say. 'I don't know what to do. As my father used to say, I'm all at sea.'

'Come on, Nicholas,' he says kindly, his hand heavy on my shoulder. 'Let's leave these decisions for another day, when we've less weighty things on our minds.'

I nod, step out into the midday sun and turn back to him. 'Best get ready, I suppose.'

'Good man.'

'You're travelling down to Mara tomorrow?'

'Indeed.'

'Karl is giving me and Lauren a lift, but I'm sure there'd be room for you.'

'No, no. Don't worry. An old friend is driving me there.'

'All right,' I say, my voice betraying my uncertainty.

He picks up on it straight away. 'Is everything okay?' he asks, with concern. 'Are you worried about tomorrow?'

'I don't know,' I say quietly. 'It's just strange, I suppose. It hasn't really sunk in.'

I let the words hang, and Murphy nods, understanding, then puts his hand to my back solicitously. 'Don't worry, Nick. It'll all be fine.'

I go down the steps, wrestle my helmet from the youngsters, and reward them with a handful of sweets. Their laughter carries back to us as they run off down an alleyway. I turn back to Murphy. 'Actually,' I begin, 'when I think of Luke – of laying him to rest – I feel more than strange. I feel . . . scared.'

'Scared?' His face is poised and still, a shadow passing over it. 'But what are you scared of?'

'Me?' I whisper. 'I'm scared of myself.'

He stands at the doorway and watches as I steer carefully along the street. I can see him in my side-mirror, his broad shoulders and solemn face, his eyes squinting in the sun, until I turn a corner and he is gone.

We get to the Safari Club an hour before the service is due to start, and join the others in Julia's suite. To anyone's eyes, we are an odd gathering, Julia, her mother and sister, tailored in pinched black suits, heels that could puncture tyre. Lauren has persuaded me to wear my wedding suit, but now I wish I hadn't – it seems disrespectful, somehow, not to mention the confusion it creates, the two events merging in my mind. Lauren stands to one side, unusually sober and understated in a dark blue dress and sandals. We haven't spoken much today – she didn't ask where I'd been all morning, and I never said.

Julia breaks free from the cluster of her family and I catch her mother throwing me a glance loaded with suspicion. It makes me wonder what Julia might have said about me. Or is it less about me and more about my brother? After all, he was the one who abandoned her.

'You've seen the room?' Julia asks me, taking me by the elbow and leading me to the window.

'Yes,' I say.

'Do you think it'll be all right?' she asks nervously.

I see all the tension, the toll these last weeks have taken on her, and can't help but feel sorry for her. So I don't tell her that I think the room is a joke, with its ostentatious displays of flowers, its sterile furnishings and manufactured reverence, like some kind of fake chapel set up a stone's throw from the cocktail lounge. Instead, I say: 'It will be fine, Julia.'

Out of the window, the horizon is blotted with cranes and scaffolding. Nairobi is a building site. It is being dug and reshaped into something else. Drills, engines and sirens fill the air, and my ears. All I want to do is block it out.

Julia is talking to me, telling me, in a voice that sounds controlled and a little cold, the order of play, so to speak, who will say what, the roles we must take. I listen to her with a kind of distant fascination, as if I'm not really present in this scene, but a spectator watching from afar – trying in an absent kind of way to stave off the anger that is building within me at the charade of grief. It's only when she hands me a piece of paper busy with words that I focus on what she's saying.

'I'd like you to say this poem,' she tells me. 'I know it's very long, and if you prefer, you can swap with my sister, Andrea – she's reading the psalm. But I think you'll do it justice.'

I stare at the paper – 'The Castaway' by William Cowper – and something in me rails against it. I look up at Julia and she sees the defiance in my eye.

'This is wrong. All of this. It is so wrong,' I say, unable to hold back any longer.

Julia's back stiffens. Behind, her mother and sister turn around.

'This isn't Luke. William Cowper? Seriously? I'm pretty sure he'd never heard of the bloke.'

'Nick, please.'

'Not him or any other eighteenth-century poet. This isn't right, Julia . . . It's a sham.'

I've said the words and they can't be taken back.

For a moment, Julia holds herself so still, her face unreadable, that I can't be sure if she's going to burst into tears or hit me. She does neither. Instead, she speaks to me in a low voice that is pulsing with anger.

'A sham? You can call it that, but to me it is trying to put a little bit of dignity to this whole mess. You can say that it isn't what Luke would have wanted, you can stand around with your hands in your pockets, like some moody teen-ager – and I really couldn't give a damn. Because this is what *I* want, Nick. This is what I need. To claw back a little bit of dignity for myself.'

Julia's eyes are wild with the rage and the injustice that has been done to her and I feel myself drawing back, mumbling an apology, ashamed of my outburst, burning with regret.

'Of course I'll say the poem,' I tell her, but I'm speaking to her back as she has turned away from me, scorn coming off her in waves.

I look at the piece of paper in my shaking hands, try to pull myself together, and from the printed words that crawl around the page, these two lines break free and catch my eye:

> *We perish'd, each alone; But I, beneath a rougher sea,*
> *And whelm'd in deeper gulfs than he.*

I read those words and all at once I'm back there, water up to my waist, the sun beating down overhead, and that girl's hair spreading out like weed in the water – and it's so real that I can feel it, soft and weighty in my hands. A voice in my head, Katie's, screaming: 'Stop! Stop! You've got to stop him!'

'Nick?'

Lauren's touch is gentle but I nearly jump out of my skin.

Her eyes are round with concern. 'You look like you've seen a ghost.'

She takes my arm, turns me to the door. 'Come on,' she says. 'It's about to begin.'

10. Katie

It happens on the morning of the memorial service.

An envelope slid beneath the door of my hotel room.

Blinking away sleep and bleary with a headache that feels like a hangover, I pad across the floor barefoot, stoop to pick it up. A brown envelope, innocuous enough, until I turn it over in my hands, see my name scrawled in the same blue marker and feel a lurch of recognition that comes straight from my stomach. The dead bird. I'd almost forgotten. Sweat on my upper lip, I open it and glance inside, try to ready myself for whatever it is I will find.

A bunch of documents. Printouts from the internet. I place each one on my bed, covering it with images of drownings. Milky white limbs submerged in water, faces still and open-mouthed beneath the surface. Some are blurry and indistinct; others have a shocking clarity. Standing in my underwear in that unfamiliar hotel room, poring over each page, each image, then dropping it onto the bed with the rest. Fear and confusion washing through me, like a cocktail that is getting me loaded in a way I don't like. My mind teems with thoughts, each one clambering over the last: who uploads this stuff to the internet? Who looks for it? Who are all these people whose death masks are tossed about from one server to another? And, of course, the question that overrides all others: who is sending me this?

I think of the day in the office, the pictures of that girl

in the swimming pool, hair spreading out in water, and for a moment it distracts me – I'm even heartened a little, thinking that this has nothing to do with me and what happened in the river that day. That this is about some sicko with a mobile phone who's pissed off that we wouldn't print his ghoulish shots of a dead girl and has decided to take out his bile on me. For just a moment, I can almost convince myself that this, the dead bird, these pictures, all of it is the handiwork of some nasty little wanker with his own personal agenda. For a moment I convince myself that I am still safe.

Then I turn to the last page and my convictions desert me. I hold it in my hand, feel the belt around my throat.

This one is different from the others. It hasn't been gleaned from the internet. A photocopy of an old newspaper clipping. Details of a gruesome find on the banks of a river. A picture of a girl grinning at a camera, the kind of school photo that stood on sideboards in homes throughout my childhood: big front teeth, a rabbitty face. Seeing that face again, after all these years, sends a jolt right through me, and I realize I'm standing straight and still as a stick, every muscle and sinew alive with tension. I can hardly feel my hands, my feet. Nerve endings prickle like a rash over my skin. That face grinning out at me from beyond the grave. Her name printed in black and white: Cora Gordon. Until now, I never knew her surname. I had never thought to find it out.

But someone had.

The fear is in the room with me now, like something crouching on top of the wardrobe, casting its malignant gaze down on me, watching for my reaction. The belt at my neck is cinched to strangling point. The paper trembles in my hands. For a moment, I can't move, but neither can I look away, appalled by what has been sent to me. And I think of my other gift from this anonymous correspondent – the little bird – and I cannot deny the connection. Those birds on the veranda. The fluttering of their tiny wings. Two little sparrows.

Someone knows. Someone has found out.

By the time I reach the Safari Club, the service has already begun. Beyond the bright noise of the lobby, I join the others and sit in the hush of the heavily air-conditioned room, trying to bring my breathing under control. The priest stands at a lectern beside an ostentatious floral display, holding forth on the mysteries of life and death. He wears an open-necked white shirt, no sign of a collar. He hardly looks like a priest at all. I sit on a fold-out chair, the plastic hot at the backs of my thighs, wearing yesterday's clothes, feeling chilly and strange and jumpy as a cat. Tanya glances across at me – an enquiry in her gaze – and all at once, my suspicions are aroused. What does she know? Why is she looking at me? I stare at my knees, push down the paranoia that keeps rising inside.

Still, it's there. Fear cementing in my gut, lodging itself within me. I'd felt it at the Meridian, pressed against the desk, wild with the urgency of my fear, the stream of words coming out of me, the receptionist telling me to slow down, to calm myself, getting to her feet and leading me to a private office as if I was a child, and all the while I'm telling her about this envelope that was slid beneath my door in the night, demanding to know who delivered it, babbling about my room number, my privacy, my personal safety, all the while my voice rising on an arc of panic that her patient responses could not seem to assuage. She didn't know who had put it under my door; there was nothing in the book about any delivery for me. She would check with the night desk later to see what they remembered. Everything she said was reasonable and steady, but all the time I stood there feeling thin and light with nothing to anchor me.

The priest continues to talk and I try to keep up but it's so difficult with this pain in my guts and all these people in the room I barely know. I see Julia, her head bent, shoulders stiff with tension, and I think of her narrowed eyes as she looked at me that morning on the beach, the coldness in her voice when she said *You and those boys* . . . Could she be the one? No, of course not, I tell myself. She's hardly going to post a dead bird to her own husband, surely. For all her *froideur*, I can sense that there was love between them and that her sadness is genuine.

There's no one here I can trust. Except Nick. But Nick has his back to me, and I feel how closed off he is, locked in his own orb of grief.

When the priest gets to the part about Luke being reunited with his parents in Heaven, I get a kind of floating feeling, as if my heart is beating somewhere outside my chest. The anxiety that has taken hold of me – it's like I'm nine years old again, waking in the night to see my father's face, bleary with sleep and love and fear, saying: 'This will pass, Katie.' The waters closing over my head. His eyes seeking out some shadow of the dream that troubled me. 'Good things lie further down the road – I promise you.'

And after he'd left, I'd try to stay awake, everything in me working to keep sleep at bay, fearful of those dark waters coming over me again, the heaviness in my chest, as if I couldn't breathe. Now, in this room, even though I'm wide awake, the dream has returned, and I feel again the water sucking at my limbs, the black boughs of the trees above me drooping down into the river.

I need a cigarette. I need a drink. Nick takes his place at the lectern and recites a poem, staring hard at the sheet of paper, his voice so low I have to strain to hear him. A jar full of ashes stands on a plinth. Within it lie fragments of hard fibres. All that remains of a life. The three of us, back here again. The belt so tight now I can scarcely breathe. My chair scrapes the floor as I get to my feet, eyes following me, but I don't turn back. Through the doorway quickly, into a room carpeted with close-clipped green nylon, like fake grass, the walls busy with twisting vines and hanging fruit. The music of a string quartet seeps through hidden speakers. I take a glass of juice and knock it back, feel the skin stretched tight across my face, nerves prickling through my skull and hair. The ceremony has ended and others have started filing in. Someone brushes against me and I spring away, as if I've been shot, my bag falling to the floor. Bending to pick it up, I can feel my legs trembling, and I can't tell if that's from the fear crawling around inside me, or from thinking of Luke, what's left of him in that jar. It hits me then: he isn't coming back. Ever. My bag on the floor becomes a blur.

'Here, let me,' a voice says.

There's a hand under my elbow, and I'm being steered to a chair in the lobby, gulping in lungfuls of air, tears streaming down my face. I'm vaguely aware of him, this person, the steadiness of his hand as he sits me down, the calm of his voice as he tells me to wait there. Faces of strangers in the lobby turn to me now as the grief flies from me, as if my chest has opened and hundreds of birds come screeching out.

'Here,' the voice says, and I look down at the brown hand extending from a white shirtsleeve, holding out a glass containing an amber-coloured liquid.

I don't ask what it is. I close my eyes and fling my head back, feeling the warmth of the drink flooding my throat. Almost a month of abstinence is thrown away in a heartbeat.

'That will help,' he says, and I open my eyes to him.

Murphy. The priest.

He sits opposite me. In his own hands he cradles a matching glass. Now he raises it so that it's almost level with his eyes: he looks like he needs it as much as I do.

'I have a rule about this sort of thing. Delay your first drink of the day until after the sun has set.' He glances past me to the glass doors that open onto a sun-soaked driveway. Then his eyes meet mine and I see the humour in them. 'I make exceptions for funerals.'

He sips his drink and my nerves begin to calm a little. He keeps a steady watch on me, his eyes frank and appealing. Large hands make his glass seem very small. There is a weariness about him, a premature hunch of the shoulders, wrinkles running through his skin as though he has absorbed all the sins of all the confessions he has ever heard: a lived-in face to rival Beckett's. Over his nose and cheeks runs a network of broken capillaries – a drinker's face.

I look again at the whiskey in the glass. 'I'm sorry,' I tell him. 'It's not like me to fall apart in public.'

'Oh?'

'I prefer to do my crying alone in an empty room.'

'What a lonely image,' he remarks, a frown shadowing his brow. Then he spreads his hands in a gesture of understanding. 'This is a memorial service. Tears are to be expected.'

'I'm Katie,' I say, smiling to cover my embarrassment and offering my hand. As he takes it, I surprise myself with how shy I feel. His is a searching gaze, and he holds my hand for a second too long, as though trying to get the measure of me.

'Katie. I remember you.'

'You do?'

'And your mother. Helen, wasn't it?'

'You knew my mother?'

'Just a little. We met once or twice when you were here.'

'Oh.'

'You're like her, you know. About the eyes, I see it – the same interested gaze.' Then, changing the subject, he says: 'It was good of you to come all this way.'

'I couldn't not,' I tell him, and sense the push of truth in those words.

'Are you travelling south tomorrow with the rest of us?'

'I've come this far, haven't I? May as well see it through.' I try to sound nonchalant, as if the thought of going back doesn't scare the hell out of me.

'Good.' He smiles and nods his approval, breathing deeply, his hand going to his chest.

'Beats me why he wanted all this, though,' I say.

'Why is that?'

'I don't understand why he'd want to come back to a place he hasn't been to in thirty-odd years.'

'Perhaps it was where he was happiest.'

I cast him a doubtful look.

He leans back in his chair, an expansive gesture, and says: 'I remember them – the Yateses – when they first came out here. You couldn't help but notice such an attractive family – beautiful, I would go so far as to say. The mother – now, she was something. Oozed class. He had it too, Ken, a kind of muscular charm, a sense of great capability. And then those two fine boys – so vital and engaging. Something so optimistic about that family. It was like being in the presence of sunshine. They thrived here in Africa. Such a shame, when they left . . .' His eyes film with a kind of sadness.

The way he says it, that faraway gaze, and I'm back in that field again – the boys in shorts, knees scabby and scraped, Luke restless and bored, turning towards the lea of the hill, saying: 'Let's go to the river – see if those girls are there.' The command in his voice, the determination in his eye. Did I feel the faintest beat of indecision? I think I did, yet I don't trust my memories of that day – ragged and worn as they are.

'I'll never forget the night I went to see them,' Murphy says now. 'It was the night before they left and I was calling over to say goodbye. He came down the steps to me – Ken. I had never seen anyone change so rapidly. The pale, hollow-eyed person that came forward to greet me. And Sally, too, all the radiance gone out of her. I didn't see the boys. And I kept asking them why – why were they leaving like this? What had happened to make them want to go so suddenly? It was almost as if they were scared.'

'They had birds – Nick and Luke – as children,' I say then, and he looks up at me sharply. 'I remember a bird-cage hanging on their veranda. Two little sparrows. Do you remember?'

Confusion crosses his face and I watch him carefully. I hadn't intended to ask him this – I'm not even sure why I have. A small bubble of suspicion, perhaps. My nervous state. Everyone's a suspect. He holds my gaze, confusion shifting to something else, a kind of understanding.

'They were starlings, not sparrows,' he corrects me. 'And, yes, I do remember them.'

The way he says it, patient, forbearing, as if he's seen it all before – people racked by grief and confusion – and the generosity of his understanding make me hang my head, a rinse of shame going through me. 'Sorry,' I say. 'It's just –'

'No need to explain. This must be strange for you, coming back here. Under these unhappy circumstances.'

'I keep thinking about him,' I say now. 'Luke, going back to that derelict house, holing himself up in that lonely place, and then . . .' I can't bring myself to say the words, emotion catching in my throat.

He nods, then spreads his hands wide. While his accent is a mixture of Irish with a peppering of South African, his gestures are more Mediterranean – that Gallic shrug.

'When something like this happens – when someone we love takes his own life – we struggle to find a reason for it because it is so tremendously difficult to think of him being in such pain that he couldn't see any way forward, except the obliteration of death. We keep asking ourselves, "Why didn't he tell me? Why didn't I notice he was in such pain? Why didn't I do something?" It's a natural response. But, Katie,' he says gently, 'it's a false path. Don't go down that road, girl. Don't torture yourself. Luke had a lot of problems – financial, emotional. He was not well. Whatever drove him to do what he did, it came from inside himself, not from anywhere else.'

Despite myself, I can't help but feel disappointed with his response, priestly as it is.

I finish my drink, return my glass to the table and thank him for his company.

'You're leaving?' he asks, as I pick up my bag, get to my feet.

'Tell Nick I'm sorry, will you?'

'Of course.'

Just as I'm about to leave, I feel it – the nudge of curiosity, of suspicion. I look at Murphy. 'That night when you went to see Sally and Ken, when you went to say goodbye, did they tell you what it was that scared them? Did they tell you why they were leaving?'

If he is surprised by my question, he doesn't show it. Instead, he says, 'No. They never did. Too scared or too proud. And I've learned over the years that some secrets are not meant to be shared. I do remember this, though. When I left them that night, and Ken walked me to the door, I put out my hand to shake his, and all of a sudden he drew me into his embrace. There was a ferocity in the way he clung to me that I've never been able to forget.'

Something inside me falters at the thought of Mr Yates, wild with anxiety, brought to the brink, and I have an overwhelming desire to be outside, to breathe in real air, not this purified oxygen. Murphy reaches out to steady me. His hand on my arm is so big and strong that it makes me feel like a child again, and I don't know whether I like that or not.

'Let him go, girl,' he says, his face old and tired. Then he withdraws his hand and sits back. I can hear his dry cough all the way across the lobby until I am out on the street.

Back at my hotel, I'm told there is no news about the envelope delivered in the night, but my bag has shown up. I go to my room, shower and dress. Just shedding the clothes I've been walking around in for the past two days is a relief. Afterwards I sit quietly, sipping a beer from the mini-bar and smoking my way through a carton of Marlboro Lights. The beer has an industrial taste that is something like guilt. The afternoon light falls in blocks on the carpet. The room is in disarray: clothes spill from the open suitcase. My phone has been ringing on and off for the last hour but I don't answer it. I've left it on the bedside table where it continues to give the occasional bleat. I'm still jumpy as hell, my mind growing tired from the endless tracks it keeps going down. The newspaper clipping of Cora's death, the images of drownings. The birds. I think of Luke – 'My past is coming back to haunt me' – and feel the slow creep of terror at the thought that keeps surfacing: *Someone knows.*

A knock at the door. I nearly jump out of the chair. I peer through the spy-hole, then open up, eager to see him, knowing somehow that he is the only one I can turn to about this – all of this.

Nick steps into the room and straight away I say: 'Someone knows.'

I put a hand to my mouth, turn from him as he closes the door and walk towards the window.

'Someone's been sending me things – threats, I suppose. A kind of coded message. I kept thinking it had something to do with work, but now I know it can't, it just can't. Pictures, newspaper clippings and worse . . .'

The words peter out as I turn to him. He's standing, staring at the generic brown furniture, but I can see how blank his gaze is, how stunned he is by his grief. The expression on his face: as if he's just witnessed an accident. Blood on the road. He hasn't heard a word I've said.

He sits on the bed and lowers his head into his hands. From within that cupped space I hear his voice, low and choked, saying: 'I'm so fucked, Katie.'

He lets his hands drop and I see the tears on his face. His vulnerability – I can't help but think of the dark-haired boy Murphy described as I sit next to him, my arm going instinctively around him, pulling him towards me. Just for a moment, I forget my panic. 'You need to sleep,' I say.

'I need a drink,' he replies, pulling a bottle of whiskey from his jacket pocket and making a sound that is supposed to be a laugh but comes out strangled and strange.

I take it from him, and go to the mini-bar for glasses.

'I'm going to nip down the hall for ice,' I tell him, the thrum of my pulse alive in my ears. 'Back in two ticks.'

He smiles drowsily at the floor as I close the door behind me.

At the ice machine, I stand with my arms folded over my chest, silently furious with myself for letting him in –

into my room, into my thoughts. I can feel how deeply lodged within me he is and always has been.

When we were children, he felt like a brother to me. Later, when we were students, on the cusp of adulthood, that same closeness was there, but it had become compromised. As our friendship rekindled and came alive again, I felt the subtle lacing of new threads of feeling between us. The young man he had grown into had echoes of the brother I'd remembered him to be: the shyness, the dark hair shadowing his face, the fierce goodness inside him — and the music. Of course, the music. But there was something else that I couldn't help but be drawn towards: a sadness that lay just beyond the corners of his smile, and I could tell that he, too, felt lost and bewildered and distrustful of his place in the world.

And there was the problem of sex, the complication of attraction between two people with an already tangled past, two people with self-inflicted scars on their palms that marked them for ever as siblings. My friends in college could not seem to understand the friendship between me and Nick. 'When are you two going to get together?' they would ask me, and I would laugh and protest that I just didn't feel that way about him, hoping they wouldn't see through me.

Then one night at a party, we ended up alone in a room together. It was late, the party well past its prime, and the crowd had dropped away, just a few stragglers occupying dim corners of the house. We sat on a bed and talked, and in the whispered darkness we returned to that field in our childhood. We went back to the river. Once only, I listened to him reliving it — what had been done; the parts we had all played in it, Nick, Luke and I. And I listened to his account of it with a kind of slow-burning shock, afraid to speak, afraid that if I said anything he would stop, clam up, return to his habitual silence. But what he said confused and frightened me. It made me wary of my own memories, casting them all in doubt.

How long did we talk that night? Hours, perhaps. The whole house silent around us as if we were the only two people left. And as the granular light of dawn crept across the sky, the talking stopped, and it was just the two of us lying on that bed. I knew from the measured way he was breathing, holding himself so carefully still, that he wasn't asleep. And I, too, feigned stillness, yet every inch of me was waiting, poised for what might happen between us. All it would have taken was for one of us to reach out, for one to turn towards the other. And yet neither of us moved. You see, it was in the room with us now – that thing from the past. Summoned like a spirit through all the talk, and it seemed to lie alongside us, that dead girl like a third party. I felt her presence and knew he did too, and it occurred to me then that it would always be like that between us. That no matter how close we grew to each other, she would always be there, holding us apart.

And now, as the ice tumbles into the bucket, I feel her again. Walking back to my room, I'm so aware of those old emotions stalking me, waiting for my guard to come down and my good intentions to crumble.

Nick is sitting on the bed when I return, reaching to put the phone down.

'I hope you don't mind,' he says. 'I just wanted to call Lauren.'

'Of course.'

We perch on either side of the bed, sipping our drinks, awkward in each other's company. He is the first to speak.

'You must be surprised to see me.'

I think about this, then say: 'No. I'm not surprised.'

He looks at me properly then and holds me there for a moment, nodding slightly in understanding. Of course he would seek me out. After all, we're the only ones left. And I feel them crowding around us in this room – the ghosts of the others: my parents, as well as his, Cora, and now Luke . . .

'It's strange,' he says, 'but ever since it happened – ever since I found Luke – I've felt this overwhelming need to talk.'

He peers at me to see if I get the oddness of that statement, and I do. Of course I do.

'But I've never been very good with words,' he goes on. 'It seems the only person I can talk to about it is you.'

'You can tell me anything, Nicky,' I say quietly.

'I wanted to tell you about what happened when I found him – Luke.'

I push myself back so that the pillows are behind me, my feet crossed at the ankles, whiskey cradled in my lap, listening.

'It took so long for them to come. The guards, the ambulance. It seemed to take for ever. And what do you do while you wait? It must have taken them half an hour to get there, and all that time I'm supposed to just leave him there, hanging from a beam?'

179

'What did you do?'

'At first, we went outside, stood by the car, trying to pull ourselves together. Then I called Julia.'

'That must have been hard.'

'The worst phone call of my life.'

'How did she take it?'

He shrugs, trying not to make a big deal of it. Still, I can imagine the shout of fright she gave, the distress and denial within it.

'After the phone call, I got a bit panicky. The guards were so long and I started worrying that Julia would take it into her head to come down. Just the thought of her seeing Luke hanging there like that –' He breaks off, drinks some whiskey.

'I got worried that I'd imagined it, which sounds ridiculous, but I started to think all kinds of crazy shit, like I would go back into that house and he wouldn't be there, or that maybe there'd still been some scrap of life left in his body when we'd found him but instead of checking we'd just assumed and maybe now it was too late.'

I tap a cigarette out of the box and offer one to him.

'So, I find myself racing back into that house and up the stairs, but he's still there and from the colour of his face, the swelling and bruising and just the sheer stillness of him, I knew he was dead. But somehow . . . somehow I couldn't leave him like that. It was so undignified. And I know I should have waited for the cops, but it just got so I couldn't stand to think of him staying up there one second longer. I kept imagining my father's face were he to walk into the room and see Luke like that, even though the man has been dead for the last decade.'

His voice, husky from cigarettes and booze and lack of sleep, cracks, and I see the tremor in his hand as he brings the cigarette to his lips. He holds the smoke inside him for a beat, then releases a plume of it into the air.

'So I cut him down.'

The words sound hollow and forlorn and, for a moment, they sit there between us.

'I took him down and laid him on the floor, then covered him up with my jacket.'

'Christ.'

'Lauren was there. At first, she stood back and watched as I laid him down. But then she knelt next to him and very gently, very tenderly, as if he were just asleep and she didn't want to wake him, she started straightening his limbs, like she was trying to make him more comfortable or something, brushing the hair off his face, holding his hand. I stood there watching her do this and it occurred to me that she had never met Luke before, that this was the first and only time she would see him, and when I looked at his ruined face, swollen and distorted – gruesome, even – all the life and the charm and the humour fled from it, I felt this surge of anger rise up in me, this fury at *her*, at Lauren, my wife, for handling him in this delicate, intimate way, like she had known him for ever when really he was a stranger to her, and always would be, so I said something to her, something terrible. I said . . . I said . . .'

'Don't, Nick. Please don't.' I'm shocked at all this talk gushing out of him and swirling around us, and even though I'm glad he can confide in me, I don't want to hear the thing he said to his wife. But he says it anyway.

'I said: "Take your fucking hands off him, Lauren."'

It sits there pulsing between us – the wrongness of it, the violence of that word, spoken in that space, the room that held the recent dead as well as the ghosts of the others. My thoughts go to that girl in the airport lounge with her straw-coloured hair and her carefree manner. He might as well have slapped her face.

We sit in silence for what seems a long time. I close my eyes, listen to the hum of the city outside, hear it breathe in and out like a living being.

Nick says, 'I had the stupidest thought on the way here.'

'What?'

'That if either of the Yates brothers was going to take their lives, it should have been me.'

I sit up. 'Nick, you shouldn't say that.'

He sits across from me, briefly returning my gaze, and I can feel the heat in it. He reaches for the bottle, his hand shaking. Catching me watching, he lowers his hand to his lap, stares at it, as if it's a foreign object. But then his face seems to warm a little and he holds up his hand to me, shows me his palm.

'Remember, Kay?'

The scar there – a white ridge of hard skin among the map of lines. I feel my answering smile and hold up my hand. 'I remember,' I say.

We regard each other fondly, and the old twinge comes back, the twinge that suggests what might have been but never was.

His mood shifts again, another thought coming at him, nudging away the momentary peace. 'Something else I can't get out of my head. It was something the guards wanted to know, or one particular detective. There, after they'd arrived and I'd made a formal identification of the body, he asked me who had cut the knot.'

'Why?'

'Because,' and it seems he is quoting from memory, 'because if you cut a victim down, you're supposed to cut *above* the knot. That's what he told me.'

'And they told you this at the house . . . right after?'

'Right there and then. It preserves the rope for Forensics if you cut above the knot, you see. Cutting below ruins it. This guy – the detective – he said if the marks around the neck, the bruising, if they follow the same pattern as the ridges in the rope, well and good. I asked what's good about that, Kay. You know what he said?'

'No.'

'He said, "Then we know it was suicide, plain and simple."'

'Plain and simple, huh?'

For a moment, his face remains the same – eyes a little too bright, though his gaze is fixed and inward-looking. Then his expression begins to change. The slow understanding of how passionate he had become, how wild his words had been, breaks through into his consciousness. He gives me a look that seems half apologetic, half resentful. Before my eyes, he is closing in on himself.

'Can I ask you something?' I say to him. 'Julia. Do you think she knows?'

His expression changes, becomes quizzical. 'About the three of us? About what we did?' He stares down at his hands. 'I don't know. Maybe.'

'Do you think Luke told her?'

He shrugs, mumbles: 'She was his wife. He could have.'

'Have you told Lauren?'

His eyes flash in a way that tells me I've overstepped the mark.

'Sorry. I didn't mean to –'

'That's okay.'

A prickly silence sits between us, and instinct tells me to let it be, but curiosity wins out.

'What about Murphy? Do you think he knows? He was close to your mum. Perhaps she –'

'Jesus, Katie! Nobody knows but us – okay? Remember the rule? *Not a soul. You can't tell anyone.* Right?'

'Okay,' I say gently, reaching forward to touch his arm, and he exhales deeply, rocking forward on the bed.

'Sorry. It's just . . . I'm so tired,' he says, even though I know there is much more to it than that.

My phone rings, interrupting the silence. He glances at it with irritation but tells me I should answer it. Then, catching himself, he explains: 'It's my tinnitus,' he explains. 'Noises – electronic noises – make it worse.' His eyes are full of injury and apology and I feel a pang of sympathy for him.

'I'll take it outside.'

In the corridor, I speak to Reilly in hushed tones. I fill him in as best I can, pitching my voice at an approximation of calm and restraint so that he won't worry about me. I almost tell him about the envelope, about the picture of Cora, but somehow telling him seems too hard, complicated and somehow forbidden – like breaking the rule that was made so many years ago. *You can't tell anyone.* Still, before he rings off, he tells me he'll call again tomorrow, and I find myself smiling at his thoughtfulness, his concern.

When I push the door open, I can hear the regular sound of Nick's breathing. He's lying on his side, his head on the pillow. I stand for a moment, watching him sleep. Then I put my phone back on the nightstand and go to the window where I draw the heavy curtains, blocking out the evening sun so that only the gentle burr of light from the bathroom falls onto the bedroom floor.

I turn off the air-conditioning, the silence in the room like a sudden intrusion. But then I lie down next to him, turning so that my back is to his, close enough to feel his body warmth, my legs curled up and my hands beneath the pillow, the way I used to lie when I was a little girl. And for the first time in such a long time, I feel a kind of peace. The fear inside me leaves — like a moth drawn to a light in another room — as we lie there in the shadows, Nick and I. For a while, I listen to the steady rise and fall of his breathing. Then I close my eyes and sleep.

11. Nick

We meet in the dark, load the truck and set off without a word. It's going to be a long trek to the Masai Mara. Karl's driving. I've got the passenger seat. Lauren has the back to herself. She stares out of the window watching the light begin to break on the horizon.

Karl hums to himself, hands me a flask and says: 'Open that for me, will you?'

I unscrew the top and the smell of hot coffee wafts through the truck.

'Help yourself,' Karl says.

'Lauren?' I say, turning to her.

'No, thanks,' she says without looking at me.

Soon, we are out of the city and onto the wide roads where the tar is chipped and uneven, no markings visible.

The truck hits a rock on the road. 'Christ,' Karl says. 'I hope this pile of junk makes it.'

The vehicle is battered. The springs poke through the seats. The steel is rusting, the joints creaking. It is, as my dad would have said, 'banjaxed', creaking like it might fall apart at any minute. But the truth is that, despite the vehicle, there's no one I'd rather travel alongside on this difficult journey than Karl.

'Thanks for doing this,' I tell him, and he grins at me before turning his attention back to the road. He drives hunched forward, leaning on the steering-wheel, occasionally tapping out whatever rhythm is travelling through his head.

'Couldn't have you two doing this on your own, could I?' he says.

I stare at the road in front of me, think about where I'm going back to, and hear it begin, the distant whining deep within my inner ear.

We drive for long stretches without talking. Much of the land is arid scrub, a harsh frontier where people eke out a living. The poverty of Kenya is immense, its scale almost supernatural, but now as light touches it and the truck trundles along, I find that there is something calming about the terrain's roughness, the lack of refinement and the heady soundscape it holds. As Nairobi disappears behind us and we go deeper into the country, I settle back in the seat and allow my mind to slip into a sort of numbness, giving myself over to the journey ahead of us.

I can see Lauren's reflection in the side-mirror. She seems distant, as if she is mulling something over in her mind, her eyes fixed on the passing landscape. Her quiet determination reminds me of a time some months ago, before we were married, when she travelled to Mara on a field trip of sorts, but when she came back, she seemed subdued, troubled for days, but wouldn't tell me why. She got over it, and I forgot about it, but now she has the same air of disaffection, the same sullen inwardness.

She looks tired. I want to tell her to close her eyes and rest, but I don't. I'm afraid if I say anything to her it will only end in an argument and I'm not sure I can cope with that right now. Everything seems shaky today, so I bide my time.

I had left Katie's room before dawn broke, sneaking out of her hotel like a thief in the night. Outside, the streets were eerily quiet, the weather uncertain and cool; even in the darkness, I could see large clouds grouping on the horizon. A stray dog nosing its way through a bag of rubbish looked up at me warily before returning to its pitiful business. As I walked home in the pre-dawn darkness, a melody entered my head: Dexter Gordon playing 'Guess I'll Hang My Tears Out To Dry'. It has been turning in my mind ever since, and with it the words: who cut the knot? Who cut the knot?

As the truck judders and bumps along a particularly battered stretch of road, I feel my head emptying of everything except those words, going around and around in my head like they would on a scratched record.

Hours pass, the sun rising high above us. Karl decides to stop for lunch at a place he knows.

'The food's not great,' he says, 'but it'll do.'

The place he brings us to — a long flat building with large windows, blue paint peeling off the walls, concrete floors giving it an industrial feel — is more like a school canteen than a restaurant. The three of us queue at a counter, then take our trays and sit at one of the long trestle tables that stretch out across the room. The place is already filling up — the faces here predominantly white and Asian, tourists heading west to go on safari. The food — a stew with a gristly meat that we guess is goat, served in mismatched bowls — is better than I expected. Lauren dips bread into the gravy, but doesn't touch the meat. She drinks her Coke and hardly says a word.

When she goes to use the bathroom, Karl says: 'Everything okay between you guys?'

'I'm not sure,' I say.

'She was worried about you. You should have called her,' he says.

'I did call her. She knew where I was.'

A call to tell her that I had gone to Katie to talk because I'd felt I had to. A call in which I had said to my wife: *You do trust me, don't you?* She had said yes, and I had told her I loved her. But now, I can't help but feel naïve and stupid, even a little reckless.

He raises an eyebrow. 'Maybe that's the problem. Maybe you shouldn't have told her where you were.'

We climb back into the truck, a little weary, but eager to be on our way.

'How long to go until we're there?' I ask.

'A few more hours,' Karl says, letting the handbrake down with some effort.

The roads are bad. So bad in places, we have to take the hard shoulder. Nairobi is already a distant memory. The landscape ahead of us rolls on and on. Shanty towns – anonymous, without a name or a mark on any map – appear out of nowhere. They seem makeshift, fragile, prone to quick evacuation. The truck rattles and shakes. It hits one pothole after another. Farmers and animals watch us pass with a lazy indifference.

Lauren shifts in her seat, but remains awake. Her anger has a slow-burning flame.

'Why were you gone so long?' she had asked, when I finally got back this morning.

A whispered conversation in our bedroom, Karl waiting in the living room, sipping coffee on the sofa.

'I'm sorry, Lauren. We talked and then I fell asleep.'

'You fell asleep?' Disbelief in her voice.

'Nothing happened . . . You believe me, don't you? We just talked, that's all.'

She held my gaze, her eye fixed on me with suspicion, and then, in a quiet voice, she said: 'If you say so.' Turning away, she reached for her holdall and stuffed the last of her clothes into it. There was something savage about her movements, something that seemed completely alien to her usual grace and self-possession, and I could see how rattled she was. I searched for something to say to her – something to dispel her suspicion.

'Katie and I are old friends, Lauren. We go way back,' I began.

Lauren didn't answer. Behind her, the bed sheets were tousled, but I could tell she hadn't slept. Her face was drawn and worried. She didn't ask any other questions. There was no interrogation. Just a steely, implacable silence.

'Maybe you should get changed,' she said quietly, and I heard the coolness in her tone. 'Karl's been here for almost an hour. We need to get going.'

I knew that it was not finished between us – this row, if you could call it that. But how could I explain why I went to Katie? How could I explain the inextricable bonds that exist between me, Luke and her? How could I explain that I needed to understand why my brother had done this and that the only person who might help me was Katie? My apology did not seem enough. And because I was so dog-tired and we had a whole day ahead of us, sitting in a hot truck, I couldn't trust myself to start explaining something that confounded me – the thing that sits in the very depths of my past, beating like a black heart.

Before we get into the truck, I say: 'Lauren . . . I want you to know how sorry I am.'

'Nick, this is hard for me too. It's not just about you and your brother.'

I don't know what she means. Besides, she says no more. She simply climbs into the back seat and stares at the clouds overhead, and I see that she is containing her disappointment. Saving it. It feels like a form of torture. Her rage would be more welcome than this. She is pensive, her brow furrowed at the glaring sun, her eyes squinting up at a lone single-engine aeroplane passing high above us. She is biding her time, and I find myself waiting too, while the words *Who cut the knot? Who cut the knot?* trip through my head, forming a music all of their own, haunting the passageways of my inner ear.

There are words too – lyrics written not by me but by my brother. His letter is in my shirt pocket – I can feel its hard corners rubbing my chest, burning a hole there, demanding to be read again. A letter written on plain ivory paper, the kind our mum used. A letter written in a jagged, hurried cursive, the rushed slant of the letters on the page, the *t*s crossed quickly, the dotted *i*s wayward and panic-stricken.

But I don't take the letter out – I don't need to. I've read it countless times since Julia gave it to me, and each time it's as if Luke is whispering into my ear, as if his breath is brushing the back of my neck, causing goose-bumps to rise all the way up my spine. I feel them now as I close my eyes and hear his voice, remember words he wrote to me:

191

Dear Nico,

First up, a confession. I'm writing this with a few drinks inside me . . . and I know, I know, it's a mistake to put pen to paper when you're three sheets to the wind, but it's been a strange day and I feel somehow compelled to write to you, even though you probably won't read this, won't answer. All the same a big part of me feels that there isn't a single person on this earth who understands what I'm going through right now – except you, Nico.

We've spent the day – Julia and I – going through Mum's things. Her 'effects', as Julia calls them – how ludicrous and Dickensian a term! As you know, Mum was a hoarder, and after eight hours of wading through paperwork and photographs, there's still a mountain to climb. Most of it's junk, though I kept finding myself dithering over whether or not I should keep something or throw it out – honestly, I was getting myself into a panic over receipts and holiday snaps, postcards of obscure places sent by people I don't even know. Ridiculous, isn't it? But this is what grief has reduced me to – paralysing indecision. And I do grieve, Nico, believe me I do. I was able to hold it together during the funeral, and for the first couple of weeks, but now, with the seasons changing, the reality of her absence is kicking in and I feel bereft, like a part of me has just leaked away without my noticing, but now it's gone I can't seem to get it back.

Today, all day, I felt the pull of the past. I'm sitting, now, at Dad's desk, writing to you on paper that I found in Mum's writing box. Even writing you a letter rather than an email or a text seems like something more real, if old-fashioned – it's like something Dad would have done. There are times I sense his presence, when I am alone here in the office, late at night, leaning on this desk of his. Sometimes I wish I could summon his ghost, even once, to put to him all the questions and doubts I struggle with, like he might offer up some sort of wisdom, tell me what to do, help me see my way through the fog.

As for Mum, I don't feel her presence now at all. Not since she passed, and I can't help think of her passing as some sort of abandonment. Like she's well and truly done with me now.

I think we made a mistake, Nico. The weather here has turned very cold, and when I think of her lying out there in the frozen earth, it seems so wrong to me that I have to stop what I'm doing, try to calm myself. I know we buried her next to Dad because it seemed like the right thing to do, but now I wonder, was it? Think of her spirit, Nick, her very essence — she was a creature of heat, she worshipped the sun. It always seemed to me that she was a different person in Africa — happier, carefree. But I suppose we were all different then . . . Anyway. Maybe it was wrong to bury her in a cold climate. Not that I'm suggesting we exhume her body and take it abroad. I guess I'm just telling you that I have regrets and that is one of them.

When my time comes, I don't want to be lowered into the cold damp Irish soil. Have me cremated, will you? And then scatter my ashes somewhere the sun shines — Kenya, why not? I said the same to Julia today but she just said I was being maudlin. I don't think she takes anything I say seriously right now, thinks it's just the grief talking. But it's not, Nico. That's why I'm telling it to you. When the time comes, I want to go back to Kenya. Back to the Masai Mara. Scatter my ashes by the river Mara. Think of it as a form of atonement.

Jesus, I'm so tired. Head swimming in brandy. But you do what you can to get you through the day, don't you? Lately, I need more and more help with the passing hours. I think I've taken on too much, Nick, but I don't quite know how to shed the load. Mum left everything in my care, but this was always

193

her thing — and while it gave her a lift, visiting Nairobi when-
ever she got a chance, it's not something that appeals to me. I
fear going back there, and yet there is the constant pull of the
place. I considered asking you to take it on. But that day — the
day we buried Mum — when you and I were here in my study,
talking, I could tell you didn't want it. That you needed to get
away. To distance yourself. After all, haven't you spent your
whole life doing that, Nico? Don't be offended now — I don't
mean that in a bad way. If anything, what I'm trying to say is:
I understand.

I think I'll stop now. It's late and I've drunk enough to sleep.
I'm going to seal this letter and maybe I'll send it to you, maybe I
won't. I'll sleep on it. But whenever you read this, wherever you are,
I hope you are happy, Nico, and I hope that you think well of me,

Your loving brother,
Luke

As we drive through the dry landscape, the letter replays
itself to me. It's there in my shirt pocket, next to my heart,
and as the day deepens, drawing me back there, I feel the
words pumping through me in an unshakeable rhythm:
Think well of me, brother.

A rap at the window. I sit up, blinking. The truck has
stopped and through the muddy windscreen the sky is
streaked with thick swathes of orange sunlight. I don't
know how long I've slept, but we're at the banks of the
Mara river and Karl is outside lighting a cigarette, Lauren
standing a little way off, her arms crossed over her chest. I
get out, feel pain travelling through my body as I stretch
and try to shake off the heavy daze.

The mourners gather in a confidential circle by the water, waiting for us. Figures darkly dressed, standing silent by the river's edge, regarding me from a distance.

The sun is slipping down, casting the trees in long shadows. Now that I'm out of the truck, I'm suddenly cold. I feel the sweat on my back drying, my shirt stiff with it, and my whole body shivers.

'Are we late?' I ask Karl hoarsely, as I close the door behind me.

'Just in time,' he says, dropping his cigarette and stepping on it. 'Come on, buddy. They're waiting.'

With Lauren, we walk through the sweet red-oat grass and the circle greets us with nods and murmurs, like a troupe of theatregoers recognizing guests who have arrived late.

'You made it,' Murphy says, coming forward to embrace me.

It's only as he draws away that I see the urn clasped in one of his hands and with it comes a rush of sound into my ears.

'Just about,' Karl replies.

My mouth is dry. I feel dizzy. I take a deep breath, then feel a hand in mine. It's Lauren. I squeeze her hand, grateful for the gesture, even if this peace between us is only temporary.

You can hear the movement of water nearby, some creature surfacing further along the banks of the river. A herd of impala are tugging at the leaves on the lower branches of the acacia trees in the next field. You can see, too, the lights coming on from lodges and camps all around us and along the horizon. But it's not how I remembered it. Not at all. It's so different I could be somewhere else. I know back then I was a child and I may have misremembered certain things. I know time can play tricks on the mind. But it's not as I remembered it. The river is wider and brighter here, the vegetation cut back. It doesn't feel like the same place at all.

I feel kind of disappointed, cheated in a way. And guilty, too, because in my mind we're doing Luke a disservice. This is not the place he thought it was.

'"Scatter my ashes by the river Mara." That was Luke's last wish and that is why we are here,' Murphy says, breaking the low murmur of unease between us.

He takes his glasses off and looks at each of us with a kind of ceremonial deliberation. We fan out around him and he begins his sermon.

'We're here where Luke wanted to be laid to rest, where he wished his last remains, his ashes, to be scattered. "Scatter my ashes by the river Mara. Carry me home," he said. We're here where Luke Yates wanted to become again part of the land he loved so much, a land he first came to as a child, and that land, here, the Masai Mara, held out its arms for him, welcomed him, his brother Nicholas and their parents, Sally and Kenneth, into its welcoming embrace, and it is with great sadness that we now bid farewell to one of Africa's returning sons. Let us pray.'

He starts the psalm: 'The Lord is my shepherd; I shall not want.'

And we, all of us, join in as a faltering chorus, our voices weak at first, but slowly gaining strength as the light fades:

'He maketh me to lie down in green pastures: he leadeth me beside the still waters. He restoreth my soul: he leadeth me in the paths of righteousness for his name's sake. Yea, though I walk through the valley of the shadow of death, I will fear no evil . . .'

The light is fading. I can see the smoke of a bonfire rising in the distance, hear the rhythmic chant of tribal music from nearby. I can't tell if the music is for tourists or not, though most things here now seem to be.

But not back then. Not when we were here: Luke, Katie and I. I wonder if some of the people with us knew what had happened here, all those years ago – I wonder if they would have come.

Not Julia. Not Karl. Not Lauren. Surely.

Maybe none of us should have come back. Maybe this is all a very bad idea and we should simply have ignored Luke's outlandish request.

Listening to Murphy's voice now, I can't help but think of that time when we fled this country, as if we left in shame and silence, and how when we arrived in Dublin everything had changed.

Shivering in the cold of that house in the Wicklow hills, all of the words locked fast inside me, swathing myself in silence. Our parents had grown distant with one another. I remember, too, Luke's sudden unnerving stammer. It seemed as if we were two different families. One family in Africa. One in Ireland. One was the negative print of the other. Back in Ireland we were all in darkness, growing quickly apart, each of us gravitating away from another.

I remember one time Luke crashed Dad's car. He was seventeen. I was fifteen. Mum was out visiting an aunt who was ill in hospital. Dad had gone to his old rugby club in Donnybrook for a reunion. I was in my room listening to

Dexter Gordon's brilliant disc *True Blue*. Luke stood in the doorway twirling Dad's car keys around his fingers. I pulled out my earphones and he said: 'Fancy a spin?'

I thought he was joking and laughed. He walked out to the car and I followed. 'Jesus, Luke, what are you thinking?' I wanted to say, but I was so pleased he had asked me that I said nothing and climbed into the old red Mercedes.

When we got to the road that leads up to the Featherbeds, he said: 'You have a go.'

I slid into the driver's seat as he stepped out.

'Clutch, brake, accelerator,' he said, and I remembered it from one of the few lessons Dad had given us under what he called 'controlled conditions'.

'Take it handy,' Luke said.

I got the hang of it without difficulty, flew up the Featherbeds to Military Road, then stopped at the Viewing Point. A rake of cyclists flew by us, and I was picking up speed as I took the corner for Kilakee, but I misjudged it and slammed the car into a tree.

Luke and I were flung forward hard against out seatbelts. Luke forced me out, inspected the damage and got back into the car. It started, but the front bumper was mashed.

On the way home, I said I was sorry. But Luke told me to shut up and let him deal with it.

He took the rap, and was grounded for months. Dad was furious. The car was repaired. But when Luke came home six months later, drunk from a night out with friends after finishing their mock exams, Dad went ballistic – only for Luke to point to me, as I came down the stairs to see what had happened, and say: 'It was him, him, he did it . . . He smashed the car. It was him, it was him . . .'

Luke was distraught, his face wretched with tears. Dad had to coax him to a kitchen chair, where he cried into Dad's sleeve, both of them looking at me – the words still echoing: *it was him, it was him.*

It was another example of how we were gradually growing apart, a process that had started when we returned to Ireland. We'd been home only a few weeks when my father told me that from then on Luke and I would sleep in separate rooms.

'You're getting older,' he said. 'The house has enough bedrooms, and with more homework in the new school year, Luke will need his own desk and the quiet to study.'

I didn't say anything – I couldn't – though I felt the words jostling inside me, pushing upwards as if they might suddenly burst out and break the silence that had me trapped.

'We're not in Africa any more, Nicholas. We need new habits, new routines. And one of them is that you and Luke are to have separate bedrooms.'

He sounded as if he was reading from a script, or that he was a robot, talking to me as if he didn't know me, that I wasn't his son, that I wasn't Nick.

'And,' he said, 'we thought it better if you went to different schools as well. You both have . . . Well, you have different needs.'

Maybe he saw my unspoken fear and confusion. Or maybe he, too, had begun to adjust to our altered state, and was starting to read my silences and the thoughts that might lie inside me. So he sat down on my bed and spoke softly, his brow furrowed with tenderness, as if he hated saying this, but knew it was for the best.

'You must understand,' he said, his voice dropping low, a new urgency spilling into it. 'I'm trying to protect you.'

That was when I started to cry. I knew he was trying to make everything right – trying to shield us from whatever dangers lay around and within us. But that didn't stop me wanting everything to be like it had been before. As he turned the light out, in my *new* room, he said, like the old Dad might have, 'Don't worry, champ, it won't be so bad. You'll be okay.'

We never talked about Africa again. It was never mentioned or alluded to in passing. Neither were the Walshes up for discussion. It was as if my parents tried deliberately to erase the time we had spent in Africa from our lives – which only forced it further into my unconscious. As time passed and I would try to remember what had happened in the days and months we spent there, the memory was never the same, but came back to me ever so slightly altered.

Maybe that's why the place seems so unfamiliar to me now.

Murphy breaks off. The low tones of the prayer fade into silence. After a time, he says: 'Please take some moments to remember Luke to yourselves and pray for his soul.' He dips his head and we do the same. I don't know whether I feel relieved or desolate that it's nearly over.

Murphy takes the lid off the urn, sinks his hand into the ashes and lets them run through his fingers. 'Ashes to ashes,' he murmurs, 'dust to dust.'

He steps to Julia, her face streaked with pain and grief, and as she releases a stream of ash onto the gentle breeze, she whispers some private message, then starts to cry and her mother goes forward to comfort her.

It's my turn. Murphy holds out the urn. I put my hand into it and feel the sandy grit between my fingers, its surprising coolness.

'Goodbye, Luke.' I toss it into the air.

I can think of nothing else to say. Nothing that would do my brother's life justice. Julia is weeping quietly now.

There's still ash left in the urn. I dip my hand in again and this time feel the hardness of what must be the nub of an uncremated tooth or bone.

Then I fling the last of my brother into the wilderness.

The group of mourners breaks up and moves falteringly away from the river. The great Masai Mara is shrouded in darkness now. You can hear the nocturnal animals rousing themselves. There are rustlings in the undergrowth, and the great chain of sound the crickets make begins to spin in one loop after another. They pick up the song the birds of the Masai Mara sing. Its verses are the same and its chorus too: *Who cut the knot? Who cut the knot?*

I stop and turn back to the place where we have scattered the remains. In the darkening light it seems too stark, too bare, too open to the elements. Fear rises in me again and the memories come flooding back: I'm five years old and standing on tiptoe in our parents' bathroom, watching wide-eyed as Luke smears shaving foam over his jaw, then reaches for our father's razor; or we're sitting side by side in front of the fire on a Saturday night, our hair still wet from our bath, eating sandwiches while watching *The Muppet Show*; or I'm running to keep up while Luke charges ahead through a field of grass, a stitch starting in my side as his whoops and calls and wild laughter ring out; or it's our first day at the International School in Nairobi, I'm sick with nerves, and Luke's saying to me, in his older-brother voice, 'Don't worry, I've got your back', or I'm standing on Killiney beach on a cold grey day, looking out to sea, when a white streak rips past me, Luke shouting with delight as he flings himself naked into the waves. I feel it all rising inside me, as if I'm brimming over with these memories of him as a small boy, before it happened, before it all changed, and with it comes the sense that, in scattering him to the wind, these memories of him are all taking flight – memories so precious to me now, because despite all that has happened, despite what he did back then, he was my brother and I loved him.

'I don't want to leave him here,' I say, my voice cracking. I can feel the answering squeeze of Lauren's hand in mine. It is supposed to be a source of comfort, but it's not. Instead it triggers in me something fearful and alive.

I'm fighting what has happened, railing against it. And yet, if anything, the fear grows. I can feel it as definitely as my fingers find the line of melody in any of the late-night gin-joints I've played in, in any of the waywardly tuned piano keys I have pressed – a fear so real and so familiar it feels like a recurring nightmare. Like *déjà vu*. I shake with that fear, look out into the darkness and it's there: the past stalking me like a late-night predator – stealthily, hungrily – coming towards me.

'Come on,' Lauren says, pulling me to her and sensing my unease. 'Let's get out of here.'

12. Katie

Funny the things you let slip when you've a few drinks inside you.

I've been to several funerals in my time, and at each and every one, no matter how tragic or shocking the loss, there always comes a moment afterwards when people have had a couple of drinks and the cold grief of the graveside seems to have been dispelled somewhat by talk, reminiscence, the closeness of the relatives and friends who remain, the bond that you feel in the aftermath, a moment when it seems okay, that the grief will be bearable, that life goes on. It's like a held breath that is now released. A relaxation that creeps in around the mourners.

I'm sitting alone in the lounge, cradling a drink in my hands. Scattered around the room are various groupings of mourners, as well as other guests at this luxury safari lodge. Outside, the dusk is gathering over the savannah, night creatures sending out their chatter and calls, their twilight song. Behind me, a conversation is happening. Julia and the priest are sitting together and he is talking to her in steady tones, much as he did with me yesterday when we were in Nairobi and I was a blathering mess. Julia is more held together, but I have seen a slump come over her in the last hour – tiredness or defeat, I can't be sure which. The slightest of slurs in Murphy's speech gives him away, and he's speaking a little too loudly, taking on the dull, lecturing tone that older men sometimes employ when they've had one too many and rediscover the importance of their own thoughts and experience.

'It was the right thing to do, Julia.'

'I know, Father.'

'The right thing. And Luke was always one for doing the right thing. For setting things straight.'

'Unfinished business.'

'Exactly. My point exactly, Julia. It was unfinished business. He wanted to return to make things right. And I knew it,' he tells her now. 'I knew it the moment Sally told me they were leaving.'

I sit up a little in my seat.

'I knew that it was not right. For the boys, for their future. To run away like that. It felt like . . . like leaving a frayed end flying in the wind.'

'They were only children,' Julia says.

Her words are a douse of cold water. She knows.

'Only children,' he repeats. 'I said to Sally that it was a mistake. And to Ken. The night they were leaving I told him. I said: "You're only going to make them feel guilty if you take them away like this."' A deadening sigh. 'Didn't listen. Didn't want to know.'

'They were scared. It was natural.'

'But *I* knew. *I* knew it wasn't over. Some things are too big to run from. Some things draw you back. It could have been different for them, Julia. For those boys. It could have been different . . .'

His words drift into a melancholy silence. But I don't feel melancholy. I feel alert, more awake and present than I have done in weeks.

A shadow moves in the doorway. I see it, and Murphy does too, because he gets to his feet, an awkward, lumbering movement, and I hear him tell Julia that someone's waiting for him, someone he must speak to. I watch him walk towards the door, an old man, tired, drunk, with a myriad private griefs and troubles.

So he did know. He knew all along. Yet he lied to me about it, and I can't figure out why.

My eyes follow him across the room until he has gone and all that remains of him is the suspicion he has aroused within me.

True to his word, Reilly calls. It's late. I sit on the steps to the terrace, the phone pressed to my ear. Light thrown from the hotel reaches across the gravelled drive to the lawn. Beyond that, the contours of the trees and bushes become blurred, the gloom turning to darkness. Reilly's voice sounds distant, a hush of air between us, like a third party listening.

'How was it?' he asks gently, and I tell him about the gathering by the riverbank, the sun setting, the scattering of the ashes. I tell him how, afterwards, we had come back to the hotel for a meal that was silent and subdued, as if we were all laid low with exhaustion and spent emotion.

I've left the others in the lounge, huddled in groups around low tables, the noise growing as the night comes on and the alcohol does its thing. Nick is at the piano, bent over the keys, slow blues numbers played with a soft hand an undercurrent to all the talk that surrounds him. He doesn't lift his head, his attention on the music, and it crosses my mind that he's hiding behind it, playing one tune after another as a means of protecting himself, keeping everyone at bay. And I am out here, talking to Reilly, the low chatter of nocturnal insects rising up from the garden and the plains beyond.

'Well, it's over now,' he says, and I say, yes, it is.

Straight away, he catches it. 'What is it, Katie? You sound strange.'

'I don't know. I just expected to feel different, once it was done.'

'How so?'

'Like I would feel some kind of an ending. Relief, I suppose.'

The air still holds the heaviness of the day's heat. It's there in every indrawn breath. Somewhere out in the darkness, Luke has returned to the earth.

'You need to sleep,' Reilly suggests. 'Perhaps in the morning you'll feel that relief.'

'Perhaps . . .'

But I know it isn't true. For years now I have been living my life as though what happened to me in Africa was over – a closed book. Our secret is out there now. There are others who know. Julia. Murphy. Who else? But also I know that I can no longer look away, that no matter how long I wait, it's not going to pass. I knew it from the moment I stood in the glow of the red sunset, watching Nick open his hand to release his brother onto the breeze.

'Remember the bird I was sent?'

'Of course.'

'I think whoever sent it is here.'

I can sense him stiffening, his attention pricked, and I tell him about the anonymous post slipped under the door of my hotel room in Nairobi. Pictures of drownings. All those limbs plastered with wet clothes, chalky-white skin, hair like weed. I leave out the part about Cora.

'Jesus,' he breathes, and I can picture him sitting there, one hand squeezing his temples. 'Did you bring them to the police?'

'No.'

'Katie! For God's sake, this isn't a joke!'

'It's not that I think it's a joke. I am taking it seriously. But I just don't think that's the right avenue to go down. I want to find out myself —'

'How? What exactly are you planning on doing?'

I pause, take a breath. The truth is I don't have a plan. The truth is that this thing requires something other than logic or reason. I need to feel my way through it, trust my instincts to lead me to the truth. I close my eyes, hear Murphy's voice in my head: *Let him go, girl.* Feel the clawing of suspicion, of something close to dislike.

'The charity,' I say to Reilly now, opening my eyes. 'ALIVE. Have you had a chance to do some digging?'

'Yes — I was coming to that. Turns out there are big problems. That accountant that Luke Yates had go over the books, he unearthed a huge hole. Unexplained disappearance of funds. From what I've heard, the accountant was urging a criminal investigation, but Luke was resistant. He even wanted the whole thing wound up.'

'Do you think the priest is involved?'

He exhales noisily, with irritation, and when he speaks again his voice is lowered. 'I don't know. But right now, we can't rule him out.'

I can feel the suspicion inside me — the instinct that

leads me to distrust, to doubt, to question. Every good journalist has it. The kernel of suspicion has been inside me since the moment Murphy took my hand in his, that searching gaze passing over my face, since he kept hold of my hand a second too long and said: *I remember you.*

Down in the garden amid the topiary and the grottoes, I glimpse the glow of a tiny red light in the darkness, then watch it disappear. The tang of cigarette smoke in the air. I train my eyes on it, the darkness composing itself into shadows, silhouettes. The bluish glow of a white shirt.

'I wish I could be there with you,' Reilly tells me, and I can't help but smile.

Even from this distance, I feel the warmth and safety of his presence, the depths of his voice, the goodness that seems to be at the very core of him.

'When I get home, let's go for a long walk, you and me,' I say.

'I'd like that.'

'Let's go somewhere that we can take the air and talk.'

'I'll take you to Dún Laoghaire – the West Pier. The East Pier seems a little too refined for us.'

'Reilly,' I say then, a sudden urgency that I find hard to understand or explain building in me, 'there are things I haven't told you . . . things I've done . . .'

'Katie, love,' he says gently. 'There'll be time enough to lay bare our souls.'

Behind me, the music keeps on and on, a swarm of conversation rising above it. I put my phone away, get to my feet, but instead of returning to the others, I step away from the terrace, and move down into the darkness of the garden.

It's quiet out here, the only sounds the chatter and call of night-life hidden in the dark foliage of the garden and, beyond it, the long grass of the savannah. The river flows along the edges of the estate, the grounds sweeping down to its banks where black trees loom large and scrubby bushes form a ragged perimeter. There's no light here, and as I advance, shapes begin to define themselves, the contours of a path like an animal track snaking through the undergrowth. My footfall is slow, deliberate: I'm anxious not to disturb, not to draw attention to myself. An animal advancing on its prey.

Two figures, near the river's edge. One short and stocky, skin as dark as the night. The other tall and white, the bluish glow of his shirt. From this distance, I can make out the stooped form of the priest, pushing his face close to the other man's, articulating his point in sharp bursts of language. Kikulu or Swahili, I don't know. Guttural sounds, sharp clicks of the tongue, whatever it is he is saying is animated, almost wild except for the whispered hold he keeps on it. Hands gesticulating, a question asked, while the other man leans back against something – a post? a tree? – staring ahead, refusing to make eye-contact with Murphy, smoking in a way that suggests the casualness is false. Here, in the shadows, observing the exchange, I can feel the charge in the air between them. Murphy is agitated: he shakes his head, baffled, then drops it briefly, large hands cupping his face. The short man – his friend? – steps forward, puts a hand to the priest's shoulder, says something low, his intonation softened with concern, yet his voice is hard around the edges. There is something familiar about him that causes my heart to thrum.

I move a little closer now, painfully aware of each crackle of grass beneath my feet, every dislodged stone. Almost upon them now, I find myself holding my breath, listening to the words coming out of the man – the stranger – an urgent throatiness coating the silence, like a layer of grease.

'No, no, no,' Murphy says emphatically. 'That was not what I wanted!'

The other man continues in his own language, persistence in his tone. I try to make out his face, but it's so dark. Small eyes, flat features, a broad nose, deep lines running to the corners of an unsmiling mouth.

Sudden movement – a creature in the undergrowth; a gasp of surprise. The talking stops. Everything grows still, and in the silence that surrounds me, I feel the nudge of fear. They have seen me. The stillness in their pose tells me as much. Instinct tells me to turn away, to run, yet there is an itch in my brain – a question that demands an answer. I take a step towards them.

Murphy's companion appears older now that I approach. He carries with him a faint air of menace. His eyes – small, obsidian, flashing in the moonlight – stir something within me.

'Did you follow me?' Murphy asks, and I turn to him. There are white bristles all over his chin, bags under his eyes; any trace of kindness has been chased away.

'Yes.'

He nods and looks me up and down.

'Why did you lie to me, Father?'

'Lie to you?'

'You know what happened. You know what we did. So why did you lie about it?'

Still he says nothing, his gaze hardening.

'I don't think you've been altogether straight with me, Murphy.'

'I don't know what you mean.'

'Dead birds. Pictures of drowned girls. Threats. Luke, too. I think you know exactly what I'm talking about. '

A hunch, that's all. The insistent voice of instinct that speaks up now tells me he knows, he must do. I think of Reilly and what he said, feel the hardening crust of distrust.

He holds my gaze for just a moment, and when he breaks it, a small self-deprecating smile comes over his wizened features. He seems to give himself a little shake as if to shrug off this unpleasantness. And it is this gesture, this one small shudder, that triggers it. All at once I'm hurtling back through time, brought forcefully to a moment in my childhood when I stood behind a door and observed an argument. I had forgotten it completely, as if my mind had tipped it out onto a floor and left it. But now I know it was there all along, lurking in the shadows.

'I remember you,' I tell Murphy now, and he raises his head, his attention snagged by the seriousness of my tone, the grain of something remembered. 'I saw you. That day in the house, with Sally.'

Close my eyes, and I'm back there. Eight years old, awkward and out of place in that house where I don't belong, seeking a pocket of coolness in those dim rooms, the window shutters closed against the battering heat of the noonday sun. Where were the others? My mother, the boys and their father? I have no idea. That part of the memory has been lost. What remains, though, is so breathtakingly clear that I can see everything in sharp focus – the dark wooden furniture, the striped ticking of the bedcovers, the lazy revolution of a ceiling fan, my feet hot and dusty in the red sandals I disliked, and the sway of Sally Yates's skirt as he grabbed hold of her arm and pulled her back to him. Behind the door I held my breath, all too aware that I shouldn't be there, shouldn't be watching, and although I didn't fully understand what it was I was a witness to, I had the sense that it was something clandestine, forbidden even. The whispering presence of a man in a bedroom that wasn't his own. His grip on Sally's arm, the way he pulled her to him, then letting go of her arm, his hand moving to her hip. I couldn't see his face, couldn't hear his words, but I heard something in the tone – an insistence, a firmness of purpose. And while he spoke, she didn't look at him, just stood there staring at the floor, as if waiting for him to finish, enduring the clasp of his hand and his river of words until the moment he released her and she could get away. The shake of her dark hair then as she vigorously denied whatever it was that he put to her. And when she spoke, her voice came out fractured with emotion.

'No,' she told him. 'You know I can't, so stop asking. Don't you know it only makes this harder?'

His wheedling tone again, the pull of his hand moving her body closer to him so that she was trapped in his embrace. Briefly, the fight went out of her and I felt a lurch of fear or dread as she seemed to lean into him, her head resting on his shoulder, her arms loosely about his waist. In my head I felt the words flowing: *oh, no, oh, no, oh, no.*

Standing there, unable to pull my gaze away, I felt the order of things changing. Sweat in my sandals, my heart beating wildly, I felt the tumult of that change come over me. I don't know why it affected me in that way. After all, she was not my mother. But standing there in the shadows, my eyes fixed on them through the narrow crack between the door and its frame, I felt something slipping away from me and it made me afraid.

She straightened, pulling herself from his embrace with a kind of determined ferocity, and when she spoke to him, the tears had gone from her voice, and her tone was upset, accusatory.

'Don't you think I would if I could?'

She moved so swiftly that I had no time to react. The door pulled back, her face as she saw me changed into a mask of anger and fright. 'Katie! What are you doing?'

I looked up at her, at the features I had once thought so beautiful, contracting now around her suspicion, and the tears welled up inside me, with the powerful need to run.

Just a glance at him was all I got. It was enough, though. His eyes, small and blue, flashing reproach at me. And then the little smile to himself as he looked down at the floor, his hands going into his pockets, and that little shake of his shoulders – the shudder repeated now, almost thirty years later – as I turned from them both, the rubber soles of my sandals slapping all the way along the tiled floor and out into the sunshine.

'It was you,' I say to Murphy now, all of it falling into place. 'You were the one Luke spoke of. You were the one he told Nick about.'

He doesn't respond, keeps his eyes narrowed, his gaze fixed determinedly on the trees behind me.

'You and Sally Yates. I saw you together that day in the house. Before we left for the safari. You were arguing.'

It must have happened shortly before we left for the Masai Mara so there was no opportunity for her to confront me again, find out what I had seen or heard.

'Did my mother know about it?' I ask Murphy now. 'Did Ken? Did they know you two were having an affair?'

'Enough!' he hisses, his anger surfacing. He holds up his hand, but I see that it's shaking.

He fixes me with a baleful look but all I see in that moment is a dry, withered old man trapped in the wasteland of his own grievances, bitterness and regrets.

Silence for a moment, the whisper of running water. Murphy's companion says something I don't understand. I'd almost forgotten him. But now, as I turn my attention to him, I see the hardness of his stare, a malignant flash in the amber light of those glassy eyes before he backs away into the shadows.

'Wait,' I tell him, but he turns on his heel.

'Tell him to wait,' I say to Murphy, but he draws in his chin, watches his friend disappear into the dark clump of trees.

'Who is he?' I ask, my heart beating loudly now. A kind of excitement taking hold of me, interlaced with fear. I'm close, so close I can almost touch it.

A tightening in his face, mouth crimped in a defiant pout. Hands in his pockets, he turns from me and starts back towards the hotel.

'Murphy!' I shout after him, but he doesn't turn.

A frozen instant of indecision, but the pull of the river is there – a path through the trees. Without stopping to think, I turn to follow the stranger.

I don't know what direction he's gone in, but feel I'm close nonetheless. A faint stirring of branches up ahead, the crunching footfall. I hurry now, the trees a hard, dark presence above me, the river bubbling. I don't know where I am but I need to move, to follow, to find. I know this man. Somewhere down the dark corridors of memory, a match has been struck. In these woods are answers to my questions and, whatever the risk, I'm propelled by something outside myself to hurry, to hunt him down.

The path thins – an animal track – and leaves become densely packed. The earth under my feet is softer, branches scrape my face, and I flick them away, pushing hard now against the growth, the dripping trees. Heat trapped in this space, musty and savage, odours rising from the river, animal and strange. The track is leading me to the water, and as I near its banks, a shape forms and moves, a lizard slipping into the depths. I stop. Feel the breath catching in my throat. The air grows still. The darkness around me seems oppressive. A threat forms in the air. It comes to me at once: no longer in pursuit, I have become the hunted one. All at once I feel it – a presence. Watchful. Disturbed. The silent power of the river. *Cora*. Her name carried in the water, dripping from the trees above; it's there in the wet mud that grips my feet. The cloying presence of her; the air clogged with her death.

I hold myself still. Senses heightened like a startled deer.

A crack behind me and I swing around. Pain breaks like a wave against my head, a thousand nerve endings screaming in chorus. Blackness sings in my ears, a wash of it coming over me, pulling me down, down. A presence at the edge of my sight, a faceless figure, my fall silently observed by him and no one else but the listening trees and the hanging vines.

13. Nick

That night my sleep is broken. The cooling air of the Masai Mara has got into my bones. Lauren stirs next to me. Her breathing is laboured. We don't talk. That can wait until morning.

When light finally breaks into the room, Lauren pulls herself from the bed. She stretches before going into the bathroom.

As I swing my legs out and go to stand up, it hits me – I feel as if I'm under water: a sucking noise in my ears.

'Are you all right?' Lauren asks, when she comes out of the bathroom. She is clutching her towel in front of her, frowning.

'I don't feel well.'

She comes forward, presses her hand to my forehead. 'You're burning up.'

'I'm fine,' I say, needing to get moving, to get away from this place. I reach the end of the bed and the room swirls around me.

'Nick, you're sick. You may need a doctor.'

'I need paracetamol, that's all. And some water.'

'I'll find Karl – tell him we won't be able to leave today.'

'No!'

My shout makes her draw back, startled.

'No,' I repeat, softer this time, but still firm. This noise in my ears that started on the journey down here has been building to a crescendo, its whine driving me to distraction. I can't shake the feeling that until I leave this place, until I start to put distance between me and the land where my brother now lies, I will get no peace. I start to get dressed while Lauren looks in her bag, then hands me some painkillers and a bottle of water. I knock them back and swallow hard.

'We need to talk,' she says quietly.

'I know we do. I know. But, sweetheart, can't it wait? I feel so strange. This noise in my ears . . .'

'No, I don't think it can wait, Nick.'

Something sinks within me. I stop buttoning my shirt, put my hands on my hips and try to steady myself, try to feel the floor beneath my feet. My head is swimming with fever, water rushing through the channels behind my ears, and even though I know she's entitled to a decent explanation, I'm not sure I have the energy to give it.

'Nothing happened, Lauren. I promise you. We talked – that's it.'

She is frowning with frustration at herself, at me, impatient. 'You know what, Nick? I believe you. I do. You went to Katie's room, you talked, you fell asleep. Fine. If that's what you say happened, then I accept it.'

'If you accept it why do you sound so angry?'

'You just don't get it, do you? You think this is just about sex. About fidelity. But the thing is this, Nick.' She draws close, close enough for me to see the bright flecks of amber in her eyes. '*I* am your wife. That means that *I* should be the one you go to when you need to talk. *I* should be the one you confide in. *I* should be the one you turn to for understanding, or for comfort. Not her.'

I feel the stab of each one of those *I*s and sit down on the bed. I am so tired of running from this thing, from avoiding it, and now with the plains of the Masai Mara swarming outside me, pressuring this room, trying to get inside my head, I cannot bear it.

'There are some things I can't talk to you about, Lauren.'

'What things?' she asks, but I can't answer.

'I see,' she says, her voice icy now. 'So you can't talk to me about it, but you can talk to her.'

I close my eyes, but that just makes the whining noise worse. When I open them again, Lauren's eyes are red and teary. My mind's on fire. There are too many things I can't figure out right now. Too many memories that clash.

A voice in my head is pushing me to tell her, whispering to me: *Let her in.*

The room seems smaller now. There's no air. I get up, cross to the window and throw it open. I feel claustrophobic, breathless. My hands are shaking and my head is full of a noise that sounds something like an untuned radio.

When I turn back, she's staring hard at me, in a way she's never looked at me before. It's as if she's urging me to say something. And in that moment, it feels as if we could kill each other or make love.

We do neither. Of course we don't.

Instead, Lauren goes to the window and stares out at the savannah beyond the hotel grounds. 'This place. What it does to people . . .' she says enigmatically.

And finally the pressure that has been building in me breaks, and I say what I have wanted to say but not allowed myself to do so until now: 'When I was eight, I watched my brother kill a little girl. It happened here in the river. I watched him hold that girl under the water until the life went out of her. I watched him do it and I didn't stop him. And Katie saw it too. That's why I went to her. That's why I had to talk to her. That's why I couldn't talk to you.'

Lauren looks at me, but says nothing. She turns, takes her bag, and leaves. The door falls shut heavily behind her.

I sit on the bed again, hang my head in my hands. My whole body is shaking.

I realize I may have lost her. The look on her face, the fear that had entered her eye. I never told her I loved her. I never said I was sorry it had happened – that it was the greatest regret of my life. I am amazed at my own reckless-ness – that I would gamble with our happiness like that, take such a foolish risk and tell her what we had done. I stare at my hands and see the dirt around my fingernails, the reddish arcs of dust beneath them, and I think of my hand going into that urn, the coolness of the ash, and feel a sudden panic. Quickly now, I get to my feet and rush for the door, feeling the spinning as if my brain is floating in water.

I'll find her, I'll tell her I love her. I'll tell her that what happened when I was a child was awful, too awful for me to think about, to look at. But I will open up to her about it, if that's what she wants, I will tell her what happened, confess my part in it, but then we would put it behind us, lock it away in the past, push it back down there into the dark, return it to its place in the shady waters, where it belongs.

But my legs buckle and my hands drop from the

door-handle. They're too weak. I'm too weak even to open the door.

I stumble to the bed, sit down on its edge and hold my head. I'm dizzy and nauseous and the world seems to be spinning in furious revolutions. The sweat is cold on my forehead. I wipe it with a shaking hand, close my eyes and try to steady myself. As I breathe in and out, it comes back to me then, like a half-forgotten melody my father might once have hummed, the day it all happened.

'We're going down to the river,' Luke says.

'Really?' I ask.

'Mum says it's okay.'

Dad has gone looking for another driver. Katie's mum has gone with him. She's in a huff, Katie says. Luke says she's 'distraught'. It makes me think of the word 'drought', and the dry expanse of desert we crossed with our parents only months before. I thought I'd seen a pool of water on that trip. But my dad called it a mirage. It's when you see something that isn't really there.

'Come on,' Luke says. 'Let's go.'

The three of us run into the undergrowth towards the river. Luke is ahead and Katie comes streaming by me. We run through the high grass and, after several minutes, stop to catch our breath and take stock. From where we are, I can see the van we came in, but not the driver. He's asleep in the front seat.

The grass scratches and tickles us as we run through it. Luke is singing a song of nonsense and I'm smiling broadly into the rushing wind. Then, as the muddy smell of the river rises, we see her – Cora.

She's sitting in a tree, her feet dangling over the river.

She has blonde hair tied in green-ribboned bunches. She's talking, not to another person but to herself. The closer we get, I realize she's not talking but singing quietly. It sounds to me like some kind of lullaby.

One hand clutches the bough she's sitting on, the other a green-leafed branch, which she is sweeping this way and that. I wonder what her song is, or where she imagines herself to be. I can almost make out the words as they leave her lips in gentle plosives.

Her younger sister, Amy, is crouched on the riverbank, entranced by a game of her own. When Luke arrives first, panting, it looks like he'll startle the girls, but he doesn't. They turn and gaze at him as if they've been expecting him, as if we're all grown-ups and he is some gentleman caller.

I wave, like we're old friends, not kids who've only known each other a short time. Yesterday we found them here by the river, and together the five of us had splashed around at the water's edge until the sun dipped low and our dad came down and called to us back to camp, it was getting late.

Luke walks to the riverbank and kicks stones, digs his hands into his pockets and looks from one girl to the other. Then he pulls off his T-shirt and walks into the water.

I follow, but Katie stays where she is, at a distance. The water is cool and clear, not cold. It feels good to put my toes into it. The water tickles. Cora jumps down from the tree – she follows us to the water, giggling. The girls wear dresses. One is pink, the other green. They are sitting by the water now with sticks and are making spells.

Luke asks if they're witches and they laugh.

'Is it deep?' Luke says, pointing into the water.

Cora shrugs. He dives straight in and the girls gasp. When he emerges, his smile is broad and the water trickles down his face.

'There might be crocodiles!' Katie shouts.

'It's not even cold,' Luke says. He waves to her. 'Come on in,' he hollers, but she doesn't budge.

I want to follow him – it's so hot and the river is begging me to come in – but Katie's caution holds me back. I hunker down in the shadows, scan the surface of the water for the stealthy glide of a ridged back. One of the sisters crosses the river – Amy, the younger one. She inches her way towards me, staring at me with curiosity.

Mum comes to check on us, her form a silhouette against the white light beyond the trees. Hands on her hips, she hollers at Luke, but he won't come out of the water, even though she tells him to. I'm not sure if she can see me in the shadows. I'm not sure I want her to.

After she goes, I follow his lead and dive in. We jump on each other's backs and splash. Cora has moved closer to us: she wades into the water, and before we know it, we're all splashing each other.

'Where are your folks?' Luke says, and she laughs.

'Folks?' she says, and giggles again.

'Parents?' Luke clarifies.

She keeps laughing. Apparently there is no answer to this question, or, where they are from, parents are hilarious creatures, or perhaps they don't exist at all. I run out of the water to pull Katie in, but she shrieks and I leave her be. Then Luke asks me to count as he plunges his head into the water.

'Now your turn,' he says.

After several attempts, it looks like there's going to be only one winner. I can't beat Luke, but Cora – she might even be older than him, she's certainly lankier and longer – says: *Let me try*. Then it's my turn again, but Luke has an idea. 'Stay down longer, I'll assist,' he says, using one of the grown-up words he has acquired from our parents. He holds his hands over my head and mumbles something that sounds, as I submerge my head beneath the cool water, like a prayer, like something the priest would say at mass as he passes his hands over the congregation, not *Body of Christ*, not *Take away the sins of the world*, but something more garbled: an underwater sermon of sorts.

The game has no name. The game is the game. The game is pulling and pushing and laughing. And taking turns. It's my turn next. I take a deep breath and look upward. I take such a big breath, my mouth wide open, I think I'm going to swallow the whole of the blue sky.

'Okay. Now teams,' Luke says. 'One boy, one girl. Hold hands and stand over there,' he tells me and Amy, and I take her hand and we walk down into the water, like Luke and I did at the pool our dad brought us to in Dublin. That was when we lived in Ireland. We now live in Africa. Luke says we're Africans now. In the swimming pool in Dublin, you have to wear goggles and the chlorine makes your skin crawl and rashes appear, like red maps, and drive you crazy with how they itch. But there's no chlorine in the water here and I can keep my eyes open, wide open. I think I could be a fish or an underwater creature of some sort.

I'm counting in my head. I could be weightless, floating

in outer space. I pull Amy's hand and we go down into the depths, my legs giving way until it's deep. Then Amy pulls on my hand and we pop out of the water without a drop of air to spare.

The water sprays from my mouth in a fountain. Amy laughs. Her hand is small in mine, and soft like dough. I feel like I can hold my breath for ever. Cora is brave too. She can hold her breath for longer. Is that because she's older than me? 'No,' Luke says. 'It's because she's brave.'

Katie is walking in circles, talking to herself, sometimes stopping to watch, sometimes with her head down. She'll get dizzy walking in circles, I think.

But I'm getting tired. Luke says: 'Another game.'

The sun gets hotter. We play until my lungs hurt. I'm thirsty too. I want to go back to the camp. Maybe Dad's back now. Maybe he's found a new driver. I look for Mum from the water. I can't see her. I wish she'd come to get us. I'm not sure where Amy's parents are. I haven't seen them. For all I know, they don't exist.

Luke says, 'One more game.' But I don't want to. 'Come on,' he says. 'You might win this time.'

I gasp for air, swallow hard, then fall, dizzy onto the riverbank. My mouth has water in it and I sound like I'm gurgling.

Luke calls the next round 'the finals'. 'Is everybody ready?' he says.

We nod and he counts us in again and we all go down, the water covering our heads. Amy and I stay down until she wriggles and struggles. I let go of her hand, pop up, and she pops out of the water after me. I don't like holding Amy's hand when she starts to wriggle like that.

Luke and Cora are still under water. Cora is trying to come up for air. Luke is holding her.

Overhead, a hawk swoops and turns. It glides through the air effortlessly. Sometimes I wish I could fly. There's a stillness in the air, and time seems to have stopped. But something does not feel right.

I'm counting: 'Thirty-one, thirty-two . . .'

'Luke,' I shout, walking through the water. I'm scared now.

My ears are full of water. I can't make out anything except that hollow sound, like the ghostly wind when a shell is pressed against your ear.

Maybe there's nothing to hear anyway. Maybe all there is is silence.

Because the girl is still under the water. Like a rag doll, she floats on the surface, face down.

She starts to turn a little in the water. I'm waiting for her to lift her head, spray water from her mouth and say: 'I tricked you.'

I'm waiting for her to move in any other way. But she doesn't. Luke looks at me and there is blood coming from his nose. He reaches for the girl and she turns in the water, a swathe of blood reaching across her face.

He takes her in his arms. She's limp, her arms draped on each side of her, her face losing more colour, her mouth puckered, her eyes open.

Luke doesn't look like himself. He looks like someone else. He doesn't look like my brother any more, but someone older. His eyes are like stunned, frozen stars.

'Help me,' he says, but I can't move. He pulls Cora through the water and lays her on the riverbank.

Why won't she sit up? I think. I'm still in the water. I'm shivering now. I want to say: 'Stop play-acting.'

But I can't say anything.

I want to say: 'Luke, let's not play this game any more.' I want to say: 'Let's never play this game again, Luke.'

'Luke, can you hear me?'

Luke is kneeling by Cora's side and pushing on her chest, up and down. He is frantic and afraid.

Her struggle and the terror she must have felt at the end are not captured in her body or in her eyes. Instead, her pale blue eyes look like they have seen Heaven.

Katie is crying out now as she scrambles towards us. Amy is nowhere to be seen.

Katie's eyes are large and afraid. My head fills with noise. I'm standing in the water, shivering.

Luke is pressing his mouth to Cora's – breathing into her.

The trees are crowding around us, black and silent.

Then we are moving through the water – me, Luke and Katie – pulling, dragging. The river water is rolling down my back, beginning to dry in the heat. Something passes over my hand; it's Cora's hair, like weed, floating beneath the surface as we take her upriver. Her wrist is gripped in both my hands. I cry out, letting go of her arm, watching it float away to her side.

'For Christ's sake!' Luke shouts.

What happens then? Shouts and murmurs. Luke saying, 'Keep a lookout.' Branches gathered – sticks, leaves, twigs. Slowly, Cora becomes hidden from view. A bird shrieks high in the branches. Movement on the bank and Katie screams. She's standing in the water, her eyes enormous, hands over her mouth. My head is filled with noise. I cannot hear what anyone is saying. I can only hear the sound of water rushing upward. She screams again, and Luke swings around, shoves her back hard so that she loses her footing, falls into the water. He turns back to the bank, his face hot and white with fury, finishes the task. Something moves on the other side of the river – Katie glances downstream. Then Luke is grabbing me by the wrist, pulling me so hard I lose my footing, bare feet scrabbling in the dirt, but still he keeps pulling. Katie is by my side and now all three of us are running.

Later, my dad asks us a hundred questions, and then another hundred.

'Tell me,' he says, 'as clearly as you can, *exactly* what happened.'

Was this before or after the police came? I can't be sure. But I can't say a word. Something is stopping my throat.

'We were playing,' Luke says.

'And then?'

'We started this game.'

'What game?'

'Just a game.'

My dad has never hit us, but I feel the great rage within him and the will-power it takes to stop himself shaking Luke or lashing out at me when I won't speak.

'What happened to the other girl?' Luke asks.

'What?'

'The other one? Amy?'

Dad tries to stay calm, but he keeps asking question after question. The hours that pass are blurred and indistinct. Some things puncture the vagueness. The policeman's height – he might be the tallest man I've ever seen. I hear my dad say the word 'accident'. Sitting in the police station, picking at the scab on my knee. My fingers still white and wrinkled from the river. The station is bare. Mum fidgets, biting her thumbnail, sits close beside me. My father writes out our statements; we sign. A swimming accident. Children unsupervised. The declarations are witnessed.

I have a strange feeling there was no morgue. The girl may have rested on a pallet in the back room of that station.

The policeman holds out his massive hands. 'A tragic accident,' he says, and sighs.

He closes his eyes.

I imagine that when he opens them, he wishes us gone.

The long drive back to Nairobi – not a word spoken.

'Jesus, Mary and Joseph,' is my dad's plaintive refrain. He says it over and over and over again; late into the night, all night, every night for the rest of our lives.

Mum cries and cries.

That night, back in our house in Lavington, we are sent to bed. Katie's bed remains empty. Tonight she sleeps in her mother's room. I can't imagine sleeping ever again. I am afraid to go to sleep. Afraid that if I close my eyes, the only thing I will see is the water, its silty murkiness and the girl's eyes wavering, staring back at me.

I trace the grain in the wood of the beams above my bed. I follow its meandering, circling, maze-like paths as it leads me out of where I am. Luke, on the other hand, has hidden himself beneath his bedclothes, buried himself completely. From downstairs, the adults' voices rise. Katie's mum is frantic, a shrill note of fear in hers.

'We need to leave here,' she says. 'In the morning, first thing. The risk is too great. Please, Ken.'

My father's voice is low, calm, yet he sounds different now, taken by a new seriousness. He urges Helen to remain calm, but she is well beyond that.

'Control myself? A child was killed! How can we possibly stay here?'

My mum makes inarticulate objections, which end up sounding like a series of buts.

'Do what you want, Sally,' Helen says sharply. 'But Katie and I are leaving. My God, I wish we'd never come!'

The argument continues through the night. I keep my eyes closed tight. In the darkness, as I drift in and out of consciousness, I think I can hear, from under his blanket, Luke counting again, his voice fragile: 'Thirty, thirty-one, thirty-two . . .'

Katie's mother goes to her room. I hear them whispering and know that Katie is awake but I can't make out what they are saying.

My parents stay downstairs, talking. I hear the murmur of their voices mingling, kept low.

'A tragic accident.' My dad's voice. 'That's what the man said.'

'Yes, but the other one. The smaller one. The way he was looking at us . . .'

'Sally.'

'If we had had more time . . . If we'd just come up with something clearer, something more solid . . .'

Dad says something then, something indistinct and muffled.

Mum's voice, prickly with fear: 'I don't know, Ken. I just wish we could be sure.'

I'm counting now in my head. I've taken over from Luke, who has fallen silent. He might be asleep. Either way I keep counting, as if counting is a kind of prayer, lulling me to sleep.

The memory fades.

I hear a car rev its engine outside. I open my eyes and see dust floating through the air. I lift myself from the bed, stand and walk to the window of the room. Outside, a shimmer of heat is rising in the distance. In it, the world wavers, like some kind of mirage. My limbs are leaden. I walk back to the bed, ready to fall onto it, but hear footsteps hurrying down the corridor towards my room.

And then comes the frantic knocking on the door. I turn.

'Nick? Are you there? Open up!'

I struggle to the door, fling it open with my last ounce of strength and there before me is Murphy – sweating and wild-eyed.

'Something's happened,' he says, reaching for me. 'There's been an accident. You need to come with me now.'

PART FOUR

Kenya 1982

14. Sally

The scream. She cannot shake the scream from her memory. It keeps coming back to her, unannounced and unwanted.

That last scream, different from the others. And she knew from it, before she ever got to the river, that it was not a child's voice. The sharpness of the note, the depth of it, spoke to something primal within her, the burning point of motherhood, and she recognized the distress within it and that was the thing that made her run, breathless and ragged, feet slapping the dry earth hard, all the way to the river. That was when she saw her – a woman standing up to her hips in water, turning about frantically to scan the surface, the riverbank, the surrounding trees. She saw the heave in the woman's chest, the craning of her neck, features stretched in desperation, in her hand green ribbons, and from her mouth, the one name called over and over in a shrill note of panic. Behind her on the banks, skulking in the shadow of the trees, the little girl, the younger of the two, watched Sally with solemn eyes.

'Everything has changed,' she tells Jim.

They are sitting outside a café near her home in Lavington – plastic tables, scalloped parasols protecting them from the sun's glare, cans of Coke sweating in the heat.

'Not everything,' he says. He's holding her hand,

kneading her fingers and knuckles, and she feels the pressure of his touch. 'We're still the same – you and me.'

Conscious that they're in a public place, she withdraws her hand from his, glances around at the other diners.

After that, he sits in injured silence for a while, ferocity in his gaze.

Before the Masai Mara, before *the thing*, he had pressed her into making a decision. An ultimatum delivered: me or him. She had come close to leaving her husband.

Now, her focus is on containing this *thing*. She cannot even bring herself to give a name to what happened. Nor can she tell him about it – not properly. The details she has given him are vague, sketchy. Even telling him that much feels like a betrayal. She looks to him for reassurance, for distraction, but even when she's with him, she's reliving it in her head. The woman's scream of fright. The solemn gaze of that little girl watching her from the other side of the river. The rise in her gorge of fear for her own children as she began to search for them, adding their names to the air in her own clear note of fear. She had tried to engage the other mother, asked her about the boys, about Katie, but the woman was well beyond that, had burrowed deep into her own fear. She held the green ribbons to her chest, sobs coming between the cries of her daughter's name. The woman wading through the water, and Sally running along the bank, searching through the trees, through the long grass of the field beyond, the pressure building in her chest, a prayer running through her head: *Not the boys, please, God, not the boys.*

She doesn't tell this to Jim. She doesn't tell him much at all. Their meeting feels flat, a little desperate, cursory too, and when she tells him she has to go, the injured look he gives her tears at her a little.

She gets on her bicycle to leave, and he makes her promise not to forsake what they have but to hold on to it, to feel the strength and depth of his love and it will carry her through this difficult time.

'Promise me,' he says, with an urgency that unsettles her.

But Sally knows that promises – after what has happened – can no longer be made or honoured.

The cycle home is mainly uphill and Sally feels it in the muscles of her thighs, staring at the blurred strip of clay road ahead of her under the glare of the afternoon sun. By the time she reaches home, she has sweated through her clothes and feels dizzy from the heat of the day and her meeting with Jim.

A jeep she doesn't recognize is parked in front of the house, and beyond it, on the veranda, Jamil stands deep in conversation with a man in a white suit whose face Sally cannot see. Her pace quickens and her heart beats a little faster. Jamil catches sight of her and points towards her. The man turns, a big man, his dark face shining under the sun. He squints and raises a hand in greeting, a smile broadening his features as she leans her bicycle against the post and climbs the steps to greet them.

'Mrs Yates,' the man says, a deep voice, a ready smile, eyes that seem bright with interest as he goes to shake her hand. 'I'm so glad I've caught you.'

'Hello,' she says, attempting a smile as she takes his hand, feels the cool dryness of his skin against her sweaty palm, and laughs apologetically. 'Do forgive me.'

'Not at all. It's a hot day,' he says warmly. 'And you have been cycling.'

His suit, though crumpled, has a sort of elegance. At a guess, she imagines him to be in his early forties. His English is perfect, his accent cultured, and there is an air of quiet authority about him, a gleam of intelligence in his soft eyes, and Sally knows, somehow, that for all his charm, the visit is official. This man is police, and she knew, all along, that this was coming.

'Jamil, could you get us some iced tea, please – I'm dying of thirst.'

Jamil nods and turns, and it is only when the two of them are left alone on the veranda that the visitor introduces himself. 'I am Inspector Atabe of the Rift Valley Police. I am the officer in charge of investigating the death of the little girl.'

Even as he says this, she feels herself drawing away, a kind of heave coming over her whenever she is brought to the brink of remembering. Hearing it again: 'Hello, lady!' in that sing-song voice. That girl, freckles on her nose. A rabbitty face.

'I see,' she says, nodding, taking on a serious look. 'Such a tragedy. We're all still in shock.'

'I can imagine,' he says kindly, adding, 'I have children of my own and it is my worst fear. That something like that will happen to one of them.'

'Indeed.'

'I was hoping you might be able to help me with my investigation.'

'Of course,' she agrees quickly. 'We gave a statement at the time to one of your colleagues . . .'

'Yes. Thank you. It has been very helpful. There are just a few small things that I would like to go over with you.'

'All right,' she says, feeling the sweat on her body, her face flushed. 'My husband is at work in the city, but I'm sure he could come home if you need –'

'No, no. That won't be necessary. I have only a few questions that I'm sure you can help me with. If there's anything further I require, I can always go into the city and meet your husband later.'

She directs him to the cane chairs on the veranda, then asks him to excuse her for a moment while she freshens up after her ride.

'Of course.'

She smiles like a gracious hostess, but once inside the house, she hurries to the kitchen and finds Jamil setting the glasses and jug on a tray. 'Where are the boys?' she asks, keeping her voice low.

'Upstairs, Miss Sally.'

'Let me take that. You go upstairs and stay with the boys – keep them in their room until our guest is gone.'

If he's surprised by her request, Jamil doesn't show it, and when she adds, over her shoulder, 'And keep them quiet, Jamil, okay?' his face doesn't betray a thing.

Outside, the inspector has turned his chair to face the garden and he sits with one leg thrown over the other in a louche manner, slouching a little in his seat. Bougainvillaea spills over the roof of the veranda, long tendrils trailing down the wooden posts. In silence, he watches the whirling spray of water from the sprinkler on the lawn catching the sunlight in a flurry of sudden stars. He accepts the glass of iced tea she offers and compliments her on the garden.

'So lush and green!' he remarks with pleasure.

'A small reminder of home.'

'Ah, yes. Although I have never been to your country. The United Kingdom is the closest I have come.'

'Well, that's very close,' she says, sitting opposite him and sips from her glass, trying to calm her nerves. She wonders how long he will be there, and strains to hear any noises from the boys in the house.

'I'm always glad to return home, though,' he continues, in a relaxed manner. 'Even coming here to Nairobi – I cannot wait to leave and get back to Narok.' He flashes her a smile, then fixes his eyes on the garden again. 'But that is just me. I'm a home-bird. Some people love to travel, don't they?'

'It's true.'

'Like the Gordons, for example.'

'Who?' she asks, and he turns to her, still smiling, although his eyes seem more serious, as if he is looking at her properly for the first time.

'The family of the little girl.'

'Oh,' she says, and feels her cheeks flush.

A flash of memory: that woman in the water, clutching those hair ribbons, anguish contorting her face, making her deaf and blind to everything except her one need – to find her child.

'The worst thing to happen to a parent. My heart goes out to them,' she goes on, but he makes no answer, just a slight inclination of his head. She feels as if she has failed the first test.

His body has grown still now that he has arrived at the reason for his visit.

'Did you know them?' he asks, and she tells him, no.

'They have been living in the valley for a while, now,' the inspector says. 'They have kept mainly to themselves. Looking for a simple kind of life, I suppose.'

'We saw the lights from their hut in the evenings, across the river. But we never saw them, never spoke to them. Except the children.'

'The children knew each other.'

'A little. They played together a couple of times over the course of the few days we stayed there. God, I still can't believe that poor girl drowned.'

'Cora.' He says her name, and Sally lifts her head.

'Yes, Cora.'

He holds her gaze for a beat or two, then turns his gaze back to the garden once more. 'She was eight years old. The same age as your son, Nicholas.'

'Yes.'

'Are they home, the boys?' he asks casually, as he reaches for his glass and takes a drink.

'No. They're at a friend's house.' She tries to make it sound relaxed, fears her own voice will give her away.

'And the girl, their friend – Katherine?'

'Katie.'

'Yes.'

'She and her mother have gone home, I'm afraid.'

He pauses, his smooth face frowning just a fraction. 'That is a pity. I would have liked to speak to her.'

'It was the end of their holiday. They were only here for a few weeks.'

'Ah. Well . . .' He allows a silence to drift in, while he gathers his thoughts.

From their perch behind her, Sally can hear the twittering of a pair of starlings in their cage. Automatically her thoughts go to Jim. A memory comes to her: the two of them lying together in that great raft of a bed, the hardwood frame that groaned, the cloud of the mosquito net billowing out, like the lazy inflations of a jellyfish, whenever a breeze passed through the open window. With the tip of his index finger, he traced the brown curve of her nipple, the gentle ridge of the areola like a ring of tiny blisters. Her hand stroking the hairs on his arms. The two of them lying there, in the swamping, limb-draining fug of this strange new love, worn out by the long months of resisting temptation, and the radiant explosion inside her once she had surrendered to it. She had felt as if that great bed were floating out on a body of water and never wanted to touch land again.

Inspector Atabe has lost interest in the garden. He turns his chair so that he is facing her. Reaching into his inside jacket pocket, he takes out a notebook and pen, and asks: 'Will you humour me a moment, Mrs Yates, and take a look at this?'

She acquiesces and he opens to a page where he has drawn a map. Examining the neat marks, the careful and deliberate strokes of the pen, she can see that he is a fastidious man, with a certain neatness, despite the crumpled suit.

'This is a little map I have made of the area where the death occurred,' he explains, and then, using the nib of his pen as a pointer, he goes on, 'This is your camp, and over here is where the Gordons have their hut. And here, between the two, is the river. You will see here this little X I have marked on the river – this shows where Cora's body was discovered. And over here, you will see another X I have marked to show where the children were playing.'

She leans over the page, following the movement of his pen, wondering where he is going with this.

'In the statement that your sons gave to my colleague in Narok, they said that they were playing here – the boys and their friend, Katie, and the two little Gordon girls.'

'That's right,' she agrees. 'I saw them there myself.'

'And, according to the statement, they were splashing around in the water, playing some game that involved holding their breath?'

'Yes. It's a game they sometimes play. They hold their breath under the water. Whoever stays under the longest is the winner.'

He smiles and nods, but she feels the undercurrent of danger.

'Then they say that at some point they noticed one of them was missing.'

'Yes.'

'Strange, don't you think? That they didn't notice she hadn't surfaced, that they weren't paying attention to her – as if she wasn't part of the game?'

'Well, no . . . I mean, they had been playing it for a while. It was a hot day, they were tired, probably a little light-headed from holding their breath for so long . . .'

He watches carefully as she offers this explanation, his face giving nothing away.

'So when they couldn't find her in the water,' he goes on, 'did they look for her along the banks?'

'I think so. For a little while.'

He watches her. Waits for her to go on.

'They were tired from the game, the heat of the day.'

'So when they couldn't find her, did they come and tell you?'

A beat. A slight flash of panic. She tries to put herself back to that day, to what she said in the police station, the statement she had made.

'They assumed she had gone home.'

'Oh?'

'The younger sister had already disappeared. When they couldn't see Cora, they thought she must have followed her sister home.'

'So they didn't come to tell you.'

'No.'

'What did they do?'

'They went back to the field. Resumed their game there.'

She says it as lightly as she can, holds his gaze. But her heart is beating fast, and she is living it all over again – the moment when she found them. Three heads close together in the tall yellow grass. Relief going through her like a flash of pain. They had turned when they heard her approach and the expressions on their faces had made her stop. Fear mingling with guilt. And that was when she had heard it. Another scream. The word 'No!' carried on the air. Felt her breath catch in her throat, understanding what it meant. When she had turned back to them, all three children were staring at the ground, not at her, not in the direction of that cry of distress. Heads bent, they

244

refused to look her in the eye, as if they knew what had happened – as if they had been expecting it.

'And that is where you found them,' Atabe goes on.

'Yes.'

'How long had they been there?'

'I'm not sure. A while, I think.'

'They didn't hear you calling them? They didn't hear Mrs Gordon crying out Cora's name?'

'No.'

'You don't find that strange?'

She shrugs. 'Water in their ears – from the river. My son, Nicky, still can't hear properly since that day.'

'I see.' He smiles, but fleetingly. 'And when you found the children, what did you do?'

'I brought them back to the camp. My husband had just returned, along with my friend, Helen.'

'You didn't go back to the river? To see if Mrs Gordon had found her child?'

She hesitates, panicked and uncertain as to what they had agreed upon – Sally and Ken – when they had gone over the story together. They only talk about it at night, when the boys are asleep in bed. Each night since it happened, the pair of them have picked away at the scab, whispered conversations hampered by grief and shock, this awful cocktail of fear and a disappointment so bitter she can taste it.

'Not straight away, no. But it was a few minutes later.'

'Why did you wait?'

'I wanted to tell my husband what had happened.'

Again, the lightness of her tone, working hard to keep hidden from him that frantic conversation at the camp,

245

Ken's eyes widening with alarm, the urgency with which he had walked away from her, his stride quickening to a run, through the field, down to the river, from where the howls were rising.

'Of course. Forgive me,' he says, and she realizes how defensive she must have sounded, despite her efforts.

He looks down at his notebook, flicks on a few pages, glancing at notes she cannot read. 'And just to go back. All the time the children were at the river, you were at the camp?'

'Yes. I was packing up, preparing to leave.'

'And you knew the children were by the river?'

'I did.'

'You weren't worried? After all, this is the Masai Mara we are talking about. There are hippos, crocodiles . . .'

'We were told that part of the river was safe.'

'I see.'

He flicks the pages of his notebook again, finds his little map, runs a finger along his brow, and nods. She senses, with a degree of relief, that this interview is coming to a close.

'One more thing, and then I will leave you in peace.' Drawing her attention to the map once more, he says: 'This is where they were playing the game, yet this is where Cora's body was found.'

She follows the movement of the nib of the pen from one careful spot to the other.

'It's a distance of ten or twelve metres.'

She looks at him, unsure.

'Why do you suppose the body would have moved so far from where they were playing?'

He holds her gaze, and she feels momentarily staggered,

confused as to what to say. Sweat breaks out anew on her back, and she swallows, leaning forward to look at the page. 'Isn't it possible that it floated away? The drag of the river . . .'

'But the body was found upriver from where the children were playing.'

She frowns and pulls at her lower lip with her thumb and index finger. 'Maybe the children had moved upriver to play –'

'No. Amy Gordon says they remained at the original spot. There is a knotted blue rope hanging down from a tree that their father had hung there for them. He always insisted that they stay there when they were in the river.'

'Are you sure? I mean, children say all sorts of things, especially when they've been disobedient. And that little girl – Amy – seemed very young. Only four or five . . .'

'Five. But I've spoken to her and I would say that her evidence is reliable. She is an intelligent little girl, and quite eloquent, despite her age.'

Sally, flustered now, struggles for an answer. 'Perhaps an animal pulled her upriver. Some creature hidden in the water.'

'There was no evidence of any animal marks on the body. Besides,' he says in a silky tone that she doesn't like, 'didn't you just say that part of the river was safe?'

'Yes. But I suppose –'

'There were leaves in her hair. And twigs.'

'So?'

'When I went back to the place she was found, I saw other leaves and branches heaped there along the bank. The same kind that had been tangled in her hair.'

'I don't understand.'

'Those sticks and leaves did not arrive there by themselves. It looked to me like someone had put them there. To conceal the body.'

'But the drag of the water, the trees nearby, surely . . .' Her voice drifts into silence.

He holds her there for a moment or two and Sally knows she has failed. She has failed this test but, more than anything, she has failed her sons. Fear grips her heart and words come to her lips, words that she had had no intention of saying.

'The driver . . .' she begins, and watches his eyes narrow, a new curiosity entering his gaze.

'What about him?'

'Have you spoken to him?'

'Yes.' He spreads his hands wide – large hands, she notices. 'There was not much he could tell us, seeing as how he was asleep in the van for the duration. Drunk, I believe.'

'Yes,' she says, but the way she draws it out slowly, speculatively, makes him sit up and lean forward a little.

'Are you saying he wasn't?'

The question is put to her softly, easily, and just as easily the lie comes.

'I was putting away the tents. My husband had gone to the village and my friend had followed after him. The children were down at the river. While I was packing the tents away, I looked into the van to check on the driver. That's when I noticed he wasn't there.'

'He wasn't there?'

'No.'

'You're sure?'

'Yes, I'm sure.'

'Did you see him anywhere?'

'No. I didn't look for him. I assumed he'd gone to find a cooler place to lie in – the van would have been very hot. But now I wonder . . .'

Her voice drifts into silence. The lie is out there.

A beat. He considers this new information. It sits between them – the seed she has planted. And, for just a moment, Sally can almost convince herself that it is true. That it really happened. Later she will tell herself it was a white lie – told to deflect attention from her sons. She will tell herself that it will come to nothing anyway – that she will not swear to it in court.

He frowns, as if this new evidence troubles him, writes something in his little notebook. All the while, Sally holds herself steady, wills him to leave, for this interview to be over.

Inspector Atabe gets to his feet and downs the rest of his iced tea in one gulp, placing the empty glass on the table beside hers. He tucks his notepad and pen back into his jacket pocket and she stands up to see him off. At the bottom of the steps, he turns back to bid her goodbye, and as he shakes her hand, he says to her: 'Perhaps you're right. Perhaps something did pull her under.' He looks her squarely in the face, his eyes plain and searching. 'There are all sorts of creatures lurking in the water.'

Just like that, the decision is made. Rather than feeling panicked in the aftermath of Inspector Atabe's visit, a kind of calm comes over her. After all the turmoil, the indecision, the sleepless nights, the endless prevarication and discussion, in the end the decision is arrived at swiftly and definitely, her mind made up by forces beyond her control.

Calmly, she picks up the phone and dials the number. In even tones, she tells her husband what has happened.

'Did he say if he's going to return?' Ken asks, in a voice kept low so that his secretary in the next room cannot hear. Sally hears the note of alarm in it anyway.

'No, but he will,' she says softly.

'Sally —'

She is there before him. 'We'll be packed by the time you get home.'

One more phone call. She keeps it short, imparting only the most basic and urgent of details — that she loves him but her boys come first. There is no discussion: she will brook no argument. Her mind is made up.

Then, quietly, she goes about it — moving from room to room, packing enough for her and the boys. They will go ahead; Ken will follow in the coming weeks. He spoke of it briefly on the phone and she had agreed: he would see out his contract, and arrange for the rest of their belongings to be packed up and shipped home. But Sally and the boys would go now, as soon as they could get flights. They would tell no one — not even Jamil. The risk was too great. But still she had called Jim. She owed him that much.

By the time Ken's car pulls through the gates that evening, she has the bags packed and is waiting for her husband to join her so they can tell the boys together. Watching him mounting the steps, his briefcase in one hand, his jacket slung over his shoulder, she notes the weariness in his posture. He hasn't seen her yet, and in that brief moment, there is something about him that is so defeated she wants to take him in her arms. The impulse passes, and instead she opens the door, takes his briefcase from him and briefly touches his arm, an unspoken resolution passing between them.

'It's all booked,' he says quietly. 'I've got you seats on an Air France flight to Paris, with an onward connection to Dublin. It leaves in the morning.'

She nods, the shadows gathering now as evening draws in – their last night together in Kenya as a family. Something inside her is coming undone.

They tell the boys together. Luke cries, but Nicky doesn't say a word. They hug their sons, telling them how much they love them, how this move back to Ireland is for the best, a new adventure in their lives, but however hard they try to reassure them, Sally cannot help but hear the hollowness of their voices, the tinny music of their forced enthusiasm.

They eat in silence, picking at their food, a collective loss of appetite in the wake of the decision made. And it is as she folds her knife and fork across her plate that Sally sees the swing of headlights across the windows, hears the screech of brakes outside. Ken swivels in his chair to follow her gaze, then gets to his feet. Already, Sally can see the apprehension in his face, the sudden loss of colour in his cheeks as he moves swiftly to the door. The boys look at her and she holds herself very still, straining to hear who it is. A car door slams, the click of the screen-door, and Ken's footsteps on the terrace, his voice raised in greeting. Another voice – a man's – low and gravelled and she knows it immediately.

'Go to your room,' she tells the boys, hearing the urgency in her own voice.

They shuffle away and she hurries to the screen-door, her heart beating high and light in her chest.

Jim is at the foot of the steps, and from where she stands, hiding, she can see his face lit from above by the lamp over the door. There is something unsteady in the way he is holding himself, his shirt untucked and hanging over his jeans, hands on his hips and a kind of wildness that seems barely contained within his body. He has been drinking. Ken stands with his back to her so she cannot see his face, only the line of his shoulders, hands by his sides, as he waits on the bottom step, looking down at Jim who speaks in a low voice: 'You can't do this, Ken. It's folly – a complete overreaction.'

'Thank you for your concern, Father Jim,' Ken sounds stiff and formal, rigid with suppressed anger, 'but we have made our decision.'

'Please just think about it – sleep on it. Don't tear the boys away from their home like this. Don't you see? After all they have been through, surely what they need now is the security of familiar surroundings, rather than being uprooted and plunged back into a life they have no memory of.'

'Please, Jim, I know you mean well,' Ken says, and she hears the strain of temper in his low voice, 'but your concern is unhelpful at this time. We need to be left in peace.'

She holds her breath, willing her lover to leave. In that moment, she sees how dangerous he is to her, brought to the brink by the decision she has made. In her head, she pleads with him to go, uncertain as to whether she should go outside and attempt to defuse the situation, or whether that would only fan the flames. Meanwhile he continues to stand there, hands on his hips, facing Ken.

'If you send them away, it will only make them appear guilty. Don't you see that?' he implores, tilting his head to one side, his face caught in the ghostly light of the lamp, a pale bewildered moon, eyes desperate. 'By making them go, you're fingering them – condemning them. Your own sons . . .'

Ken, a hand held up in warning, says: 'You've said your piece. Now you should leave.'

But Jim is rooted to the spot, as if stepping away would leave him coming apart at the seams.

'What about Sally?' he asks desperately. 'What about what she wants?'

Sally stiffens.

'She wants to protect her sons.'

'She's just doing this because of the pressure you're putting on her.'

'You're overstepping the mark, Father.'

'Am I?'

'Don't presume to lecture me about my wife.'

'Why not?'

Consternation rises in Sally, like something hard in her throat.

Recklessly, Jim goes on: 'I know her better than you think, what she wants, what she desires –'

It happens quickly. Ken steps down, places his hands on Jim's chest and pushes him. Her lover staggers backwards, shock on his face. Ken pushes him again and, moving quickly now, Sally comes out onto the veranda and down the steps while the two men grapple and grunt, trying to gain some kind of purchase on the other. Wild swipes that barely connect, an awkward dance of grabbing and shoving, and she is there at the edges, trying to pull them apart, an ineffective plucking and pleading. A gap opens and she puts herself between them, her back to her husband – a protective pose – the two of them breathing heavily while they face Jim down.

A moment to catch her breath. Behind her, she hears Ken say: 'Get rid of him.' All the fight gone out of him, he turns away.

At the top of the steps, he stops to look back down at them. A searching gaze, full of pain and confusion. It is not for her, but for Jim, as is the question he asks.

'Tell me this much, Father. How will I ever forgive her?'

She feels the heat of it scalding her.

Everything is changed.

The screen-door slams behind him leaving Murphy and Sally outside.

For a moment, they stand there, looking at each other. In the lamp-light, she sees his face is white with shock, despite the scuffle with Ken.

'I'm sorry,' he says, composing himself. 'I didn't mean it to come out that way –'

'Don't,' she says, her voice barely controlled.

He heaves in his breath, his eyes imploring, but she doesn't move, doesn't say anything.

'Don't you see?' he goes on. 'I couldn't just let you leave. Not after everything . . . I couldn't just let you go.'

'You don't have a choice. Neither of us has. The boys –'

'I'll take care of them. I'll take care of all of you.'

She stares at him, aghast. 'You can't protect them. What they did —'

'It was an accident. Anyone can see that. They're just children.'

'This country can be harsh. It can demand that children be treated as adults. That policeman who came today . . . he frightened me.'

'We'll find a way, Sally. God will help us.'

Still, he speaks of God, as if he retains that authority.

'Please, Sally. You can't go. You can't do this to me. I know you won't. You can't.'

'I have no choice. It's too risky for the boys to stay.'

'Then let them go!' he bursts out. 'Let their father take them home. But you and me,' he comes forward, takes her hands in his, 'we need to be together. How I feel about you . . . how we feel about each other . . .'

She is bewildered. 'I'm their mother. They need me —'

'*I* need you.'

He pulls her towards him so he is staring straight at her, close enough for her to catch the wildness in his eyes. How to explain to him the difference between his need for her and the all-encompassing pull of motherhood? She looks at him now, the shadow of stubble running over his jaw and neck, how deeply set his eyes are, startlingly blue beneath brows that are thick and dark and a little unruly. Such a serious man, capable of volcanic anger and extraordinary tenderness. She sees the yearning in his eyes — and the fear — and with it, she feels an answering disappointment inside herself. This man, whom she had always considered so strong, now veers towards desperation, and their bond is coming undone.

'Please don't do this, Sal. Please don't shut me out. Not after all I've done. Not after the sacrifices I've made for you.'

'Sacrifices?' The word scratches at her – a match to tinder.

'Yes! I've made sacrifices. I've broken my vows for you!' His voice rises now. 'Do you think that was easy for me? Do you think I held them so lightly that breaking them was just a casual thing, like slipping off a coat?'

His eyes flare with fury, the veins bulging in his neck.

She thinks of all she knows about him: his long struggle with his faith, arguments with his superiors, an endless battle between stifling clerical duties and the pull of his earthly desires; and always that silent but insistent pressure from his family back home in Ireland, the unspoken rule that he must never shame them. She'd known it was wrong from the moment it started – a terrible sin – but somehow the wrongness seemed to stir her desire, a jolt that went straight to her groin the first time she opened herself to his embrace. And now, in this garden filling with darkness, she feels at once how reckless she has been, how naïve, to think she would not have to pay for what she has done, that there would not come a time of reckoning.

His grip around her wrists tightens.

She pulls her arms free, takes a step back. She says nothing. Taken by a cold anger, she backs away, turns to the steps.

Furious at her silence, he shouts after her: 'For Christ's sake, woman, what do I have to do?'

A movement of wings catches her eyes. Flutterings

from the cage on the veranda: the birds on their perch, witnesses to this unravelling.

She has a sudden flashback to an afternoon at the start of things between them. He had come to the house, the cage in the back of his car, a gift for the boys. Two birds with bright plumage – petrol-blue feathers and orange breasts, twittering, black eyes gleaming like brightly polished seeds.

How many times has she allowed him in her house? In her bed? With a sudden glare of clarity, she sees the foolishness of her behaviour – the immense selfishness of it – and all the destruction it has wreaked. In this darkening house, a home she will soon leave, each member of her family is nursing a wound that she has, somehow, inflicted.

She casts one last look at Jim, then goes to the cage, opens the little door and reaches in with both hands. She catches one bird and releases it, followed swiftly by the other. They take to the wing at once, fluttering briefly about the veranda before powering their way high above the roof and disappearing into the darkness.

She does not look at him, does not want to see the pain crossing his face. Instead, she goes into the house, closing the door softly behind her.

PART FIVE
Kenya 2013

15. Katie

Light breaks through the darkness. It's fleeting at first, glimpsed through gritty eyes, a fog in my head keeping me under. But something pulls me towards it. Dark silhouettes announce themselves as trees. The long knotted hair of some demon woman reveals itself as a hanging vine. The coil of roots in the ground beneath me presses into my flesh. Ragged breathing, stones embedded in my cheek. A smell like decay rising from the earth. Shadows deepen, the light becomes true and clear, the slow creep of reality trying to break through.

Voices then. Someone saying, *She's had a fall.* The metallic taste of blood in my mouth. My tongue, swollen and thick, like a foreign object. The chirrup of insects, the nearby swish of water as some unseen creature launches itself into the river. The river. Something sparks in memory. Then another voice, *Let's get her to the car.*

Hands under my arms then – the shock of human contact. I'm on my feet, held up by strangers I can't see, yet I can feel their blocky presence against me. Feet stumble and drag along the ground. Roots, like ancient fingers in the soil. My head lolls – I can't seem to hold it up. A pain blooming deep within my ears. Feet stumbling over rocks, floundering, trying and failing to gain purchase. We break clear of the trees and, Jesus, how the light cuts through me, the backs of my eyelids singing with hurt.

I can't get a handle on my bearings. The pain, like a heavy stone in my head, making me stupid. Long shadows and the nip of cool air. Early morning, then. Still, it's too bright, I can hardly stand to open my eyes to it. Lungs working like a wheezy organ. A thought surfaces: *I might have died out there.* Grit and red clay on the ground in front of me. Then the jarring sight of a dusty wheel. Everything is distorted. The creak of a car door scraping through my head.

Next thing I know I'm sitting in a car. Legs stretched out and aching in the foot-well. A bottle of water in my hands, a voice telling me to drink, but I'm so weak and the bottle is so heavy. Water in my mouth, cutting across the dried membranes of my lips and teeth and tongue. I might cry, I feel so fucking grateful. A shiver that comes up from my bones. My heart a dull thud in my chest. *More*, the voice instructs, and I feel the water reaching down towards the dryness in my throat, the parched plains of my insides.

The thump of a door closing. Low voices in conversation outside. I tilt my head to see but the pain comes in my ear like a swarm of black flies, and I hold myself still. Close my eyes, feel sleep coming.

Movement wakes me. The jolt of the car going over a pothole. The landscape a smear of colour seen through a windshield speckled with dirt. My head feels heavy and dull with sleep, but the pain has subsided. My breathing has calmed. A mess of filth rises up over my feet and ankles, the tideline skirting the legs of my jeans. The car bumps over uneven roads; the dream-catcher dangling from the rear-view mirror jumps and spins with each bump.

'You're awake,' Lauren says.

She drives with a committed air, both hands on the steering-wheel, her eyes narrowed on the road ahead.

I try to say something, but all that emerges is a strangled croak. She glances across. 'You shouldn't try to speak,' she tells me. 'There's more water. You should drink.'

It is warm and tastes of plastic. I drink as much as I can, but I'm starting to feel strange again – thinned out and stretched, the water sloshing inside me, like seawater in a cave. Part of me craves a cigarette, yet the thought of dry smoke curling around my insides makes me nauseous. We drive across land that is spartan and bare, save the occasional acacia tree or thorn bush, the grassy scrubs in clumps over the dusty plain. No sign of civilization.

It hurts to speak, but I manage to ask where we're going.

'You shouldn't talk,' she says again. 'You've had a shock.'

And all at once I'm back by the river, something stirring behind me, turning to the darkness, and that sudden wash of violence breaking over me, like a wave. I squeeze my eyes shut against the memory, queasy.

Opening my eyes, I see a sticker on the dashboard in front of me – an anti-nuclear sign in black and white – and a tatty fringe in a colour that was probably once red but now has faded to rust. The steering-wheel is covered with a greyish wool. It's like someone has tried to soften the contours of this pile of junk, make it homely. The car squeaks and groans over the uneven surface, the springs beneath my seat jumping enthusiastically, adding to my nausea.

'The hotel,' I say.

'Soon,' she says.

Over one wrist, she wears a band of cheap bracelets — leather ties and plastic beads in orange and turquoise. They wend their way up her arm, which is tanned against the deep purple of her open-necked blouse, a tie-dyed blue skirt stretching down over her knees. Her feet on the pedals are brown and strong, as if she has spent her whole life barefoot or in flip-flops. This is the first time we have been alone together and I'm not sure how I feel about that. I draw my gaze away and stare out of the window.

A heat haze lies heavily on the land blurring it. Inside the car, it is hot and oppressive. No air-con in this rust-bucket. I lean my head against the window and allow myself to become distracted by the dancing dream-catcher, its beads and feathers hopping around crazily.

'My father used to have rosary beads hanging from his rear-view mirror,' I say. My tone is dreamy, calm, almost dazed by the heat, the fatigue left in the wake of all that adrenalin.

'Where is he?' she asks, and I tell her he's dead. My mother too. My voice coming back to me.

'Just like Nick's parents,' she says.

She looks across at me, a levelling stare, and adds: 'Something else you two have in common.'

I shift uncomfortably in my seat. My head hurts. There's a lump at the back of my skull from the force of the blow. I put my fingers to it, a tentative exploration of injured flesh, the sharpness of a graze. Taking my hand away, I see dried blood caught beneath my fingernails. Suddenly it feels like we've wandered far from the town.

'Where are we?' I ask, as she drives off the road onto a track that is barely passable.

It is now that the thought occurs to me: finding me by the river was no accident. She meant to bring me to this place.

'Sit tight,' she says, with an air of calm authority. 'We're almost there.'

She parks the car and gets out, slamming the door behind her. It disturbs the peace, and a flock of birds rises, twittering, from a nearby tree, swooping in a broken cloud and passing over the long grasses to the field beyond. Once they have settled on new branches, the air falls silent again.

I sit in the car watching. Something is holding me back. I'm not sure I want to be alone out here but, for all my reservations about her, curiosity pushes me to follow. Gingerly, I get out of the car. There's a murmur in my ears, and the landscape around me seems shimmery, indistinct.

'Come on,' Lauren says, finding a narrow track through the long grass and beginning along it, not looking back to see if I'm following.

The heat hangs thickly around us, like something viscous you have to wade through. Soon enough, I'm perspiring through my clothes, thin as they are, legs like rubber, beads of sweat running down into my eyes. Lauren pauses once to tie her hair back in a messy knot at the nape of her neck. Otherwise, she seems unperturbed, pushing on with a silent determination. We don't speak as we walk. All my energy is required to keep pace with her. As I follow her up the track, I consider what I know of her and realize it isn't much. Every time Nick spoke of her, I had the impression that his knowledge of her is almost as limited as mine and confined to certain things. Even I can see the romance in that.

'You and Nick,' I say, once her pace slows enough for me to walk alongside her. 'How did you meet?'

A little smile, one hand reaching out to touch the tips of the long grasses as we pass through.

'I sought him out.'

'You did?'

'I heard about a guy who was playing jazz piano in a bar in downtown Nairobi.' She shrugs, as if that's explanation enough.

'From what Nick says, you hardly knew each other five minutes before you got hitched.'

A puckering of skin between her eyebrows – the tiniest frown before it's smoothed away.

'For some people, love comes quickly. Especially if they're not afraid of it.'

She glances at me in a way that I don't like and I stop. 'Why have you brought me here, Lauren?'

But she keeps going, never once breaking her stride. 'It's this way,' she calls over her shoulder and, to my annoyance, I find myself hurrying to catch up.

We reach a clearing, and I realize that the track has been leading us slowly uphill. Now we stand on the lip of a wide field that ripples with long grass, dipping down to a copse at the side where dark trees clump together along the perimeter and birds call from the leafy black boughs.

I stop, hands on hips, and look around me. Lauren has continued into the field, but I stay where I am. There is something about this place, something familiar.

There is a bald patch of land at the side where it seems as though the grass has been burned away. A structure of one sort or another once stood there. Slowly now, with caution, I move into the field in Lauren's wake. She has come to the middle, and stands there in the full sun, idly swatting flies from her face. From the ground around us I hear the low murmur and rustling of insects. I glance at the surrounding lands where the grass grows waist-high and could easily conceal a creeping predator. This nervousness is not new. I have felt it before.

With a jolt I look down to the copse, bending subtly towards a river that I cannot see yet I know is there. The bald strip of land is where we pitched our tents. Here, in the grass, Sally Yates lay sunning herself. And down there, where the dark trees bend in towards one another and the water bubbles beneath, that was where we went to play, where the game took shape, where those little girls stood knee-deep in that brown water, grinning up at us with curiosity.

'Oh, God,' I say, the jolt ripping through me. It is as though the whole field is tilting, as if I could lose my footing at any minute and go hurtling down to the river and see again the skinny ankles dangling above me in the dappled shade of those ancient trees.

Lauren is close to me now and I can tell from the look on her face – patient and inquisitive – that she understands that I know where she has brought me. What I don't know is why.

'Oh, God,' I say again, as the tears come quickly.

In the bright sunlight, I shudder, trying to dispel the memory. The air seems to carry the poison of the blighted thing that happened here. I can hardly breathe, as if I'm crouched in the shadowy chamber of the past – the cramped, airless room that should remain sealed for ever.

'Nick brought you here?' I say, disbelief seeping into my tone.

And I do find it hard to believe – that he would want to open the lid of the past for anyone, even his wife. To bring her to this place and show her the site where all of our innocence was lost seems too painful to contemplate, like tearing the wound open.

'Nick?' she asks, but it is hardly a question. There is no puzzlement in her voice. 'No. It wasn't Nick.'

'Then who?'

'My mother told me about this place.'

Something is nudging at the edge of my consciousness – some hidden and crucial truth that is close to my grasp, yet still it eludes me.

'Your mother? I don't understand.'

Her face is clear of all expression – a deep, concentrated gaze. 'They lived just over there.' With one hand, she gestures to a place beyond the copse, a place I cannot see.

Something slips in my mind then, the sudden slide of truth falling into place.

'Those little girls,' I say, understanding now.

'Yes,' she answers, nodding slowly. 'My sisters.'

I bend over, my legs suddenly weak, clasping my thighs to steady myself. Some part of me – some cold, dark part – had always known I would come back to this place. Things like that don't just go away. For years now – almost a lifetime – I have been kidding myself that I could keep it there, locked away in the past. But the hard, honest part of me knew that one day it would jump up and bite me.

I look up at Lauren, standing in the sun, so cool and untouched.

'Does he know? Nick?'

A shadow crosses her face. 'Not yet. But he will soon.'

I stand up straight and look her full in the face. 'How could you keep something like that from him?'

'I don't expect you to understand,' she says coldly, but there is defiance in her tone. 'It's not an easy thing to explain to someone.' Her voice tapers off, her gaze drifting to the distant trees, some private thought taking her over.

'I don't remember you,' I tell her.

She turns back, gives me a sharp look. 'I wasn't born when it happened.'

A quiver of heat in the air. We stand there, regarding each other. Across the distance, I feel the stirring of nerves inside her – the build-up of all these emotions, all this information, the welling up of her story inside her. And now that it comes to it, now that she has me here, in this place, her captive audience, I sense she feels the nudge of stage-fright. But then, finding her voice, she says: 'After what happened to Cora, my mother left here. Took Amy with her. Left her husband and got on a plane back to the States, a place she'd sworn never to return to. But I guess when you're hit hard by something, home takes on a different meaning.'

She pauses briefly, before going on.

'She met my father not long after she returned. They weren't exactly love's young dream, but it's not like that for everyone, is it? My dad says she cured him of his loneliness, and in return he offered her protection, the security of home. My brother Daniel was born not long after they got together, and I followed some time after that.'

'Did you know about Cora – about what happened here?'

'Not for years. My dad treated us all the same – me, Dan, Amy. I assumed Amy was his. I think even she forgot after a while that he wasn't her real father. She was so young when it happened. And my mother never said anything.'

'When did you find out?'

'When I was in high school. I got it into my head that I wanted a passport – some stupid notion of travelling the world although, up to that point, I'd barely been outside the state. I went looking among my mom's things and found her marriage certificate. Only my dad's name wasn't on it. Some guy I'd never heard of – the marriage dating from years back. That was when I found out that my mom and dad weren't actually married to each other and that my mom had this husband living in the back of beyond in Africa. That my sister was actually my half-sister.'

'And Cora?'

She pauses. I watch her carefully.

'Yeah. That came out too.'

Concentration clouds her face.

'There were times while we were growing up when my mother would be so totally absorbed in her own sorrow that she was hardly able to get through the day. It wasn't all the time – but still. She'd go through these phases of turning inwards. It wasn't just that she got depressed – it went so much deeper than that. Like she was infected with sorrow. It was in the meat and bones of her.'

The rippling of the grasses has stopped, the air around us grown still. There's an ache in the back of my head, a trickle going down my neck that makes me worry about the wound. I cannot break my attention, though, riveted by her account.

'From the time I was a small child, I knew that she was not like other people's moms – she was broken in a way that couldn't ever be fixed.'

'I can't imagine what that must have been like.'

'No. I don't suppose you can.'

Her tone is hard and pointed, and I feel the threat in it. But she seems to lift herself, and her voice when it comes again seems matter-of-fact.

'It was weird for a while, but we carried on. I finished high school, started in college, but it was always in the back of my mind – this curiosity. About Kenya, about this other sister, about this whole other life my mother had lived.'

'Is that why you came here?'

She nods, fiddling with a stem of grass she has picked.

'My mother got a letter one day, informing her of her husband's death. Strange news for her after all those years – something and nothing, you know?'

'And that's when you decided to come here.'

'I needed to see for myself.'

'And the letter your mother received?'

'Father Murphy sent it.'

'Murphy? But how did he know?'

She seems to consider my question and, as she does, her gaze drifts upwards.

'Rain is coming,' she tells me.

Following the line of her vision, I see a swathe of iron-grey cloud, ponderous but approaching fast from the horizon. There's a weakness in my legs now, a pounding at the base of my skull. 'We should go back to the car.'

'No,' she says firmly. 'Follow me.'

We move quickly. Rain in this part of the world comes

swiftly, clouds scudding across the sky or moving in great bulky masses, crowding out the sun and dumping rain on the parched earth below. As we walk, I try to take in all that she has told me, but in truth it seems too vast to contemplate. Instead I consider her marriage, the schism at the very heart of it – the pull she must feel between her love for her husband and the pain of her family history. How has she managed to conceal it? To see your husband every day and know that the great sorrow that laid your mother low was his responsibility. The straightness of her back, the relaxed set of her shoulders, you would never think that such conflict might exist inside her.

She leads me down towards the trees, along the jagged edge of the river. Under that dark canopy of leaves, there is coolness. I shiver, which has more to do with memory than the dip in temperature. Despite myself, I peer up into the boughs, hoping to see what? That little girl perched on the edge of a branch, swinging her feet and grinning down? With a flash of startling clarity, I see her smile, the gap where her tooth had fallen out, the bright white square of a brand new adult tooth next to it. But the memory fades and I'm staring at an empty branch, hearing the rustle and shush of leaves overhead, the lonely sound of moving water.

On the other side of the stream, a dirt track leads up a sharp incline and, breaking clear of the trees, I find myself in another field, smaller this time, where a hut stands – a low, squat thing – no more than three metres squared, with a flat roof, a curtained window and flimsy door. The type of hut you see in the townships and villages, makeshift and poor. There's a weathered look about it, paint peeling at the edges, a strip of felt coming away from the roof.

'This is where he lived?' I ask, and she nods, running her eyes over the poverty of the place.

I want to ask did he die here, but the words stop in my throat. Perhaps it's because I'm weakened by what happened last night, or perhaps it's because of the distrust that bubbles between us, but I experience a rush of fear at the thought of being alone with her. There is nowhere out here I can run to, no nearby house or village, no one, apart from the animals that stalk in the surrounding plains, to hear me scream.

She reaches for the handle, opens the door and steps inside. Turning to me, her face is in shadow. 'Are you coming up?'

I hang back, hesitant now.

She shrugs. 'It's your choice.'

But I have no choice. I need to know.

I hurry up after her, into the tiny confined space, and she closes the door behind me.

For a moment, I stand there, adjusting to the dimness after the glare of the afternoon sun. A musty scent invades my nostrils, the smell of too much living inside too small a space. Curtains are drawn over the window and below them I see the gatherings of a rudimentary kitchen – a tiny fridge tilted at an angle, a one-ring burner on a Formica-topped table, condiments sitting in neat order alongside stacked plates and a thin clustering of cups. Behind me, I am aware of a narrow bed pushed against a wall. A blue plastic basket hangs from a hook, spilling over with clothes, sleeves dangling down, like ghostly forms.

Lauren says nothing, and I can see that her face has changed. She is regarding me with an expression so grave and intense that it feels threatening. All the danger that has been hovering at the edges of our contact comes flooding into this room.

'There,' she says then, pointing to the wall behind me, and loath as I am to turn my back to her, I do as she asks.

I draw in my breath.

Over the bed, plastered the full length of the wall, are a mass of paintings and photographs. They crowd the entire space as if each one is fighting for supremacy. Blonde girls, hair in bunches, grin down at us, caught in the bleached light of a 1970s summer. Polka-dot dresses in the long grass. A blue swimsuit, a chubby arm holding a crab aloft. A woman with the same white-blonde hair, sunburned face running to tan, teeth slightly crooked, staring back at the camera, a baby held to her shoulder. I look at that baby and see the tenderness of her bald head touching her mother's cheek, so real that I can almost smell the newness of her scalp. But it is the paintings that bring the tightness across my chest: a child's artwork, great big daubs of gaudy colours on paper that seems to crackle with age. The whole wall is taken up with them, in varying degrees of ability and imagination. On the bed, I see a gathering of toys – dolls and teddy bears, soft bunnies and Barbies with raggedy hair. Something about the way they sit tells me they have been carefully arranged. All of it – the paintings, the photographs, the dolls – preserved as if time had stopped on the day she died. In that one small space, the child's life has been carefully sealed in aspic. I stand there, taking it all in, the enormity of it. I am observing far more than just pictures and keepsakes. I am beholding a life's work. I am staring obsession in the face. And when I turn to Lauren, her gaze seems empty, as if she has seen this room so many times, she has become inured to it.

'He even kept her clothes,' she says, in a deadened tone.

'But why?' I ask, and turn with a sweeping gesture that encompasses the whole room.

'He lost the only thing that mattered to him. He needed to fill the emptiness.'

Something seems to heave within me – a kind of dread. I want to know what happened. I want to understand, and I don't know if it's being in that room with its ghosts, or the lingering memory of violence from last night, but I feel afraid. I can sense the danger.

Just then there is a screech of brakes, then the slam of a car door.

Lauren goes to the window and peers behind the curtain.

In a voice that betrays no emotion, she says: 'They're here.'

16. Nick

'Is it Lauren?' I ask Father Murphy. I see worry in his eyes; his face is drawn and haggard.

I think about what I told her then, about what Luke did, and my ears fill with a noisy clamour.

'It's Katie, she's been hurt,' he says, leading me down the hotel stairs and into the lobby.

'She's been hurt? But how? What happened?' I ask, stalling on the steps to the hotel.

'There's no time for explanations. Please just come. I'll take you to her,' he says, guiding me to the car.

The windows are rolled down and the back door is open. A man with a black leather cap is leaning against the bonnet. He watches us approach with a lazy indifference. There's something about him I recognize, a local, perhaps, but I can't think how I know him or where from.

Murphy nods to him, but the man makes no sign. He simply spits whatever stalk he's been chewing onto the ground and climbs into the driver's seat.

I get into the back and Murphy takes the passenger seat. He says something to the driver, who turns on the ignition, and we pull away with a stutter.

'Tell me, Murphy,' I say, my head pounding. 'What's happened to her?' My voice sounds shaky and tense – it's full of the same unnerving echoes it contained when I asked all those questions after hearing of Luke's disappearance.

'I don't know the details, Nick, but it sounds like she had some kind of fall,' Murphy says slowly, keeping his eyes on the road while the car travels at a steady speed.

I stare out at the land around us. The houses have fallen away, and there is only the wide expanse of the plains, broken here and there by a clump of trees, a scrub of bush. The road is narrow and dusty – a track the car rattles and lurches over. We're the only vehicle for miles. I don't know exactly where we are and my brain's sucked dry and addled with memories I don't want to relive.

The driver lights up and smoke from his cigarette wafts through the car. A silence comes over us as we travel further inland – it reminds me of the silence of waking alone in a small hut on the outskirts of a nomadic village in Mozambique, in the years before I met Lauren, a thread of raindrops falling onto my face as dawn broke, the village quiet, the wildlife about to stir.

A moment of beforeness, like the one into which my tears fell after my dad had said to me, one night in Wicklow: 'It's not your fault. You were only a child.'

I had woken up from a nightmare and cried out in fright. He came to my bedroom door. I was shaking with fear.

'What is it? A bad dream?'

I nodded and told him what I had dreamed, told him about the river again.

He came to my bed, sat down. He didn't want to hear the details of the dream: he had stopped asking by this stage what had actually happened. He only asked us to forget. 'It was an accident,' he said, 'time now to put it behind you,' all the while rubbing my back and calming me until I finally fell asleep again.

I've tried, Dad. I've tried to put it behind me, to push it down, to forget, but it catches up. It won't let me alone.

There's only me and Katie left from that time, and now that she's in trouble, hurt somehow, I'm filled again with a paralysing fear, and my mind rushes to what might have happened to her. Could she have walked down the wrong street and met a renegade militia, been overtaken by the heat, consumed some heady cocktail of alcohol and prescription medication, all to stave off the awful time we are having by being back in what is to us a blighted spot?

My hands shake as they do before I go on stage. 'I hope she's okay,' I say, but no one answers.

We drive on in silence. I peer out of the window. The landscape unfolds before us, the same undulating vastness — we're in the middle of nowhere. Then, after some time, the car slows with a judder. The driver takes the cigarette from his mouth.

'Look,' he says, pointing, his voice deep and gravelly. 'Two lions.'

I can't help thinking that there's a glimmer of recognition in his eyes: a challenge, even.

Beneath the branches of a large acacia tree two young lions are resting, sheltering from the sun. They eye us with threatening curiosity, the paw of one lying on the head of the other. The two are so close in size and age they could be brothers, and the way they shift about with such ease and grace only hides their power.

'Why have we stopped?' Murphy asks, agitated.

'To watch the lions,' the driver answers gruffly.

One of the animals moves towards us, watching us closely to see what we might do, padding with slow, deliberate steps – a ferocious strength in its limbs. They seem relaxed, but they are aware of everything around them. They are predators, after all, and later today, in all likelihood, they will kill. And with that thought comes the image of us on safari all those years ago: we're in the van, my dad has his arm around me and I can feel the heat of his body against my face as I lean into him. 'Look,' he says, pointing to a lion in the distance chasing down a hyena. The van races after them and I throw my arms around his waist and hold on for dear life. As quickly as it arrives, the image fades: my dad's wild smile vanishing with it.

We're closer to the lions here than I'd thought. If they decided to take an interest in us, we could be in real danger: the car might not start quickly enough, they could attack and, as predators, they would show no mercy.

We watch them for a time, in silence, the driver blowing out one mouthful of smoke after another. His nonchalance is infuriating – Katie's hurt, and he's admiring the wildlife. Then one of the lions comes closer to the car. That's close enough, I think. Time to reverse, time to drive off. But the driver does nothing and the lion lifts his front paw onto the bonnet and raises himself up and onto it. The car creaks and sweat trickles down my brow into my eyes. I want to tell the driver to start the engine, but the words catch in my throat.

The lion peers lazily at us. Even Murphy seems rattled.

'Mack . . .' he says nervously.

But Mack doesn't answer him. Instead he turns to see my reaction, as if I am the one who has spoken his name. He smiles, his gaze resting on me, and I can't help thinking that he's enjoying how I'm shifting in my seat – frightened and defenceless.

And as he turns to me, something passes between us – an acknowledgement of sorts. He smiles again, but there's nothing joyful about it. 'You know me now, don't you?' he says.

It hits me then. 'It's you,' I say, and just like that I can see myself on tiptoe all those years ago peering through the window of the van watching a younger Mack sleeping, his cap pulled over his eyes, his arms lying slack by his sides, his mouth open – the rise and fall of his chest steady and deep. Luke coming up behind me, peeping into the van as well, then falling back and laughing at the state of the driver. I can still hear his mischievous chuckle – the rat-tat-tat of it tapping out its tune in my inner ear, like a little drum-beat.

The lion on the car is approached by the other, which begins to circle us.

'Murphy,' I lean over to whisper in his ear, 'ask your driver to get us out of here.'

'Mackenzie, time to go,' Murphy says. But Mackenzie does not start the car.

'You know him well?' I ask Murphy.

'I know him from years ago,' Murphy says a little distractedly. 'He's one of my lieutenants – a wayward lieutenant.'

His words fill the car, but he is staring out of the window with a kind of wistful inattention, none of the purpose and focus he normally commands. Sweat forms over my lip and the dryness in my mouth is chronic. The humming in my ears starts again.

I think of when I went to visit him in his office only the other day: his irritation on the phone, his annoyance and distraction were the same as they are now.

'Why wayward?' I ask, despite myself.

The second lion comes to Murphy's door and pushes its head against it, shaking the car.

Murphy says something to Mackenzie in his language, which I'm not supposed to understand. He turns to me. 'Mack has a habit of taking things into his own hands. He has a problem sometimes with authority, with not doing what he is told.'

Mack grunts back, 'I do what you tell me to do.'

'But not now?' Murphy says.

The driver gives him a hard, serious stare.

'Mackenzie has had his fair share of injustice, his fair share of misery. I shouldn't be so hard on him,' Murphy says.

My heart starts to beat a little faster. 'What do you mean?' I say, but Murphy doesn't answer.

The lion on the bonnet lets himself down and walks to my side of the car. I can feel it rubbing its haunches against the car's panelling; I can hear its heavy breathing.

'I remember you,' the driver says coldly, 'and your family. They complain. They don't want Mackenzie to drive.'

'History, Mack. Ancient history,' Murphy says.

'Look, maybe you should start the car, Mackenzie,' I say. 'We've seen enough of the lions and it's time we got going. Katie's hurt, for Christ's sake.'

He swings around to me, his voice leaden with fury: 'You dare to tell me what to do? You? After what you have done?'

'Me?' I say.

'I lost everything because of you – my job, my family, my home . . .'

'Because of me?' I don't understand.

'My life was ruined because of you and your family.' His voice is filled with bitterness. 'I lost my job. I lost my family.' He spits the tiny stub of a cigarette from his cracked lips onto the floor of the car.

'It was very unfortunate,' Murphy says. 'Very sad. Everything that happened . . .'

'I had a family to provide for. Mouths to feed. So when I lost my job, my family went hungry. You understand?' he says, raising his voice, but he's not looking for understanding. That's not what his tone suggests at all. He's looking for someone to blame.

'Driving was a good job. But I lost everything,' he says, through gritted teeth, his anger escalating. Even if Murphy has given him some work recently, it's obvious he hasn't let go of what happened to him.

'They came for me . . . they arrested me.'

'Arrested?' I say, the word hitting me like a gut-punch.

'Yes,' he says, squinting harder at me, 'arrested me for the death of a girl who drowned!'

'You mean . . .'

'The police came for me late at night. They took me to the station, kept me awake until morning, told lies to me . . . They said I had killed her. I said, "How?"'

His voice is forlorn, his tone bordering on hysteria, his jabbing finger coming at me again and again, each time with greater force.

'They said, down by the river . . . down by the river, because I wanted to do bad things to her. I said, "No!"'

His 'no' is wild-eyed, his hands reaching out to me, beseeching, threatening.

Now he straightens his back, leans towards me, lowers his gravelly tone to an even deeper bass register: 'I said, "Who says I do such things? Who says I went down to the river?"'

His face comes close to mine. I can smell the stale tobacco, and last night's putrid alcohol on his breath. 'They say you, your mother, Nick. They say she said so.' His eyes are so wild and his anger so palpable, I want to run from the car. But I can't. Not with the lions out there. 'They say your *mother*,' he repeats, his eyes bulging out of his head, his breath threatening to suffocate me.

He nearly shrieks in pain, grits his teeth. 'My wife came to visit me in jail. She said to me: "What have you done?" I told her, "I have done nothing wrong, nothing,"' he exclaims, shaking his finger in front of my face again and again. 'I told her, "I am innocent."'

Years of pent-up fury are finding their voice, seeming to embolden him to the point that he's going to jump into the back seat and attack me. 'When I am finally released, my family is gone. I have no job. No one will give me a job – no one will give a job to a driver to take white folk around Mara when they think he has killed a little white girl.'

His stare is so intense that I can tell he has lived with this awful truth for many years and it has been gnawing away at him, literally eating him up inside.

I look to Murphy for help, but what he has to say is of little use to me: 'It seems Mackenzie was wrongly implicated.'

'One year and seventy-two days in prison before they

283

dropped the case. One of my children died while I was there,' Mack says, saliva gathering at the corners of his mouth, his voice cracking.

Murphy lowers his head.

'All because of you,' Mack says, continuing to jab a finger at me. 'You know how many years I had been driving the safari van?'

I say nothing.

'Five years. Five. Never once did I have a problem over those five years. Not until you and your family complained. Not until that girl died, not until you all fled, not until your mother said to the police that it was me. Do you know what it is like in a Kenyan prison? Do you know what they do to child-killers there?'

With the lions lurking and Mack squinting at me, the fear is peeling off me in waves. That this man has spent time in jail for something Luke did, for something I was involved in, for something my mother accused him of, makes me weak with shame.

'Enough,' says Murphy. 'Please. Apportioning blame is not going to change anything.'

Mackenzie turns back to the front windscreen and lights another cigarette; he's not dropping the subject, I sense, just taking a break, weighing up what to do, his eyes on the big cats outside, staring them down to gain some kind of manic strength from their very presence.

Murphy coughs violently, rubs his temples. I'm desperate for him to take control of this man and his anger, but he's so tired that what he says has nothing to do with Mackenzie losing his job or going to jail or whether my family had anything to do with it.

'Do you remember the starlings, Nick? The ones in the cage?'

'Yes, I do,' I say, hoping to win him back onside so that he can protect me in some way.

'I gave them to you – a gift for each of you, a bird for both of Sally's boys. Superb Starlings, they were called.'

He smiles then, a private smile at his own recollection, and the uncomfortable thought comes to me that maybe Katie isn't hurt. Maybe this is not about her, but about me – that Mackenzie and Murphy are colluding in some way. The light strikes my eyes in a way that makes me think of the moment I stepped into my parents' bedroom to see Luke dangling from the end of a rope. I shiver.

Murphy continues, lost in his own private reverie: 'I was very lonely after Sally . . . after your family left. I wrote to her.'

'You did?'

'She never replied.'

'You wrote to me too.'

'I did.' He turns to smile at me again, but it soon vanishes. 'You never wrote back,' he says sadly.

'My dad thought it inappropriate,' I say, remembering him holding a letter I had received from Murphy, reading it, and bringing it to Mum to see. I heard them arguing – the actual words are forgotten, but the tone was sharp and unforgiving.

'No more letters,' Dad said then to me. 'Not from him.'

I couldn't think why he was so furious at the time, but it's obvious to me now. He didn't want Murphy dredging up the past. He wanted to leave in Africa the things that had happened there.

One of the lions is scraping at the driver's door. Then it swipes the car with such force that it shakes. For a moment, I think it's going to topple over.

Murphy, woken from his daze, shouts: 'Mack! Get us out of here.'

Mack guns the engine and we speed off, the wheels spinning dust in our wake.

I look out at the passing landscape: more dust, more grassland, a herd of wildebeest scattering from the speed and noise the car is making. A red hot-air balloon rises in the distance, but I don't know where we are, don't know where Mack is bringing us. I wish I was in the balloon, for the landscape and sky to swallow me. At the same time, I want to say how sorry I am to this man, to make it up to him – which I know is an impossible task. I don't know how to help him, how to offer recompense. What can I give him that could in any way atone for what has happened?

'Where are we going, Jim?'

'Down to the river.'

Not the river. Not again. Once the river rose to meet us and we ran to it – now all I want to do is run from it.

'What about Katie?'

'She's with Lauren.'

'Lauren?'

'Nick. There's something I must tell you about Lauren . . .'

I listen as he says the words, as he tears apart her past, the past I had understood her to have, and recreates a new one that is more shocking than I could ever have imagined.

'There's something you don't know about her,' he falters,

but he steels himself to go on. 'Her mother lived out here once, before Lauren was born. She was married to another man, who was not Lauren's father, but he was the father to the girl . . .'

There's something weirdly recognizable about what he is saying, but also something so frightening that it's as if I am being dragged down under the riptide of truth.

' . . . who drowned,' he says finally.

I flinch – just the sound of the word makes me crazy. I have spent my whole life trying to outrun the past, trying to outplay its ragtime rhythms, to swallow its white noise, and here it is again, spilling from the mouth of Murphy.

I'm like a man who has fallen from that hot-air balloon, a man who is rushing towards the earth without a parachute.

'She never told me . . .' I say, and before Murphy can answer Mack swerves the car violently out of the way of a wild dog sauntering down the road. I am thrown across the back seat.

This time Murphy speaks to his driver in English: 'Careful, Mackenzie, please.'

I sit up again, and even though this news of who Lauren really is will turn my world upside-down, what goes through my mind is my dad, speeding through the Wicklow hills, past the Featherbeds and through the Sally Gap, his own ending just up the road ahead of him. Did he see it coming? In that last moment, as the car swerved around the corner, did he try to control it, to steer it out of danger? Or did he fly into Death's waiting arms, eager to embrace it after all that life had done to him? Was he crying as the car hit the wall, or did he let out a great sigh of relief that it was all over? Did he think of us, of me and Luke, of what we had done?

I hope he didn't. And I hope he didn't think of Mum and the whispered arguments he'd had with her, arguments I'd overheard more than once late at night. An argument that seemed to pivot on one thing: who to believe? Me or Luke?

'He says he didn't do it,' Mum said about me.

Murphy turns back to me. 'You know, I've thought about her, Cora, down through the years. She's always been with me in a way, passing in and out of my thoughts, like a ghostly figure. Her death touched so many lives, Nick, and we've all been hurt by what happened. Now at last there's a chance to commemorate her passing and find, if we can, some healing in that commemoration. This is my last chance to make things right, Nick. I'm an old man. That is why we need this, you and I . . . and Mackenzie. We have all suffered. And I don't want to do this in a church or a chapel. You know I lost all faith in the structures of religion, its buildings and outhouses. For me, God resides out here, in the air, in the soil, among the people and the beasts of the savannah and its rivers. Here's a real chance to heal for all of us.

'It will also be a chance to remember the girl who drowned there,' Murphy continues, 'to commemorate the passing of a life. No one's assigning any blame, Nick, but saying some prayers for one taken so prematurely would be an act of kindness, don't you think? There's nothing wrong with that, surely. And it will certainly mean a great deal to Lauren . . . and to Mackenzie.'

Mack is driving faster now, blowing smoke more furiously and nodding in exaggerated agreement. 'Prayers,' he says aloud, and coughs harshly – or is it a volley of scornful laughter?

'Jim, this is crazy,' I say, and yet part of me, the part that lived under the shadow of my parents' doubt, almost aches for a ceremony like this – even if it scares me to my core. And if it can, even in the smallest way, act as an apology to Mack, well, I'll go where Murphy wants me to go and say the prayers he wants me to say and beg, on Luke's behalf, forgiveness from Mack, and from Lauren too.

'My days are numbered, Nick. I'm very sick. I don't have long and I need a day of reckoning – before I meet my Maker. We all do. Today is that day.'

Murphy is dying. I see him in a different way. His strength and vigour have diminished, almost without my noticing. He is a pale shadow of his former self. It's difficult to see him in this new light, and I feel his words threatening to break me down again, to obliterate my composure, but still something in me fights against what is happening. 'It was a game that went wrong. An accident . . .' I say, but there's no time to discuss it, because the car has puttered to a jerky stop.

We are here.

As Murphy climbs out, he says: 'Don't be afraid. This is all for the best.'

Mackenzie glances into the rear-view mirror, his face swathed in smoke, but he says nothing, just smiles disdainfully and follows Murphy.

In the clearing, there is a hut – a poor wooden box, lonely and forlorn out here on its own amid the sprawling grasslands.

Now that we have stopped, there is no breeze rifling through the car to keep me cool. There's a rumble in the distance. The weather is changing.

I look out at the long grass, the trees, and the forlorn hut ahead of us.

Here I am again.

The river is not far from us and the sky is a brilliant burning blue. My hands are shaking and I'm too scared to move. I can see from where I'm sitting the door of the hut opening. I watch as Lauren steps outside, and feel the shock of strangeness between us. Everything has changed.

A mangy black mongrel weaves its way out from behind the hut to see what's going on and sits down to watch. Its tongue lolls over its tarry lips; flies circle its head. Time seems to stand still. A wind is picking up. Overhead a flurry of bee-eaters passes.

I imagine my mother running towards us on that day. I see the limp body of the girl in Luke's arms. I hear him counting again.

'Thirty, thirty-one, thirty-two . . .'

A terrible ache spreads about my temples. Something I have been holding in threatens to burst its banks. There's an awful pain in my chest and I'm short of breath.

I imagine Mackenzie sitting in a cell, weeping into his hands, before being dragged out by the police to be inter-rogated, threatened, beaten.

Above us there is a loud crack of thunder. The wind picks up. I want to ask Lauren why she kept this secret from me. Both of us felt a need to keep something of ourselves apart from the other. I had seen it as an expression of love and trust, but now I see it as something else – I see it as a mistake, a terrible mistake. I'm struck dumb at the vast chasm opening between us, and the tinnitus in my ears swells, like a tide coming in.

I'm scared, unsure exactly of what is going on. There's another wild crack in the sky. My hand is on the door handle, but I can't bring myself to use it. Lauren raises her arms in appeal.

Before I can do anything, the car door is flung open.

Mackenzie stands broad and menacing before me. There's a shot-gun in his hands and he's pointing it at me. 'Get out,' he growls. 'Now!'

17. Katie

So this is how it happens.

There are three of them, two standing alongside the car, the one with the gun screaming at a third who remains inside. I look at the gunman, feel my legs buckle, air escaping my lungs in short bursts of fear. It's him. Jesus, it's him. I can't see the person in the car, but I know it's Nick. Soon enough the gunman reaches in and hauls him out, a handful of Nick's shirt caught in his grip. For a moment, Nick just stands there, stunned, hands out by his sides. Murphy is saying something I can't hear – his voice is too low and I'm too far away – but I can tell from his gesture, his hands pushing down the air in front of him, that he is trying to placate the gunman. The air around us crackles with danger. Even without the gun, I'd feel it. It's coming over me again, that wash of pain, the crack against my skull, a searing blackness, almost as vivid in memory under this hot sun as it was in the pitch darkness of the previous night. My assailant, the man who attacked me: I know it's him.

Lauren takes a step forward, her eyes fixed on the tableau by the car. I can feel her hesitation. Nick hasn't looked at her – not once – and there's something very deliberate about that. I can tell she feels it too.

It's so hot. Too hot to think. Standing in this baking field, paralysed by indecision and fear, I feel the scald of the sun, think about the shade of the trees by the river.

The bank of grey clouds approaches from the west, slanting rain visible in the distance, a rumble of thunder disturbing the air.

Murphy is by the gunman's side now, plucking at his sleeve – an ineffectual gesture, easily shrugged off. The three stand there, locked in a tense negotiation. We wait, Lauren and I, nothing but the hush of grass around us, the passing shadow of a bird high in the sky. The plains around us stretch for miles – all that empty space, the rolling silence, the shimmering heat. Nowhere to run.

Movement then. It happens swiftly. A raised hand, the black shape of the gun, the butt brought down heavily and the sickening crunch of impact. A shout, then Nick staggers backwards, holding his face.

Lauren streaks past me, terror in her flight. I can't move, the fear inside me solidifying. Up ahead, I can see Nick on one knee – a strange genuflection, his hands on his face – the gunman taking a tentative step towards him before Murphy grabs him back, barks something at him. By the time my legs start working, Lauren is peeling Nick's hands away from his face to reveal a mash of gore, blood blooming on his T-shirt, a livid red flower burning through pale cotton.

'What are you thinking?' Murphy is shouting at the gunman. 'This is not what we agreed! Not at all!'

But the gunman is oblivious, staring down at Nick, nostrils flared, breathing heavily.

I know who my assailant is now. Of course I do. Memory lashes like a whip, the scent of it ripping through me, the tang of sweat, acrid smoke from roll-up cigarettes, my mother's whispered frustration, *I do wish he wouldn't smoke those vile things.* Our driver.

Lauren presses a corner of her T-shirt to Nick's face in a bid to staunch the bleeding, and for a moment Nick remains still, silently bearing his wife's ministrations. There is something vulnerable about him that cuts through my fear to a softer place. It lasts until he gets to his feet, pushing her away — a brush-off that is dismissive and curt. She reels back from it.

He knows about her, then.

The hurt is in her face as she says his name and goes towards him, but he holds up his hand in warning, and she shifts from one foot to the other, racked with indecision.

Something of her restlessness takes hold of me. The dryness of the land, the sense that, for all you can see of the fields and plains, most of the life here is hidden, skulking in the undergrowth, camouflaged and waiting, but I can't stand the waiting any longer. The shadow I have been living under since the morning Reilly told me Luke was missing — how long ago that seems — now I feel crushed by the weight of it, dried out by fatigue and sick of it hanging over me. I think of Reilly's words of warning, 'Father Murphy? I'm not sure about him, Katie,' and turn towards the priest. 'What are we doing here, Murphy? What is it that you want?'

'Quiet!' the driver barks, and I feel my face grow hot. His eyes burn with fury and shift between me and the others, deep-set eyes that try to observe everything. Impossible to slip past.

Ignoring me, Murphy faces Nick, eyes narrowed as he assesses the injury, murmuring, 'You'll be all right, son,' but his frown betrays his anxiety. As he reaches up to clasp Nick's shoulder, the old man's hand shakes. He is visibly trembling. Nick's face is pale and there's a greyish tinge to his skin.

'What is it you want?' I repeat, despite the driver's presence, his dark frown. My tone is hard and insistent, seeking to cut through the infuriating vacancy in Murphy's voice and eyes.

His gaze is on Nick, concerned, loving, like that of an anxious parent. 'For too long I've stood by and watched Nick suffer,' he says, 'pushing down the past, thinking it can be obliterated. But something like that is too big to be squashed. It's like a tumour. It grows silently in the dark.'

There's a drumming pulse of blood behind my eyes. The hard sun beats down from above and I long for the rain – I can almost taste it. The driver has taken steps towards me, the gun at his side. He is so close that I can smell his sweat.

'When a man is facing his own mortality, he feels a great need to put things right.'

I look at Murphy, the gaunt features, the boniness of his face and wrists, the yellowness at the edges of his eyes, and I see it all at once: the lurking shadow of Death that stalks him. How had I not noticed it before?

'I wanted to put things right,' Murphy says again, his face pained. 'All these fractured lives. The ripples sent out by this terrible thing. I knew somehow that if we all came here together, back to this place, if we brought it out into the open, it would draw out the poison and the healing process might start.'

'A catharsis?' I say, and I can't keep the sneer from my voice.

He goes to answer but is interrupted by the driver.

'Enough of this talk!' Words spoken right into my ear, the heat of his breath on my neck.

He indicates with the gun that we are to move down through the field. Down to where the black boughs lean towards the creek.

'Please, Mack,' Murphy says, his voice weary.

'No!' The word fired out. 'No more talk! Move!'

Something passes over the priest's face then – a flash of irritation. He lets it go, nodding peaceably, that remoteness coming over him again. He turns away from his companion and walks with his hands behind his back, his eyes on the ground in front of his feet. I almost want to laugh at his foolishness: to think that he could control this man, this loose cannon.

But the laugh doesn't bubble up. It's swallowed in the acid of fear churning in my stomach. We walk through the field in an odd procession – funereal, except there isn't a body, yet. The dry grass prickles underfoot, the earth hard and unforgiving, pain travelling up the backs of my calves. Ahead of me, Nick walks with a pensive air, the blood on his T-shirt a shocking reminder. I cannot fathom what thoughts are passing through his head. Lauren catches up with him, reaches for his arm, but he pulls away from her savagely.

'Please, Nick –'

He cuts across her: 'You knew about this? You were in on it?'

'It's not like that,' she says, urgency in her voice as she hurries to keep up with him. 'There wasn't supposed to be any violence. I would never have agreed if I'd known –'

'I don't understand you,' he goes on. 'I don't know who you are.'

'I'm the same person, Nick. I'm your wife –'

'You're a stranger, Lauren. A phoney.'

'No!'

'Tell me this. Was any of it real, what we had between us?'

'Of course!'

'What was your plan? To get close to me and then, when my defences were lowered, you'd strike?'

'I love you, Nick, you've got to believe –'

'Love! Honestly, I don't know what that is any more.'

The contours of the land are changing, dipping as we get closer. I can hear the swish and movement of water now. My pulse quickens.

'I was trying to help you. The way you've changed since Luke killed himself . . . it frightened me.'

'Why didn't you tell me about your mother? About your sisters? Why did I have to find out like this?'

I can see her searching for words, the regret visible in her. 'I wanted to tell you myself. I kept waiting for the right moment, but it never seemed to come. And then things got serious between us so quickly and I was frightened that, if I told you, you wouldn't want me any more.'

'You lied to me –'

'I didn't mean to! I didn't want to, but it got so that things were so complicated and messy, I just didn't know how. And when Murphy said there was a way I could help you, a way we could bring the truth out into the open, I thought it might be a way of letting go of this secret. Because I hated keeping it from you, Nick.'

He stops, looks her square in the face. There is naked disappointment in his gaze, such surprise and hurt that it is as if all his beliefs have been kicked out of him.

297

'You spoke to him about me like that? You went behind my back? Lauren –' He breaks off and still there is pain in all he has left unspoken. Lauren glances behind her, catches me looking, and I am ashamed for being a witness, listening in on this most private exchange, the breaking of something that was precious and intimate between them.

It lasts but a moment, and then the gunman barks a command and we do as he says and march towards our fate.

This is how it happens. This is what comes in advance of the headlines screaming of bodies found by a river, the lurid details of bullet wounds and carnage, an inventory of the dead, analysis of an execution. Photos of the victims from a time before, when they had no knowledge of the terror that lay ahead. I think of Reilly hunched over his desk, trying to choose a picture of me to print, and in that moment what I feel is not fear but a strange sorrow. I see the trees looming.

I always knew it would come to this. Deep down, I knew that we couldn't get away with it. You find ways of coping, ways of forgetting. You bury yourself in work, striving to be successful, wealthy and powerful. You engage in philanthropy, in charitable works, as if that might alleviate the guilt. Or you run away, explore the four corners of the world in an endless quest for meaning. You look for temporary solutions to deaden the memory – alcohol, drugs and a string of ill-advised romances. Or you let that memory become a black hole, a vacuum within your soul. But you know – deep down, you can't escape it – that one day there will come a time of reckoning.

Murphy stops. He has reached the river.

We stand there, watching his back, the droop of heavy

shoulders, the deliberate way he steps out onto a rock in the water, then straightens.

The blue knotted rope hangs from a branch high above. Unnerving to see it still there. I remember the hut and all it contained – that mausoleum, a shrine to the dead. The colour of the rope, although faded with time, is still vivid in the shadows, the frayed ends, a slight sway from a passing breeze. It makes me think of Luke and his own lonely end. I blink the thought away.

Somewhere above us, a bird flutters in the branches. A breeze reaches us briefly, then dies away. The only sound is the flow of the river, until it builds inside me again, the need to know, a question bubbling to the surface.

'What about the birds, Murphy?'

He turns to me. Something in his face changes.

Nick looks up sharply.

'It was you, wasn't it? You sent those dead birds.'

'Birds?' Nick says.

'No,' Murphy says, but his face tells me that this is not wholly true. 'That wasn't me.'

His eyes dart to Mack, whose jaw tightens, then lifts defiantly. There isn't a jot of apology or regret in his face.

'You?' I say, addressing him for the first time. 'Why? I don't understand.'

'It was a sign, a message,' he says, in a strident voice. 'A calling.'

I laugh suddenly, but feel the thump of fear inside. The way he is looking at me – so cold, so committed to his own path, his own truth. It's fascinating and deeply unnerving.

'The starlings,' Nick says to Murphy, confusion clearing from his gaze. 'The ones you gave me and Luke.'

'A gift for each of you,' he answers quietly. 'One for each of Sally's boys.' He lowers his head, puts a hand to his temples as if in pain. There follows a moment of silence. Above us, the wind wafts lazily through the trees. 'Sometimes things happen,' he says, 'things that make us stop in our tracks, make us sit up and take notice. Things so unusual that they make us believe there must be a God and that this is his signature. Some months back such a thing happened to me.' He swallows hard, and looks at us in turn, but when he speaks, he is addressing Nick alone and the rest of us are spectators. 'I was sitting in my office in Kianda when a man came rushing in. He was agitated, very worked up, telling me that I needed to come quickly, that something terrible was happening. I didn't want to know. Not on that particular day – a hard day for me. That morning, I had received my prognosis and it wasn't good. An inoperable tumour, a ticking clock. So there I was, sitting in a pool of self-pity, shocked, angry, fearful, when this man came and told me that there were birds falling from the sky. Reluctantly, I went with him to a patch of scrubland where rubbish was piled high and there I saw it, birds, dozens of them, maybe even a hundred, lying dead upon the mound as if they had been shot down in a flurry of bullets.'

He pauses, a frown of concentration on his face.

'But they hadn't been shot, those tiny starlings, some of them still flapping pitifully, as death overcame them. "They fell from the sky," Hamisi said. He was wild-eyed in amazement. "They just dropped from the sky. Like rain." He looked at me as if I could interpret what had happened.

'Various reasons were put forward, that they had been

attacked by hawks and in their panic had flown into a tree
or building, or that they had feasted on grain or plants that
had been treated with a pesticide that had poisoned them.
We went over the mound, picking up these tiny feathered
bodies, and all at once I thought of Sally.'

'My mother?' Nick says sharply.

'The starlings I had given you. She set them free – it was
the night she broke with me.' And I see it happening:
something shutting down behind his face, a hardness coming over him. But then he seems to shake himself. 'I picked
up a couple of those little birds from the mound, and took
them back with me to the office. I don't know what I
intended to do with them. Nothing, I suppose. I went back
there, laid them on my desk and took out a bottle of whiskey. I felt . . . I felt overcome. It was all too much – the
cancer, and all these memories of Sally filling me. And that
was when Mackenzie came.'

He looks across to where his companion stands under
the shadow of dark foliage, the gun in his hands, his
expression unreadable.

Murphy lets out a puff of air and I can see how close he
is to coming undone, the toll this is taking on him. He
glances up at the sky peeping through the leaves and blinks
away sudden tears, then gives me a watery smile. 'They say
things happen in threes, don't they?' A stab at humour, but
the smile dies on his face. When he speaks again, his voice
is low, wistful with memory. 'I hadn't seen Mack in over
twenty years. Isn't that right, my friend? Both of us adrift,
wrestling with our own demons. But by the time Mackenzie
stepped back in through my door that day, I had pulled
myself together, reassembled my life into some sort of

order. I had my work, and with ALIVE I had a goal, a sense of purpose. Sally was dead, but I was managing to cope. At least, I thought I was . . .'

He drifts for a moment, then addresses his next words to Mackenzie. 'We must have talked all night, until the whiskey was gone and the dawn had broken. No one there to hear us but the birds on the desk. One of those rare conversations full of confessions and doubts and broken dreams. I told him about Sally. About what we had shared. I told him about the starlings I had given her boys, the ones she had set free. I told him about ALIVE and the work we'd done together. I told him about the boys – about Luke and Nick – about what they had done. And I told him what little I knew of you, Katie, from what Sally had told me. I told him all about how your lives had carried on after that day by the river. I told him all of this in good faith, not knowing . . .'

His voice breaks a little then. Mackenzie stares at him, impassive. Still I can feel the jittery presence of nerves beneath the calm exterior, the sense that at any moment he could explode.

'We talked of our various disappointments,' Murphy continues, 'the ways in which our lives had gone off-course, our challenges, our regrets. I do believe that I confessed more to you on that one night, my friend, than I have done in a lifetime to my confessor. It was a long dark night of the soul, wouldn't you say, Mack? For both of us. But now . . . now, I realize, I said too much.' He looks at Mackenzie, his eyes narrowing. 'I didn't know . . . your dark heart.'

The air around us seems to hum with moisture and heat.

A muggy blanket pulling at my limbs, creeping into my lungs. I can see the sweat on Mackenzie's face, droplets glinting in the light, one tracking down his cheek, like a tear. But he is not crying. His expression is of quiet fury, eyes fixed on the priest.

'You and your words,' he says, so softly it's almost inaudible. There is something menacing in his stillness that frightens me more than when he was shouting, threatening us with the gun. An eerie quiet fills the space around and between us – a slinking animal rubbing its hide against our rigid bodies. 'I have not come so far for this.'

'You came here for the truth,' Murphy says.

'A debt must be paid for that girl's death. And I, too, am owed for all that I have lost.'

His eyes go to Nick, who stares at the river, a frown hovering on his face.

'Now it is my turn to be priest,' he says darkly. 'You will give me your confession.'

'You shouldn't have sent those birds,' Murphy goes on. 'It was not what I wanted.'

'Oh, I know.' Sarcasm makes his voice heavy. 'You were happy to sit in your little room, feeding your anger with whiskey and thinking of all the wrongs done to you. Luke, the boss-man, doesn't trust you with his money. Your woman left you because she loves her boys more than she loves you. Please,' he says, his dry lips cracking into a grin of disgust, 'you talk about pain but you don't know what it is. None of you do.'

Eyes flashing around at all of us.

'So I do what you are too yellow to do. I send those birds. Put them in a package and send them. Pictures of drownings too. I send them a message, make them scared. Dead birds don't sing. Taste a little of what Mackenzie has gone through.'

'You took care to cover your tracks,' I say, and he turns at the sound of challenge in my voice. 'The English stamps.'

'I couldn't make it too easy for you, could I?' There is a hint of humour in his eyes, as if some part of him is enjoying this. 'So I sent the package to my friend in England. He found your address and sent it on.'

Throughout this exchange, Nick's face has kept his eyes fixed on the river. But now he turns back and I see that his expression has changed. All this information is coming at him too quickly. Confusion slips away to be replaced by horror. He addresses Murphy. 'You and my mother?'

'Yes, Nick. I loved her,' Murphy says simply. 'I loved her with all of my heart. And she loved me.'

'No,' he says, shaking his head.

But Murphy goes on: 'She was going to leave your father. We were going to be together, but then . . .' He lets out a sigh.

'But then it happened,' I say, finishing his sentence for him. 'Did you really think she would go with you? That she would choose you over her own children?'

He offers me the weakest of smiles. 'A foolish dream. That's all.'

I can feel Nick looking at me, and when I turn to him, his face has darkened, something twisting inside him.

'What?' I ask.

'You knew about them?' he asks. 'You knew about him and my mother?'

'Your mother!' Mackenzie exclaims. 'Don't talk to us

about your mother!' The way he says the word makes it sound like an obscenity.

Nick is not listening to him. Instead, he is staring hard at me, an unspoken accusation of betrayal, an accusation that confuses me.

'Yes,' I tell him. 'We all did. Even you.'

'What?' he says, as he reels backwards.

'You don't remember?'

'What are you talking about?'

'When we were here before as kids? What Luke told you in the tent that night? You really don't remember?'

I know the answer from the blankness of his expression. He could be a small boy again, the way he stands with that dazed look on his face.

'When we were coming down here the first time,' I begin, 'all those years ago, don't you remember how sulky Luke was? So quiet and withdrawn?'

That's the first thing I remember of it: Luke's sourness in the van during that long, difficult journey. For three days, he kept it up, staring glassy-eyed out of the window during the safari, refusing to react at the sighting of lions, elephants or hippos.

'It drove your parents crazy. All through those days we spent here, he didn't speak to your mother – he would hardly even look at her. Your father lost the plot with him one day. You really don't remember?'

He is staring at me wide-eyed, utterly bewildered. I can feel Mackenzie's growing impatience. He holds the gun in two hands now. Still I go on.

'On the last night, we were in our tent, the three of us, supposed to be asleep, but really we were eavesdropping, spying on the adults. They had gathered around the campfire. Your father had a guitar and he took it out, began playing some fast-tempo folksong, lots of yelping and rude lyrics. Your mother got up and began to dance.'

I remember it so clearly, the sway of Sally Yates's hips, the curving line of her body caught in the light of the campfire, the glow of her cheeks and the private look that came over her face as if she were dancing for herself alone and not for anyone else's pleasure. I was mesmerized. I must have said something then, some breathy and admiring comment, something foolish, because Luke snorted. 'Her?' he said, his lip pulled back in a sneer. 'She's a slut.'

That word hit me like a slap to the face. To hear him say it about his own mother. But before I could react, Nick had sprung upon his brother, sitting on his chest, catching Luke's neck in the vice-like grip of his knees. 'Take it back!' he shouted. 'Take it back, or I'll kill you!'

They scuffled for a few minutes, pulling and kicking and screaming at each other, until their dad came into the tent and dragged them apart. Two mutinous boys, refusing to say what they'd been fighting about.

When he had gone, the three of us got into our sleeping bags. I turned my face away and tried to sleep. But in the quiet of the dark, I heard Luke whispering to his brother, and even though I couldn't hear the words, I knew what he was saying. I had seen Sally Yates with the man in her bedroom. I fell asleep that night to the sounds of the crickets clicking in the dark and of a small boy weeping.

'You really can't remember?' I ask Nick, but he's moving backwards, his hand going up to his head, and I can't tell if this is because the memory is leaking back to him, or if he is reeling from the blow to his head.

'Nick,' Murphy says, and goes towards him, but Nick shakes his head violently.

'Stay away from me,' he says, his voice low, but the threat is within it.

'I'm sorry, Nick. I truly am. That's what this day is about. It's about atonement. I've paid for my sins for a lifetime now,' he says, his voice cracking.

As Murphy moves towards him, Nick takes a step forward and strikes him cleanly in the jaw with his right fist. Murphy reels backwards, stumbling over the rocks, loses his footing, then slips and falls into the water, his face white with shock.

Nick is breathing heavily, for all the world as if he's going to wade into the river just to strike him again. But he doesn't.

A noise behind us, the switching sound of a bullet sliding into the chamber. I turn to see Mackenzie, the butt of the gun hard against his shoulder, one eye closed, the other staring down the barrel of the gun. Lauren holds her hands to her mouth. Nick straightens slowly, raising his hands in surrender. 'Please,' he says. 'Please don't shoot.'

Mackenzie says nothing, just stares at him.

My heart is beating hard now. This is when it starts, I think. Everything stills in this moment. A tremor in Nick's hands, his fear palpable.

'What do you want from me?' he asks then.

A simple answer: 'Your confession.'

The gun is held in place, ready to fire.

'It was a game,' Nick stammers. 'It was just a game. A stupid game that went wrong.'

He pauses, waits for some reaction, and Mack's voice, cool and dry: 'More.'

'Okay. Okay,' Nick says, his voice quivering, something wild in his eyes. 'Four of us in the water – two teams. Whichever team stayed under longer was the winner. We played for ages – until my lungs hurt and there was a pain in my head, like my skull was too tight. I wanted to stop, but Luke wouldn't have it. He had to win, you see. He always had to win.'

A hush has come over the trees and the water. Murphy glances at me, sees the pain in my face. I am straining towards Nick, every fibre of my being fixed on the words coming out of his mouth.

'I was so tired. I wanted to stop, but Luke . . .' He trails off, and I can tell he is back there on that day, the trees closing in around him.

'More!' Mack commands, his voice snapping Nick out of it.

When he continues he sounds rattled and scared. He is telling us now how the teams were paired up – Nick with the younger sister, Amy, Luke with Cora – and I am on the riverbank, the others waist deep in the water, hands gripped tightly, that wild intake of breath before the sudden plunge. I think of those pairings, and something jars. I look closely at Nick.

'I told him I'd had enough, that I wanted to go back to the camp. "One more go," he said, "just one more, and then we're quits."'

Lauren has her arms crossed, listening intently to the words spoken about Cora – the sister she never knew. And as he tells the story, Nick's voice grows more forceful. He is propelled by something inside him to keep going to the end.

'That time – that last time – when I came up for air, I could see her hand waving. Cora's hand. She was still under. He was holding her down. He always had to win, you see?'

His voice breaks, and I feel a great sadness coming over us, pouring down through the trees, emerging from the murky waters of the river.

It's not just sadness I feel, but a growing frustration – it builds within me, frustration that is fast becoming a kind of anger.

'He held her down and I did nothing,' he says again. 'I was so tired, and I didn't realize . . . I watched my brother as he killed that girl and I did nothing, and for that, I am truly and profoundly –'

'No!' I shout. The word ricochets off the trees.

My hand is covering my mouth, but it's too late. They are all looking at me now as I feel the words swelling inside me.

'I need to do this, Katie,' Nick tells me. 'I have to make this right.'

'No, Nick! Just stop! Christ, would you just stop? All these years, all this time, and still you persist with this?' I put my hands to my head, feel the pain there, made worse by Nick's stare, blank and infuriating.

'I'm telling the truth,' he says.

'No!' I say again, lower, more serious, my hands in fists by my sides. 'Oh, God, you don't know, do you? You really don't remember.'

Nick stops. Murphy raises his head and looks at the sky, sees the clouds scudding high above us. Lauren and

Mackenzie, both watchful and still. And she is here too: Cora. Her ghostly presence high in the trees above, waiting.

'Luke was with Amy,' I say.

Lauren looks at me sharply.

'I was sitting on the bank,' I go on. 'I sat there and watched. I saw you, Nick. You were with Cora.'

'No,' he says quietly, and there is a tug of resistance, an understandable reluctance to face the stark, cold truth.

'Luke didn't kill that girl. He didn't hold her under. It was you, Nick,' I say softly. 'It was you.'

18. Nick

I want it to stop. All of it. The wave of words coming at me, followed by another and another, an endless series of crashing waves, filling my ears with their bass roar.

Katie opens her mouth and they come tumbling out at me – *it was you, it was you, it was you* – and I want it only to stop.

'All these years, you've persisted with this version of events,' she says. 'And I, like a fool, went along with it because I cared for you, Nick. At some level I understood that this was what you needed to do to cope. But now I see how wrong that was. A massive mistake.'

'What are you talking about?' I ask her, bewildered and afraid.

She's talking now of a time when we were students, some rare occasion when we spoke of what we had done that summer, and how startled she was by the account I'd given, the shock it had triggered within her.

'You're not a bad person, Nick. You have a good heart, I know. But you were a child. And you were so upset that day. I suppose I've blamed Luke, and your mother, and him,' she says, glancing at Murphy, but I can't bring myself to look at him, or the others. Instead I stand stock still, hardly blinking, waiting for the terrible pressure in my head to ease.

'But the truth is we're all to blame for what happened

that day,' Katie says, her hands held out, talking to me, but to Lauren too, wanting to share something with her of what happened to her half-sister.

'But, Nick, it wasn't an accident. It wasn't part of the game. It was your anger that did it. An anger she tapped into, not knowing how raw you were, how shocked to the bone over what Luke had told you. She didn't know it. She was an innocent. It was frightening to watch and frighten-ing to remember, but you have to try, Nicky – you have to try to remember – because the anger that came out of you that day, it killed a little girl.'

I have a strange feeling of vertigo, as if the world is tilt-ing, as if I'm back in the water, my footing unsure as the riverbed sways and pulls away from underneath me. I need to anchor myself, find a way of rooting my thoughts, sav-ing myself from this dizzying doubt. Instinctively, I look to Murphy.

He stands at the edge of things, thin, withered, shoul-ders slumped in weariness or defeat. Mack, beside him, is a panther waiting to pounce, the shot-gun an extension of his arm, while Lauren looks at me with pity in her eyes. All four of them, expectant.

I try to remember, but it's so dark in the river, the water murky with the mud stirred up by our presence in it. Hid-den rocks slippery beneath my feet. The shock of movement, the feathery brush of something against my ankle – a fish or some water-borne creature nipping at my heels.

I can see Luke standing with his hands on his hips, shoulders squared, his desire to win pulsing through the water. And that girl – her square face pale under the trees, a spray of freckles on her upper arms, hair in bunches that made her seem younger than she was, her nose wrinkling as she grinned – mischief in her laughing look, mischief that masked the vacancy in her understanding.

Still it's all so unclear. Was she standing beside Luke? The grin she gave me – her stuttering laugh. I remember it with a sudden push of irritation.

Then, straight as an arrow, it comes at me – another image – writhing limbs, an entanglement – Luke whispering in my ear at dead of night: 'They were humping – do you know what that means? Climbing on the back of her, his thing in hers, like the dogs we saw on the street. I saw them.'

The mouldy smell of the tent against my face, smoke from the campfire beyond, the murmuring of the adults, the rise and fall of Katie's breathing from her sleeping bag on the other side of Luke. All of it comes back to me now. My mother. The priest. A boiling mass of wrongness. It stirs inside me as it did all those years ago, and with it the great swell of anger.

That girl's face – freckles on her nose, new front teeth, a stupid grin: I see it again and feel an overwhelming desire to crush it.

'Nick,' Katie says desperately. 'You must remember?'

'No!' I say wildly.

The 'no' is not a denial and I think she knows this: she says nothing. It's the need I have for it all to stop – to hold back the flood of memory, not the false memory I have lived with all these years, but the horrible reality of truth.

'Please,' I say to her. 'No more.'

I look up, see the trees and sky, feel my brain rocking in

my skull, and a sinking in my chest, as if everything inside me is on the verge of collapse. Mack steps back, lifts the shot-gun and blows on the rifle-sights. The butt is stained with my blood. Instinctively, I brush my fingertips over the cut on my cheek and feel it sting.

'Is he going to confess?' Mack barks at Murphy.

Murphy clasps his hands but says nothing.

I remember the first day we scampered down here to explore as children, while our parents set up camp. The three of us perched on this bank peering down into the murky waters, the river dark, Katie asking: 'Do you think there's anything dangerous in there?'

Why is that memory so clear, while the one event I need to recall remains swathed in a cloud of forgetting?

Fear, I suppose, but I detect anger too, anger for allowing myself to forget, and for creating a false memory to rely on, as if it could in some way dispel whatever guilt I'm feeling.

The water is still and cool in the dappled shade. Mack is still bristling, clutching the shot-gun, but at this moment I don't care. The water draws me to it. I lean forward and dip my hands into it, watch the surface break and settle, forming its own silence around the stillness of my hands. Everything slows right down – the beating of my heart, the furious trajectory of my thoughts, my laboured breathing. And it is then – right then – that it begins.

The memory starts in my hands. Just as when I sit at the piano and feel my fingers reaching for the music, so it comes to me now: I feel the coolness of water about my hands and watch it tracing a line around my wrists, feel the faint pull of surface tension, and this time when I look down, I see again my hands as they were when I was a boy – smaller, smoother, without the coarse hairs that sprout from my forearms. I see those hands, the veins thin and blue, hands that hold a girl under water, the water cold and heavy, and in a sudden uncertain shimmer of memory, I trace the hand to its arm, and from the arm to the shoulder, from the shoulder to the neck and from the neck to the head.

It could be either of us. Me or Luke. Of course it could. We're brothers. We're made of the same stuff, the same muscle and sinew, the same blood.

And yet.

And yet this time what comes back to me is not what I remembered in the hotel room only a few hours ago, or what I've been telling myself for a lifetime, but something else – something more frightening than the calamity that has for years shaken me. I feel it in my hands, the way the water holds them, as if they're trapped, and something pulses along my veins – the ghostly flicker of an old rage and how it was sparked to life that day in the water. I sense the pull of truth in it and, despite my fear, I remain still and in the moment, because I know the importance of it now.

I am standing in the river, shivering. Luke is shouting at Katie. Amy has left and he wants Katie to take her place. I can hear the urgency in his voice although his words come intermittently, water having leaked into my inner ear. I watch him moving towards the bank, towards Katie, but she is refusing to come in.

Then Cora snickers. I look at her, the grin on her face. She is low down in the water, so low only her head and her hands are above the surface. Through her open mouth she is taking in water, then spitting it out, grinning all the while. I don't like her much and don't want her as my partner. Her and her stupid laugh — hak-hak-hak, like something's stuck in her throat.

'Luke!' I shout. 'Just leave her! Let's go!'

'No!' comes the furious reply.

'Aw, come on. I'm freezing!'

I can see Katie stirring on the bank, her eyes darting between us.

He's shouting at her again, and I can't hear what he's saying — the water in my ears makes a sucking noise and I try to shake it out. Movement behind me, that girl and her rabbitty teeth, spitting out water, saying something I don't quite catch.

I turn to her. 'What did you say?'

Her eyes, round and staring above the water, a smirk on her face.

'Your mum's a slut,' she says, her mouth opening in a gaping smile of delight.

'Shut your mouth,' I say quietly.

'Slut,' she says, lowering her mouth into the water.

'Take it back.'

She bobs up, the word on her lips again. 'Slut, slut, slut.'

'I said take it back,' I say, my voice louder now.

She gives me the full beam of her moronic smile and submerges her whole head. I'm left staring at the place where the water ripples and grows still, until she bursts from it in a spurting upward movement, and screams with delight: 'Slut! Slut! Slut!'

'Shut up!' I roar. 'Shut the fuck up!'

'Your mum's a slut! Your mum's a slut!' she says, in her sing-song voice, and I reach out to grab her but she backs away.

I spring after her, driven by rage, lose my footing and fall into the water. When I emerge, gasping, she is standing, laughing her stupid laugh – hak-hak-hak! – and I lunge for her again. I grab a fistful of hair, bunched behind her ear. I yank on it hard, and she gives a little cry, then starts laughing again.

'Take it back!' I scream at her, but she just keeps on laughing, and I see her big teeth flashing and want to smash them with a rock from the riverbed.

I don't know where Luke or Katie is – they have faded away, leached out of this scene along with all the colour. There is only me and Cora and her toxic laughter touching every sore spot inside me so my insides are prickling from a thousand needles, alive with pain and fury. My mother and Father Murphy, humping, fucking. So wrong. So utterly and completely wrong. The sting of betrayal lashes me, flays me to the quick.

Slut. All day the word and its poison are seeping inside me, getting into my bloodstream, but it's a silent passenger, and I've hardly felt its slow colonization. Even when I have my hands on her shoulders, pressing her down now into the water, even when I feel the emotion boiling in my temples and in my throat, I still don't realize I've been taken over. That I'm not myself. All I want is to silence her. All I want is for her to stop saying that word. And even though she has stopped, even though she can't say anything because I'm holding her down so hard while she thrashes and flails, still it's not enough, because the word is out there now. She has sent it out there, screaming into the world.

I need her never to have uttered it. So I push her down with one hand and I bunch my other into a fist and I send it into her face again and again.

The water slows the speed at which my fist travels, so I exert even greater force, spread my fingers and scratch and claw at her face, as if I'm a wild animal.

Because, right then, I am.

I was.

Somehow by holding her under water and scraping at her face, as her thrashing dies away and her limbs grow still, it's as if I can take the word back, take the act back, and erase it completely. That is all that matters.

And I do.

And the blood that's released from her mouth, a ribbon of red, acts as her surrender.

But the word is still out there, so when my brother comes and pulls at my arms, screaming into my face, and I elbow him, it's because I have to blot out the word. That is all that matters.

When Luke finally shakes me free and drags me to the bank, I'm hardly aware of him wading back into the water and pulling the girl out, of the moments while he drags her onto the bank with water streaming from her hair, her face scratched and bleeding, her mouth hanging open, her eyes staring up at the sky, and him screaming into her face – 'Wake up!' I watched it all as if from afar, as if it wasn't happening to me but to somebody else. As if it was happening to the one I knew best – my brother.

To Luke.

And then Katie runs to us, crying and shaking. And I remember the panic. Luke's shock, his anger. 'Jesus, Nick, you killed her. She's dead.'

How scared I am. Katie's screams filling my ears.

'Shut up, Katie!' Luke shouts, and her screams subside.

'What will we do?' she says. 'What's going to happen? What's Mam going to say? What's . . .' The questions spill out of her until Luke finally speaks.

'Shut up!' he says again, taking control. 'We can't leave her like this. If they find out what's happened . . . what's really happened, we're dead . . .'

'What do we do?' Katie says again.

'We have to cover it up,' Luke says, suddenly sounding older.

We pull Cora back into the river. She's heavier than I'd imagined, her body sinking quickly into the water, then coming back to the surface, strands of hair over her cut face.

Slowly, quietly, the three of us take her, pulling gently so she moves slowly through the river. Katie is crying and Luke snaps at her to stop snivelling. Already I feel myself retreating into my shell – where there is silence, where no one can touch me. Luke snaps at me, tells me to stop being so useless, says we need to bring her upriver to where the river widens, where a stray hippo might come and find her, or even a lion venturing to the banks might sniff her out. Here on the savannah, all manner of birds and mammals seek out flesh to consume – hyenas, vultures, marabou storks.

But when it comes to it, we don't leave her out in the open waiting to be discovered. Instead, we cover her up.

And he is gentle, my brother, as he lays her down on a muddy flat above the water's surface, tucked into the lip of the bank. He takes care to make her comfortable. I know that sounds wrong. But he does.

Luke and Katie scramble about, bringing branches and sticks to cover the girl: cover Cora. Thinking back on it, I can't quite believe they acted together without saying much to each other, as if they both knew they had to do this, as if our lives depended on it. A sudden movement, and Katie screams – the sound so loud it fills the air.

'She moved!' Katie says, pointing at the bank, at Cora, and we all turn and stare.

Luke goes to her, touches her, and I feel the breath I'm holding in my chest grow large and sore, pushing at my ribs as I wait for her to move again, to sit up and grin at us, to tell us it was all a joke, all part of the game, and that she, Cora, is the ultimate winner.

Luke reaches for her arm, and it falls by her side, hand plunging into the water with a splash, and Katie screams again. This time, Luke swings around and pushes her, and she falls into the river. 'Shut up! Just shut the fuck up, would you?'

Then he turns. His face is white, eyes blistering with a look I've never seen before. For just a moment, I don't know him. I don't recognize my brother. I stand in the water as Luke throws the last handful of leaves and dirt over the girl's outstretched hand. Then the three of us wait for somebody to say something. But there is no sermon, no word of comfort. There is only one word and it comes from Luke: 'Quick!' He grabs my hand, waking me from my catatonic state, and we run.

We ran – Luke and I – Katie coming after us, the wind filling my ears with a strange silence, pushing any words I looked for further into me, further than I knew was possible – and still we kept running.

It's like I've stumbled onto a hidden place, a place I had known about for years, but denied to myself existed, a place where all of these memories waited. I have pushed the rusty gate to this secret garden and walked in. But no flowers grow here. There is only decay.

Shouting. Urgent, arguing voices. I'm back. Only now do I realize I'm crying, that I've been lost in a reverie while the others have waited for me to remember. But they haven't just waited, they've been arguing. Mack must have been recounting his grievances for Katie, detailing his litany of bad luck, his lost job, his lost family, his time in jail, and she has listened, I can tell, but is wary of him, suspicious, and defiant, too, in the way she is standing up to him because now he is ordering her about, pointing the gun recklessly to where he wants her to stand and she is saying: 'You can't tell me what to do.'

Lauren reaches for my hand, but I pull away. My hands have killed a child. How can I ever let anyone hold them again? I try to explain, but the words are swallowed by the heaving sob that comes out of me. There, on the banks of the river, I stand as I did when I was a child, but I'm not a child any more. I turn to Mack: 'You want my confession? Well, here it is.'

His face tightens, eyes squinting, and still he holds the gun high, keeps it pointed at me. But he's listening now, waiting to hear. And so are the others, because I'm telling them too, as I let it all out.

And with my words, with the confession I make, there comes a hush — as if it's not just the people around me who are listening, but everything around us: the animals and birds and insects, the dust on the ground, the limbs of the trees, the running water of the river, other ghostly presences, all urging me on, accepting my words as a final testimony, so that by the time I finish there's a kind of awed silence.

Murphy looks relieved, as if he has finally let out the tension he has been holding inside himself for a very long time – his body goes limp. Lauren's eyes are filled with pity. Only Mackenzie looks unmoved. The butt of the gun is held tightly under his arm, his fingers supporting the barrel.

'I don't know why my mother said anything about you, Mackenzie, I honestly don't,' I say, hoping to alleviate the man's grievance. 'It was dishonest of her. It was wrong. But she's not here, and I can't speak for the dead.'

His nostrils flare, and the edges of his mouth pull into a kind of sneer. 'Thirty years,' he snarls. 'Thirty years, and this is all I can expect?'

'I also have a confession.' It's Katie. Her voice is resolute, firm and clear. She looks to me – and there's support in her eyes. She straightens her back, suggesting a kind of solidarity between us. 'You see,' she says, 'in a way, I started it.'

Her dark eyes are fixed on the water below, staring back into the field of memory.

'I was the one who told her. That day, in the river, before it happened . . . Your mum came down to check on us. She told Luke he wasn't allowed in the river, and he argued with her until she gave in. Do you remember?'

I think of my mother, standing under the trees in her navy sundress, tiny white polka dots speckled along the hem. 'Yes,' I say faintly, wiping the tears away with my sleeve.

'The younger sister, Amy, was sitting alongside me, watching your mum and Luke talking. And after Sally left, Amy turned to me and said: "Why doesn't he like his mum?" And I said . . .' she falters, swallows hastily, then goes on '. . . I said, "He doesn't like her because she's a slut."'

The light swirls about us. The sky darkens. My mind goes to the undergrowth, as if something there is watching, waiting for its prey.

'Cora was there too. She heard what I said. And if I hadn't said it, if I'd kept it to myself, then maybe, maybe . . .' Momentarily, she is overcome. But then she finds her voice again, more resolute now. 'I put the word into Cora's mouth. She wasn't trying to wound anyone. She was simple, innocent. She had no understanding of what it meant. But when she heard me say it, she just repeated it. That's all. There was no intent. But you couldn't see, Nick, because of how mixed-up and vulnerable you were that day. And I was the one who gave her the word so, you see, we were all to blame.'

She stops, biting her upper lip, fighting tears. But she can't hold them back and I watch the movement of her shoulders as she cries silently. Even after this show of solidarity, I don't offer any words of comfort – I have none to give. Nor do I reach out to touch her. It's as if some canker has been taken from my body by the most awful medicine and now I can only stand there, exhausted and spent.

Katie steps next to me. She wipes the tears beneath her eyes and turns so that we are both facing Mack. 'There – you have the truth now.'

Murphy raises his head, stops mumbling whatever prayers he has been saying to himself, and looks to Mack, his two hands clutching the shot-gun. I feel the defiance in him, the disgust. If he feels disappointment in the confession he has longed for, if he feels that it is a frustrating anti-climax, he doesn't show it. The danger that has been rumbling inside him seems to build into a crescendo as he takes a step towards me and I see the tremble of anger passing through him.

'The lies you people tell. Your mother. You! You are just as bad as her! Letting other people take the blame for your actions.' Standing close to me now, I can smell the acrid stench of his self-righteous indignation, see the danger of his intent in the curl of his lip.

'Thirty years I have lived under the lie your mother told. Thirty years.' He whispers it, and within those hissed words, I can feel the terrible weight of what he has suffered, and the longing within him to face his accuser, to exact his revenge. But my mother is gone. There's only me now.

'You killed that girl,' he says to me now, and we are so close that I can feel the heat of his breath on my face. 'You killed her. Not me. So tell me this: why is it that I'm the one who has had to pay for it?'

I know that whatever I say is not going to be enough. I can also tell from the way his shoulders are set that he wants more than a confession, some form of restitution that Murphy had not reckoned on. And I have an idea of what it is . . . and I'm ready.

The clouds are low and thick and dark above us. There's a dense and moving beauty to them as if the heavens have something to say about all of this and the only way to express it is through the elemental movement above us. Yes, the clouds are heavy and beautiful, threatening at the same time to burst at any minute.

Lauren looks to me, and the distance seems to grow between us. Is this the woman who had said she would share her life with me no more than a few weeks ago? Her eyes say it all: they are reflective, sad. There is something within them – not forgiveness, but understanding. I think of all the time she knew who I was and feel a wave of shame wash over me. Now, more than anything, I want *her* forgiveness.

Whatever prayers Murphy wanted to say to bless this cursed place cannot absolve me. Within those ancient invocations, there can be only a cold comfort, the comfort of finality, captured in the fateful cadences that have been spoken over and over again, year after year, to an unseen God.

A crack above us and rain comes down in warm, heavy bursts. I want it to pound me into the earth and wash me clean away.

Then Mack raises the shotgun slowly to my head, so that I'm staring down the barrel and beyond it to Mack's deadly gaze, ready now.

There will be no prayers after all.

I see again the fleeing figure of Amy, a shadow from the past, race across the riverbank. I see, too, the vacant eyes of Cora beneath the water looking straight into mine – not with anger or malice, but with a simple lack of understanding – asking not *stop*, but *why*.

325

Why?

'Give me one good reason why I shouldn't kill you,' Mack says calmly, his aim fixed and sure.

The trees around me seem to close in and out like a terrible wing-beat. The grey sky rushes towards me and contracts; the river in my wavering mind appears to break its banks. Murphy's eyes open wide, Katie says something I can't make out, and Lauren is transfixed. It feels, too, as if other presences have gathered here, finally, to witness the end.

'One good reason,' Mack says again.

I watch his finger tighten on the trigger. Silence around us. Listening ghosts.

'No,' I tell him, and close my eyes. 'I can't think of any.'

AFTERWORD

Nick

A light rap on the door. I know who it is: Karl.

He has been coming every day, stopping by to help. I think he knows that without him I would crack.

This morning, he is supportive and business-like.

'Tord Gustavsen,' he says, holding up a disc. 'Can I put it on?'

'Be my guest,' I say, and he kneels down to the stereo. Soon enough the gentle jazz piano comes on, something to soothe the troubled mind.

'I'll brew the coffee,' he says then. And I'm grateful again for his kind ministrations.

'Strong,' I call after him, as he enters the kitchen.

'Would I brew anything but strong coffee?' he calls back.

I start to place Lauren's things in the first box. Some books to begin with – in they go, one after another.

I can smell the coffee brewing, hear the drip of the filter. So many times I've smelt the same rich roast and heard the same comforting sound, but that was when it was me who was making the coffee and Lauren was waiting, chatting to me about her research or her colleagues at the university.

Karl returns with two mugs of steaming coffee. 'Now, what's the order of the day?'

'Boxes.' I point and he nods.

Karl has been a good friend. Over the past couple of weeks I've made several fairly serious attempts to drink myself to death. If it wasn't for Karl, perhaps I would have succeeded. He came to my aid, nursing me like I was his own child, denying me booze and forcing various teas down my throat. 'Swallow it, brother,' he would say gently. 'It will do you good.'

And if he noticed the terrible despair his use of the word 'brother' brought out in me, he never let on. In many ways, I owe my life to him.

There's masking tape on the floor beside me, but I'm reluctant to start sealing any boxes yet – the gesture feels too final. Besides, it's not clear where Lauren wants me to send them. It seems she hasn't settled on one place. She is visiting her mother in Michigan, she has told me, but isn't planning to stay there.

I bought the masking tape at the shop across the street. Life goes on in all its frantic mayhem – but not in the still space the apartment has become. The delivery truck still stops outside the bar downstairs each week with a screech. The street vendors gather, call out and do their business, and the bar below maintains its custom – a steady tide of people coming and going. There remains a military presence throughout the city.

Everything is, in many ways, as it was. Life goes on.

That's what I have to tell myself. That's what Karl says.

And yet how can it?

'How can I help?' Karl asks, and I tell him that we'll just have to go through as much as we can.

It is already two months since Lauren left for the States. Part of me wanted to beg her to come back to me, but the other part – the better part – knew she needed time away from me to think about us. When she came to Nairobi to get some of her things, I pulled myself together for the few hours she was here, tried to make a show of decency, of sobriety, so that we could talk, if nothing else.

I remember leaning against the door-frame, hands in my pockets, watching her silently travelling around our bedroom, putting things into the holdall open on the bed. I watched the careful movements of her hands, the grace with which her body moved, her composure and self-possession amazing to me while I could barely hold myself together.

We hadn't talked about things – not to any real or meaningful extent – and there were so many questions I had for her, so many wonderings and confusions, that it was hard to know how to start, and I was fearful of approaching it, as if the first thing I put to her would lead to a great unravelling. In the end, it all came down to one question: 'How long have you known?' I asked.

She stopped what she was doing, looked down at the T-shirt in her hand. 'For a long time,' she said quietly, putting it into her bag.

'From when we first met?'

'From before. I sought you out . . .'

'You sought me out?'

Her eyes were gentle and full of pity. 'Yes, Nick. My mom told me something of what had happened . . . I became so curious about her other life, her life in Africa, her husband here, my sisters, that I asked more questions,' she said, speaking faster now, her voice low but urgent, as if she were reliving an exciting episode in her life. 'But the answers only fuelled my desire to know more. Instead of satisfying my curiosity, what my mom told me only fed it. Even before she heard of her husband's death here, I'd planned to come to Kenya, to study, to visit his house and see his grave . . .'

'Unlike Amy?'

'Amy never wanted to return. She prefers to leave things in the past. She's married to a dentist in Ohio, has two children, and that's her life . . . Funny how things work out.'

'And me? How did you know I was living in Nairobi?'

'Father Murphy told me. He told my mother her husband had died, so when I arrived in Kenya, I came to him and gradually he told me about you, your brother and your parents,' she says. She's taking her time, choosing her words carefully. 'And knowing that you were living in the same city only made me curious. Murphy told me you were a musician – he even told me what club you played in.'

Her eyes light up and she smiles, but then the seriousness returns to her features. 'And when we talked, I still couldn't believe that you were the person I had been told about . . . I didn't know that I would fall for you, Nick. I didn't want to, but it happened.'

I thought of a night, not long after we'd met, that we'd spent lying together in each other's arms, the night air bearing down heavily, how I'd felt so utterly at peace with this woman, as if for the first time in my life I could be myself without apology or pretence. And even though I had known her only a few weeks, already I was sure that what I felt for her – the love that had blown up inside me – would last my whole life.

I remember thinking that there was no way I could tell her what had happened back then. So I kept it secret.

When I told her about myself, living here as a youngster, returning to Ireland, then travelling and coming back, I remember how still she was in my arms, as if she was holding her breath.

I thought at the time that it was the attentive awe of new love.

Little did I know it was because of what she knew about me. How dangerous that must have felt to her . . . how utterly strange to be held by the hands that had done that terrible thing.

'So why didn't you tell me? Why didn't you say something?'

'I was afraid,' she said, sitting down on the bed now, knowing it couldn't be avoided any longer.

'Of what?'

Her brow furrowed with consternation, and I saw her struggle, for a moment, with her thoughts.

'I felt so strongly about you. Even then, I knew you'd had something to do with Cora's death. And to know this thing about you – that you were there when Cora was killed – it was so huge, so difficult to fathom. And I didn't want to believe it – I really didn't,' she said. 'I knew it was true but I persuaded myself that it didn't matter. That what happened was in the past – that you were only a boy then, too young to know or be motivated by any real malice.' She steadied herself. 'I told myself it had happened so long ago – before I was even born – that what's done is done. I made a decision that I was going to try not to let the past get between us.'

I nodded and remained standing, but inside I was starting to collapse.

'It's late,' she said then. 'I'd better go.'

I watched her get to her feet, pull her bag to her and zip it closed. Something in me rose against her leaving and I had to stop myself barricading the door, refusing to let her go. But I knew she had moved on and I couldn't blame her.

She leaned in and kissed me briefly on the cheek – not the mouth – and it seemed dismissive, somehow final. Then she passed me, and before she reached the stairs, she stopped at the piano, touched the lid. 'It's closed,' she said. 'Aren't you playing?'

'No.'

'But why not?'

How to explain it? That my hands no longer worked – that I no longer trusted them? That since they had been the conduit of the memory in the river that day, they had seemed filled with brackish water, lifeless. Sometimes I caught myself looking down at them as if they were not my own. The hands that had taken the life of a young girl.

But I didn't say any of that to Lauren, although I think somehow she understood.

'Take care of yourself, Nick,' she said, then descended the stairs and left.

Karl finishes his coffee and places the cup on the table:

'Let's go out tonight,' he says, looking at his watch. 'I have to go now, but I'll stop by at, say, seven thirty. It'll be good to get out.'

It's not a question and, despite my reluctance, I know he'll insist.

'Goodbye, my friend,' I say.

He grins at me. 'See you later.'

It was Karl who finally tracked Murphy down to a small hospice outside the city, during those first weeks when I was barely holding it together.

'How did you find him?' I asked Karl.

'Persistence,' he replied.

I took down the address from Karl, fired up the motorbike and drove to where the graffiti spreads like wildfire.

'Father,' I said, entering the small yellow-tinted, acrid-smelling ward.

He was lying on a narrow bed, his head propped on a pillow, a thin white sheet covering his shrunken, skeletal frame. His eyes were half open, sunk deep into his skull. 'Nick,' he said. 'Nick, you came.'

'You didn't make it easy,' I said, sitting down on the wicker chair next to the bed.

'I'm so sorry, Nick. I didn't want to cause anyone any more trouble.'

'No trouble, Father.'

'There's not long for me now, Nick,' he said, in a frail whisper.

'I want to thank you,' I said.

Instead of answering, he waved a hand.

'You saved my life, Father. By the river. I thought he was going to pull the trigger.'

'I think you called me an iconoclast once.'

'But not an arms-carrying one.'

He smiled faintly. 'Funny the things you do. Things you

never expect of yourself. Perhaps God has a sense of humour after all.'

'Perhaps.'

'It was something a friend gave me after the office was broken into one time. A small pistol for security reasons. For show, really. I never kept the thing loaded,' he said, breathing heavily. 'I'm not even sure why I took it with me to the Masai Mara. But that day something told me I should.'

'You had no idea you would have to use it?'

'No,' he croaked.

I remembered his hand trembling, the pistol wavering as he took aim and told Mack to put his own gun down.

'My fear was that I would have to pull the trigger . . .'

'But you didn't.'

'It was enough to have the gun,' he said, looking past me. 'It turned him away.'

'Enough to scare him, yes,' I said. 'It was a brave thing to do, Father.'

'Call me Jim.'

'I'm very grateful, Jim.'

My mind turned again to that day, and the moment when Mack looked at Murphy, the pistol held tightly in his shaking hand, the slow spread of a smile crossing Mack's face – the sight of a priest with a gun ridiculous to him. He gave a hollow laugh, and realized, perhaps, that he could never exact his revenge, because I was not Sally. I was just a substitute – a poor one at that – and killing me would not satisfy his desire for justice. He lowered the shotgun and turned away from us, the rain coming down heavily, hitting the trees and the surface of the river, pelting the land and all who stood there. I saw the defeated slump in his shoulders, the fight gone out of him. One last look back at us, water streaming over his face, before he disappeared into the trees. I never saw him again.

Murphy coughed and reached for a glass of water.

'Let me,' I said. I picked up the glass and offered it to his parched lips. He sipped a little water, some of which dribbled onto his chin.

I took a napkin from his bedside table and wiped his mouth gently. He breathed in deeply and sank further into the bed.

'I don't have much energy,' he said.

I took his hand in mine and we sat there for a time, neither of us saying anything, the ceiling fan turning in steady revolutions as the traffic streamed by outside.

'May I ask for your forgiveness, Nicholas?' he asked.

'What for, Jim?'

'For any pain I've caused you over the years.'

I didn't need to say anything. Murphy's eyes closed, and when he had fallen asleep, I left. It was later that night when I got the call to say he had passed away.

Another funeral. This time in a cemetery next to the hospice: me and Karl, dozens of locals from Kianda, clergy and aid workers gathered with the hospice staff to say farewell to Father Murphy.

In the months that follow, life falls into a pattern. I go to the office every day, sifting through documents, trying to understand the accounting nightmare, negotiating with the banks, attempting to bring calm and order to the situation. It does not come naturally to me, this line of business, but I can dig my heels in and be diligent when I have to, and something deep within me is driving me to do this.

When I am alone in the office, and the street outside has fallen quiet, I sometimes catch myself engrossed in these lists of figures, and it comes as such a surprise to me, that I wonder what my father would make of me now. Dad, the prudent accountant, and me, his renegade son. I can't even call myself a musician any more. The piano lid remains closed.

I find that, as the days go on, a sense of nervous excitement builds within me in the hope that Lauren might call. And she does — every so often. Our relationship has changed and there is a maturity to it, in the sense that we are no longer wide-eyed innocents. But, still, I have to be realistic. Lauren is back in America. A reconciliation is unlikely, and I wish her well, though I find it hard to let go.

One day shortly before the start of the rainy season, Julia rings. It's been a long time since I heard her voice, but I recognize it. The Dublin accent, the mellow tones.

'It's good to hear you,' I say.

'And you.' Her voice is quieter, calmer than before, suggesting she has accepted Luke's death and is in the process of moving on. 'I thought you'd like to know,' she says, 'that the house — your parents' home — is finally going to be demolished.'

'Oh.' The news takes me by surprise.

'The builder went bust, as you know,' she explains. 'The bank has sold it on to another developer.'

'When?'

'I understand that the sale has already gone through and

planning permission has been applied for. The word is that the bulldozers will be in before the summer.'

'I'll have to come over,' I say instinctively.

I hear her draw breath in surprise, and the truth is, I've surprised myself.

'Are you sure you want to?' she asks gently. 'That house holds so many memories – good and bad.'

'I think I need to, Julia.'

And so I make the arrangements, book the flights, and find myself, once again, in the chill climate that is Dublin.

Everything is familiar. And everything is different. I feel older returning. I know I am, but this time I feel much older. As if my youth has passed me by. I may not be middle-aged, but my youth is gone. It's not just the lines about my eyes, or the way the clothes hang on my body, it's the slight stiffness that has grown into my joints, the weariness of my movements.

Before I go to the house, there is someone I must meet.

At a café on Dawson Street, she is waiting for me. I see her at the back, her chin resting on her hand, the ghost of a smile on her face as she watches me negotiating tables and waiters wearing long linen aprons. When I finally reach her, she gets to her feet and, without saying anything, I hold my arms open for her and feel her come into my embrace. For a moment, I just hold her there, my eyes closed, thinking: This is what it feels like to come home.

She pulls back to look at me. 'Nick,' she says happily.

'It's good to see you, Kay.'

As I take my seat opposite, my eyes pass over her and notice the changes. She seems stronger somehow, as if she's been working out, making herself fit. The shadows under her eyes have faded and youth has come back to her face. She's cut her hair short, a cropped bob that skims the line of her jaw, and its sharpness suits her, sitting well with the crisp white shirt she wears, the minimal jewellery. I take in these changes, and wonder if there's a new love in her life. But I don't ask.

Instead we talk about the house that's to be demolished, and when I skirt around her questions as to how I feel about it, she takes the hint and backs off.

'Where are you staying?'

'I'm at Julia's,' I say, and watch her eyebrows shoot up in surprise. 'I know, I know, but what can I say? She offered, and I'm broke after the flights, so . . .' She laughs, and I go on, serious now: 'Besides, it felt like the right thing to do.'

'And how is Julia?'

'She's okay. Still upset obviously, but better than I expected.'

In fact, Julia has been something of a revelation. She has surprised everyone with the way she has taken on Luke's business debts, tackling his arrears, battling tooth and nail against repossession.

'So what about you?' I ask. 'What about your shining career?'

She rolls her eyes and looks down at her cup. It's coffee today – not a whiff of alcohol between us – and judging by Katie's fresh-faced appearance, my guess is that lately she's cleaned up her life. Not once in the hour we spend together does she duck outside for a smoke.

'It's fine,' she says, and heaves a dramatic sigh. Then, flashing me a smile, she says: 'I'm working on a – a little sideline.'

'Oh?'

'A book about the financial crisis.'

'Really?'

She shrugs, then grins. 'Everyone else is doing it. I figured I'd throw my hat into the ring.'

She says it casually, but I can tell that she's excited about her book, enlivened by it.

For the rest of the time, we talk around the edges of what happened – I tell her about Murphy, about the work in Kianda, what I'm doing now.

'And Mackenzie?' she asks.

'There's neither sight nor sound of him. Perhaps he's gone back to his own village.'

She considers what I have said, looks at me with concern and says, 'But aren't you afraid he'll come back and seek you out?'

I think back to those fearful eyes, the hesitant retreat of the man, his pride broken, his anger misdirected, his disappointment evident in the way he carried himself away from us that day . . . how he skulked off into the wilderness. And so I say, with little reservation: 'No, I don't think Mackenzie will be coming back.'

It seems that neither of us can bring ourselves to discuss what actually happened by the river. Nonetheless, an understanding has crept into our conversation – the sense that we have forgiven each other, even if we aren't all the way to forgiving ourselves.

As the hour draws to a close, and Katie looks at her watch, I realize I probably won't see her again – not for a very long time – and despite the joy I have felt in her company during this brief visit, or maybe because of it, I can't help the wave of sadness that surges over me as she prepares to leave.

'Have you heard from Lauren?' she asks.

It's a question I've been waiting for. Only the other day, Lauren had rung me and there was a nervous urgency to her words. She wanted to know how I'd feel about her coming back to Nairobi. She said where she was just didn't seem like home. What did I think? Was it a crazy idea?

I had tried to remain calm. I had tried not to read too much into what she might have been suggesting. So what I told her was this: 'I don't think it's a crazy idea, Lauren. Not at all.'

But I'm not ready to discuss the possibility of a reconciliation between Lauren and me, not with Katie, not yet.

'We've been in touch from time to time,' I say. 'We're still talking . . .' I leave it at that and my tone suggests, I think, that that's as far as I want to go with it.

Her phone buzzes and she reads the incoming text. 'I've got to go,' she says. 'I'd love to stay longer, but someone's waiting for me.' Her eyes go to her phone. The tenderness she cannot hide confirms my suspicions. A man.

We hug, but I sense the hurry within her now, the desire not to linger, and I remember that, like me, she was never one for goodbyes.

This place has large windows running the length of one wall, and as I wait to pay the bill, I see Katie walk past, her arm looped through a man's. He's older – and from the way he is leaning in towards her, I can tell he is listening intently to what she is saying. As they disappear from view, I briefly wonder about him, about what she's telling him, about what words they whisper when they turn to each other at dead of night.

Another taxi then, another journey home, through

Dundrum, up Ballinteer, to Ticknock, Three Rock, and further on up the Dublin mountains and into Wicklow. The place names reel off like a prayer of sorts.

The greenness is electrifying. It seeps from the fields into my vision. I have known another kind of landscape, ever changing, with dust-bowls and savannahs, wildebeest and lions, paupers and kings, but here I am again in the docile port of Dublin, and the question I have asked myself many times since that day in Nairobi is: how do you rub out an event like that from your life – or how did I?

The obvious answer is that it must be some kind of survival mechanism, a way of coping. Well, that's what I've told myself, and that all those years of inarticulate silence somehow sucked the memory out of me, how my time in the trenches of the minor keys mutated in my mind what had happened so that I misremembered.

I'm sure we all do it to some degree, but with me it was not a small thing. I was not denying maltreatment or some misdemeanour for which I was responsible but the most serious sin of all: the taking of another's life. Thou shalt not kill, we learned in school. Thou shalt not . . .

Slowly, like chinks of light flooding a cave, I had begun to see part of the picture of what happened. I have slowly come to accept the facts. And what am I left with now? Fragments, echoes, dreams, but also the realization that home is not a place. Home is a state of mind; it is the most honest state of mind where we face ourselves and accept who we are, no matter what.

There is no real way to atone for what I did but I do what I can. My work in Kianda, for a start – it's a sort of penance, I suppose, something to make amends. If there is a way to make up for one's sins, it could be by helping others. But I don't think there is a way to atone properly, not in this life, not for what I did. I think we toil and sin until the end. And that is all.

The car pulls up higher into the hills and closer to the house, and there, sooner than I reckon, I see it, its modest facade, its rendered exterior, grey, mottled, unassuming. It is, in other words, how I remember it. My heart lurches. I'm relieved, you see, that I recognize the place.

After everything that has happened, after the uncertainty of my mind, I worried that what I knew as home, once upon a time, was something else and would be so different from what I knew that I would be thrown into the depths again and not even know it.

I pay the driver and watch him leave. The grass is overgrown; of course it is. The fence is rusted. The gate does not creak. It does not open at all.

I climb over. In my mind's eye, I can see Lauren that day, pushing the back door open. No need to do that today. The front door has toppled and is lying at the threshold.

Some young rebel has been in with a can of paint and decorated the walls with graffiti. But there are no words. Images, squiggles, who knows what – intelligible only to the initiated. For all I know the graffiti says: *stay out*, or *condemned* – either of which would be suitable, either of which could be right.

The hallway is a mess. The kitchen too. I teeter on the threshold to the living room. The stippled ceiling. The shadowy squares on the paintwork that marks the places where paintings once hung. It's obvious others have been

344

through this house – squatters, developers, prospective buyers – their footprints staining the floors, their disregard and rubbish littering what was once a family home.

I remember one Christmas dressing the tree with Luke in this very room. My parents watching, amused but distant. It's amazing that one place can hold such memories: my mother bringing dry toast to my bedside as I stayed home from school, hanging onto the banisters when I had whooping cough, my father falling asleep with a bottle of whiskey at the kitchen table. I have to take it as real, even in the light of what I remember in Nairobi.

I walk towards the stairs, place my hand on the rail and shiver. Up there is where I cut Luke down. And as I make my way towards it, I feel myself drawn upwards, so that when I finally stand in that empty room, I feel no ill will, no unhappy presence, only the sharpness of a breeze blowing through the cracks in the broken windows, only the fresh air of the hills, and what it says to me is *forgiveness*.

I wasn't sure what I would feel coming back. But now I'm glad I have. It feels like the right thing to do, to say goodbye once and for all to those memories.

And for the first time in my life, I can rightly say I'm looking forward. There may yet be a fresh start for me – that's how it feels right now.

I have this thought, even with the stark fact confronting me of where I am: this is the place where I cut Luke down. I can't ignore it. My gaze comes back to it again and again. How I cut him down.

I can't help but put the questions to the empty room, to my brother if he's listening: 'Why, Luke? Why did you do it?

'Not because of me, I hope.'

I walk to the window – the boards have all been taken down – and look out past the garden and the fields to the city sprawl. I've been here long enough. I'm not sad. It's time to say goodbye. I love you all, I want to say: to the shadows, to the ghosts, to every echo of this old and lovely place.

All my worry about where to be has been shadow-play and nonsense. Maybe there is only one home, one resting place. It is, after all, where we all end up. My mother and father are there. Murphy is there. My brother too.

Before I turn to leave, I whisper one final prayer to the place we once lived. I say to myself, to the house, to whoever is listening: 'Lord, have mercy on my soul and on those who have gone before. *Wait for me.*'